Kas Skoros, his marriage to Alex's former fiancée now annulled and no longer intimidated by Athena's psychic gifts, begs her to move to San Francisco and manage an art gallery that his family's company owns. However, burned once, Athena holds him at arm's length.

Athena is enticed to consult in another serial killer case. As time passes and secrets are leaked, others—including the killer's brother—find out that Athena is the one who's helping the police. Meanwhile, a strange young woman on a motorcycle appears to be stalking her. Warning bells go off as Athena realizes the woman is not who she seems to be.

Athena's Fears
Copyright © 2019 Donna Del Oro
ISBN: 978-1-4874-1244-9
Cover art by Martine Jardin

Published by eXtasy Books Inc or
Devine Destinies, an imprint of eXtasy Books Inc

Look for us online at:
www.eXtasybooks.com or www.devinedestinies.com

ATHENA'S FEARS
THE DELPHI BLOODLINE BOOK 2

BY

DONNA DEL ORO

DEDICATION

To my husband Joe, my wonderful son and daughter, who encourage and support all of my endeavors, I give a hearty thanks! And to my two grandsons, who love books as much as I do, you inspire me.

CHAPTER ONE

A memory surfaced as the cool air whipped his long hair about his face. Huh, his new face. He'd been pumping into a whore, one of the Amsterdam whores he'd chosen. She'd thought she was doing the poor tranny a favor. One last fuck as a man before he crossed over — ha. The bitch's eyes had popped open with shock when he plunged in the icepick. Her mouth, lips smeared with red lipstick, sucked air like a damned fish sucking O's. Funniest thing he ever saw.

His new disguise always caught the bitches off guard. She'd looked at him with amusement, even a hint of sympathy when he dropped his pants. Like *life is a bitch. We're all in this damned mess together but I'm sure as hell not as screwed up as you.* She liked the fact that he could screw like a male. Something new for them, kissed by a bitch but screwed by a man. At the same time! *Crraa-zzee.*

He was imagining now the feel of his hand on the hilt of the icepick as he'd jabbed it into flesh and tissue. Felt the scrape of metal on bone as he thrust it upward with all his force. That always jarred him, like hearing nails scraping a chalkboard. The stab was heart-stopping, but for him it was a huge turn-on. The thrill made him harder than a steel rod, so he always kept on pumping. His climax always came right after. Like an explosion — one life ending, another recharging.

With one hand off the handlebars, he touched his chin. The feel of it had changed. His face, his smooth cheeks, all had changed in Amsterdam. That doctor had remade him, damn him! Now he was an effing freak, male from the neck down and a weird looking broad from the neck up. He even had to cover up his Adam's apple. No cosmetic surgeon was going to touch that.

But the facial surgery was necessary. It had made it possible for him to return to the States and to his brother. According to his smart-as-hell brother, no EuroPol or cops' facial recognition software would pick him out of a fugitive database. His brother, the only person in the world who cared whether he lived or died. A fake passport and money from his brother had done the rest.

Amsterdam turned out to be a blast—that was the kicker. But things were getting too hot there. He'd finally made it home, after two terrible years wandering from South Africa to Europe.

Not his fault that he'd learned some new skills along the way, like how to jab an icepick through the rib cage directly into a bitch's heart. It was quick, easy, and the look of surprise on the cunt's face always gave him a thrill. Easy, just find the bottom of the rib cage and move your thumb up two ribs. Thrust upward. All the way to the hilt of the icepick. Like that last time he used this new skill in Amsterdam. Red light quarter where anything was allowed—ha ha, even murder. But now he had to control those impulses, now that he was back. *Gotta stay out of trouble. Least, for a while.*

Yet the old excitement was back—the thrill of the hunt, the explosive high he got was better than a rush from a meth hit. Even with the cool air in his face, his body pounded with the heat of excitement. His brother warned him to lay off the dope, and he did. He said to lay off the thrills, too. But he wasn't sure he could do that. Not for long, anyway. No way.

Not his fault, anyway. He was wired for the thrills of hunting and killing.

Mangez merde! An expression he'd learned from a French whore. That one he liked. He'd left her alone. *If you don't like it—if you don't like me—mangez merde!* Eat shit. Ha, ha.

The rush of air in his long hair cooled him a bit as the memory receded. Night air.

Tonight, his face was covered by his helmet's tinted visor. He loved to ride at night between the hours of midnight and four in the morning. Up and down the vacant streets of the city. The only humans out this time of night were like him. Predators, lone wolves, misfits looking for trouble. Even the cops avoided this neighborhood of shabby tradesmen's shops, run-down apartment buildings and flop houses that rented by the week and day. One of them was his crash pad. Just temporary, his brother said. Until they could make plans and get away. Get out of DC. Find some hick town where no one knew them.

Yah!

He laughed out loud as he slowed and turned at the lighted street corner, hugging the asphalt as he tilted his bike dangerously close to the road. Yep, all this was temporary, and then they'd disappear like ghosts in the night. Ha, ha.

Ghosts in the night.

He cocked his head and swept a lock of long dark brown hair away with his gloved hand as he pulled up to the curb. Time to sleep. Then tomorrow he'd look for a job where he could blend in. And he knew just the place.

Athena awoke with a gasp.

That was all. Then blank darkness. The channel closed. Like wind sucking out through a tunnel. A dank, putrid smell faded as well. Then nothing. Groggy with sleep, she pondered what had just happened.

The Flow's channel had opened, allowing her mind to enter another's. But this mind was dark, ferocious, sick. Boiling over with vengeful urges. She realized it was a man's mind, a disturbed mind. He hated women, that was apparent, but why, she didn't know. A chill ran through her, making her skull shiver with dread. Were their paths about to cross? Good God! Was the Flow warning her? Her pulse began to pound. Bargaining, even pleading with The Flow didn't help. Wanting a way out of the man's black, murderous thoughts made her subconscious beg for mercy.

She called out in her mind, *Kas!*

In the dark of her bedroom she finally opened her eyes. Furniture emerged as shadows in the dim light from a plugged-in night light. Automatically, her hands fluttered over the bed covers, searching in vain for the human touch which was necessary for her clairvoyance to open the channel. No one, nothing except the dark mound on the opposite side of her queen-size bed. Dan was sleeping.

A moan escaped her open mouth. She would have to let The Flow do its thing, take over her mind. When Athena was asleep, she couldn't conquer it, not like when she was awake and her conscious mind could willfully close the channel. Now she was at the mercy of The Flow's power.

A dangerous mind.

Why? Why did The Flow allow her in?

What did this creep have to do with her?

Mercifully, her heartbeat slowed as her subconscious mind relaxed. She grew weary and closed her eyes. Within minutes, she fell asleep again.

CHAPTER TWO

The frustration roiled inside Kas Skoros, turning the cold blackness to orange heat. He coiled it all deep within and brought it under control. Flinging off a thin coverlet, he sprang to his bare feet. The sofa he'd been sleeping on was a disheveled, tangled mess. Something had awakened him from a disturbing dream . . . a sound.

A woman's voice, like a scream followed by a sad moan. Athena? No, not possible.

Upstairs. Little Alex. Maybe it was the child calling out in the night.

Where's his mother? Sleeping off another night of carousing?

The dream still held him in its gossamer web. Fuzzy headed, he paused to recall what it had been. Athena . . . was she calling out to him? After all this time?

Oh yeah . . . fuck it.

He fought the feelings the fleeting dream had conjured up and kept his feet moving. Life goes on. *Gotta do what I gotta do.* His new mantra.

His head clear now, Kas stopped at the kitchen fridge, took out one of the bottles he'd prepared the night before, nuked it for one minute and then tested the temperature of the milk on the sensitive skin inside of his wrist. That was what he'd been told to do by his sister-in-law, his brother George's wife. She had three kids, so she should know.

Though he was a fake husband, he was Nikki's part-time live-in babysitter and had been forced to learn the rudiments of baby care. Nikki Skoros—Jeez, even thinking his family's name as part of hers made him shudder. Gorgeous, socialite Nikki couldn't be bothered to get up in the middle of the night. She always said to let Alex cry himself back to sleep.

Hell, what kind of a mother would do that? When Nikki took off with her BFFs, Kas had finally enlisted his sister-in-law's help in hiring a daytime nanny so he could work on the family's big project, a high-rise, multi-use tower in San Francisco.

Kas scrubbed his face with his free hand.

Why now, Athena? Why call my name in the middle of the night?

She was long gone and hated his guts.

Kas would be free in a few months. Free to do what? Pursue that strange, clairvoyant girl once again? Or was that a hopeless cause? What the hell was that bond they had all about?

Kas trudged up the carpeted stairs in his t-shirt and briefs, scrubbing his face as he did, his grizzled beard itching his face. He'd grown the beard simply because Nikki hated it. Childish, maybe, but his little rebellion made him grin.

Meanwhile, he tried to keep his thoughts of Athena at bay. Who knew what *she* was doing or who she was doing it with? She wouldn't answer his phone calls, wouldn't return his texts or reply to the college graduation card he'd sent her. Almost two years ago, he'd taken her virginity, fed her girlish fantasies of a knight-in-shining-armor, let her into his mind and heart, encouraged her to dream of a happily ever after. Then when she was expecting a commitment, he'd let her down, like dumping a ton of bricks on her head. She hated him, and he could understand why.

All this shit he'd gone through to appease Nikki's family's sense of honor and to ensure the Skoros name for little Alex, his nephew and the embodiment of his brother's genes.

For his brother's sake, Kas had done this.

He owed him that much.

The little boy, dark-haired and a pint-sized double for his

brother Alex, was standing at his crib, shaking the railing. He beamed when his big blue eyes alighted on Kas.

"Daddy!"

The toddler was speaking already, so bright and verbal. Just like his father.

Kas's heart twisted and melted. He couldn't help but smile at his son. His brother's genes, but *his* legal son. In every sense of the word, *his* son.

"Hey, bud, what're you doing up so early? It's four o'clock, for pete's sake. Don't you know I gotta work today?" His tone was mild and matter-of-fact, not scolding.

Little Alex had his brother's curly dark brown hair and even his impish nature. He was a natural charmer, just like Alex. Amazing, the power of genes.

"Daddy, up." The tyke smiled and looked at the bottle. "Daddy bring botta milk."

"You bet. Now, how did I know to do that?"

Kas lifted the little boy into his arms, felt his flannel sleeper for a wet diaper, made his assessment and the necessary change, then drew aside the curtains and settled down into the padded rocking chair next to the window.

Alex pawed at Kas's dark beard, his blue eyes searching the face of the man who'd cared for him most nights over the past two years.

"Yep, Daddy's beard."

"B-bid," the child said, frowning. "No bid, Daddy."

"Well, I'll get it cut. One of these days. Daddy's gotta go to work, gotta do a lot of things. Nanny Ruth and Granny's gonna sit today so Daddy can make some money in a big city called San Francisco. Gotta oversee final inspections today on the Skoros tower hotel floors." Kas spoke to the tyke as if the boy could understand him, enjoying the puzzled look on little Alex's face.

"Work, Daddy. Daddy gotta go to work."

"Yeah, gotta go to work."

Now Director of Operations for Skoros Enterprises, Kas had an hour drive ahead of him later that morning. If he was lucky, an hour. He oversaw the management of the new residential tower Skoros Enterprises had recently finished in San Francisco. The three-year project was nearing completion. At thirty stories, the Stargazer Tower was one of the tallest in the city.

"San . . . cisco." The baby, uncomprehending but trying to imitate Kas's speech, swiveled his head and looked out of the nearby window. The moonlight shone in his eyes. He pointed. "Star. Sing little star, Daddy."

Kas cleared his throat and did a hoarse rendition of *Twinkle, twinkle, little star.*

The toddler gave him a smile filled with little white teeth while twining his tiny pudgy fingers through Kas's beard with one hand and grabbing the bottle with his other. Transfixed by their mutual admiration, Kas inhaled Alex's scent — baby powder, shampooed hair, sweet baby flesh. Kas's voice seemed to soothe little Alex almost as much as the bottle of warm milk the baby now latched onto as if for his very life. He used a sippy cup during the day but still clung to his bottle at night. The little boy had a big appetite, just like his brother Alex, whose appetite for life, wine, pretty girls, adventure, and fun was like no one else's Kas'd ever known.

"Fill your belly, then go back to sleep, little guy. Your daddy needs a few more hours of shuteye. Okay?"

Your daddy.

Oh Alex, I wish you were here. You should be here. Not me. He's your son, not mine. But now he is mine. I just wish I could feel it. I love the little guy, but I'm not good at this. You would be so much better.

He looked down at the baby. Little Alex stopped sucking for a few seconds and, the nipple still in his mouth, smiled up at him, as if he'd read his father's mind and was showing his disagreement. Showing him that he *was* a good father.

Well, maybe I'm not traumatizing him too much. He seems content, even happy with his bumbling stand-in for a father.

Something felt strange, like a sense he was being watched. Kas turned his head and scanned the room. No one there. He didn't even know if Nikki was asleep in her room. He heard nothing. Yet, that sensation persisted.

Am I going nuts?

A moment later. *No, not nuts. You're not going mad, Kas. It's just me, being a voyeur, a Peeping Tom. Don't you hate that? Sorry, but I can't help it. I'm asleep but my subconscious goes where it wants. You know, The Flow. When I'm asleep, I'm its captive. It's taking me to you . . . and this little child.*

Kas grew still, listening to her voice. God help him, but he was longing to see her, touch her. *She's here, in my head. Athena? Is that really you?*

She'd been in his head before many times, Kas knew. During their jet ski ride on Folsom Lake. During the crash that had killed his brother, she'd been there, watching, feeling, attuned to his thoughts and emotions as everything was happening. He'd felt her presence, there in the smashed car. Was it possible again? Of course.

But why?

She hated him, and from all reports, from her mother to his mother—cousins and modern-day descendants of their incredible, ancient bloodline—Athena had moved on with her life. She had graduated from the Art Institute, moved in with a friend, was painting . . . had a boyfriend.

Kas's heart sank.

Silence. He dismissed the eerie sensation and her voice in his head with a soft snort. He'd be the last person on earth that Athena Butler would visit telepathically. Though God knew what she was capable of. He looked down at the handsome toddler in his arms. Little Alex had closed his eyes and was no longer sucking, his little mouth pursed still. Kas gazed at the little boy, then looked out of the window at the starry night.

I'm a stargazer.

And I'm going crazy.

CHAPTER THREE

Athena sat up in bed and rubbed her temples. It wasn't a dream. As had happened before, she'd traversed the distance, three thousand plus miles, to California, and had entered Kas's mind. Her clairvoyance had expanded into a kind of remote viewing. She could enter his mind from such a distance! For many years, she had to physically touch a person before she could enter that person's mind. Of course, with Kas there was a special connection. There always had been, from the first moment she'd seen him.

She couldn't stop it. But why was her subconscious so perverse?

Why enter the mind of a man she wanted to forget? And, blimey, why the creep with the helmet and visor?

Bollocks. From hell to heaven in one night.

Damn The Flow.

The telepathic night visits she occasionally had with her mother, she could understand. Her mother was a powerful descendant of what her Nonna called the Delphi Bloodline. But why did she have this special connection with Kas Skoros? It wasn't just the sexual thing — their brief sexual fling of five days couldn't explain why or how her mind could enter his. How long had it been since she'd even thought of him? Not long enough. The way she saw it, it was an unpleasant reminder of a man who'd caused her excruciating heartbreak.

Bloody hell, Kas Skoros.

Athena closed all thoughts of Kas and the child and looked over at the warm, sleeping form of Dan Grantham. His

11

slightly open mouth and soft snoring left her untouched. Outside the coverlet, his bare chest and arms drew her attention. Objectively, she studied his body. His muscles were long and refined, his flat chest hairless. Tall and slim, his legs stretched out under the covers. His lank dark-blond hair hung limply around his head, plastered down from the night's warm bed.

She liked him but didn't love him. She trusted him, too, but only so far. There was a streak in his character that was foreign to her. What would she call it? Callousness? Ruthlessness? Larcenous? Having grown up in a poor, working class family, he'd taken a huge risk in choosing art as a profession. Although she admired his talent and dedication, she realized that same passion had also marked him.

Dan was different from most other young men she'd met. He was a painter, like Athena, and devoted to his art. Easygoing most of the time, he could erupt in a rage when a painting wasn't going well. She'd seen him knock over a worktable that sent bottles of brushes and jars of paint flying in all directions. He'd often rail against the public's lack of appreciation for talented artists, the lack of money.

She gazed at his bare shoulder as he turned over to his side. He was tall and slender, not as muscular as Kas. A man who lifted nothing heavier than a canvas on a wooden stretcher.

"Go to sleep," he muttered. "You woke me up."

"Sorry, I had a bad dream." She patted his shoulder in apology.

As a lover, Dan was different than Kas, not as passionate or as gentle. Dan made love in a detached way, more mechanical, more egocentric. Still, her sexual experience with only two men hardly qualified her to be a judge. Erotic passion was lacking in Dan, though, that much she knew, for he seemed to spend it all when he painted. That was Dan's true love. His art.

Then again, it was hers, too.

12

Wasn't it?

Her mind kept churning. She sighed and silently rolled out of bed. In the apartment's little stainless-steel galley kitchen, she poured herself a full glass of cold water and drank it slowly. Her mind couldn't shake loose the memory of her telepathic visit into that stranger's dark mind. He got off stabbing people with icepicks?

Bloody hell!

Rising from the shadows of their open living room, Athena's current works in progress stood in rows around the walls like sentries at attention. She'd better get a little more sleep. They awaited her first thing in the morning.

She finished drinking the cold water, felt better as she censored her thoughts, and went back to bed.

CHAPTER FOUR

Four hours later, Athena left the loft apartment with Mikayla, her good friend from the Art Institute and her apartment mate these past two years, to have lunch at their favorite deli.

Athena smiled at her best friend. "This is my treat. To celebrate your new modeling job with City Chicks." The photo shoot with the prominent women's magazine would take her to the Caribbean island of St. Kitts for two weeks, and the photographer was a man Mikayla had worked with before and even dated for a while. Barry had taken the place of Mick's ex, Jerry. Athena teased that her next boyfriend would be a Larry or Harry.

Mikayla was practically skipping beside her. "Okay, but your next sale is my treat."

Athena worked part-time at nearby Visions Gallery in exchange for having the owners exhibit her original artwork. Once in a while, one of her one-of-a-kind paintings sold for enough money to pay her bills for a month or two.

She laughed. "Okay, that's one way to get out of it."

Mikayla playfully slapped her arm. "C'mon now, you sold one just a week ago."

"No, more like last month."

"What about those pastiches you paint? You make a lot more money from those, don't you?" Mikayla kept eyeing a car that had slowed alongside of them.

"I'm waiting for Martin to call us together and give us another assignment. You know how that is." Athena stopped as she recognized the car. Detective Ochoa's unmarked police car pulled up along the curb where the two young women were walking. Her flat mate paused with her and frowned.

"That's a cop," said Mikayla, "Now what? Just because I'm African American, he wants to bust my chops?"

"No, no, don't be so paranoid, Mick. It's that homicide detective I used to do sketches for a couple of years ago. I don't know if they ever caught the bloody wanker, that killer of young girls. I did sketches for a couple of eyewitnesses who saw a man in a van. The descriptions, unfortunately, were too general to be of much help."

Lying to her friend of four years made her twinge with guilt, but telling Mikayla the truth would've complicated their friendship. Not because Mikayla wouldn't have believed her. It was always easy to prove to someone that she was indeed clairvoyant. But Mick would have resented Athena's lying to her for the past four years—since midway through art school, when they'd grown closer and had shared intimate secrets with each other. Athena's most important secret—her clairvoyant power—was the one she'd kept hidden. And she'd explained her previous consultation work with the cops as a part-time sketch artist.

Mikayla was holding her ground. "Hey, listen, if you ask me, you're making enough money doing those pastiches. Why get involved with the cops?"

Athena shrugged lamely. "I really don't mind helping them, Mick. I'm just one of their sketch artists. And the hourly pay helps pay for our nights out. Which you find awesome."

Mick grinned. "Well, if you put it that way . . ."

Detective Ochoa parked his unmarked sedan curbside, smiled and called her over, so Athena couldn't see any way out of the meeting. A part of her was curious, too. Almost three years had passed since the D.C. Metro police had started looking for that serial killer, less time since Athena and her mother had identified a possible suspect. She hadn't seen Ochoa in over two years, not since she'd used psychometry and touched those jackets to get a small glimpse into that killer's twisted mind. Athena hadn't heard from either Ochoa or Detective Palomino since her parents had left D.C. for her father's Consular General posting in Milan, Italy.

Now, staring at the handsome Hispanic man and his sudden appearance in his unmarked sedan, Athena noted the dusting of gray at his temples, the extra few lines on his face. Evidently, the job had taken a toll on him. Now, too, she had to brush off her friend with another white lie.

"It's hard to explain, Mick. It's interesting work, and who knows, I might help them catch a bad guy."

Mikayla looked a little perplexed but then shrugged. "Well, they could've just called. Why show up like this? The neighbors all know he's a cop." They both glanced around their short side street, Athena pausing to gaze for a moment at a motorcyclist idling in front of the coffee shop across the street. Finally, her friend shrugged in an exaggerated fashion, clearly put out by the cop's intrusion. "Your call, Thena. I'll see you and Dan later tonight, 'kay?"

Athena nodded, then slid into Ochoa's passenger seat and waved at her friend out of the open window. Now that Jerry was a fading memory but Mick's new guy, Barry, hadn't yet declared exclusivity, her flat mate was always anxious, lonely and on the prowl. She and Dan had agreed to accompany Mick to a club that night. A club where Barry was known to hang out.

"Yes, see you later."

"Seven? First round of drinks, I'm treating."

"Sounds good. Wait for me if I'm a little late from work." Athena waved at her as Ochoa pulled away from the curb.

Her shift at Martin Larsen's gallery in Georgetown, just blocks away, began at two. Martin and his partner had opened a thriving business with Genuine Pastiches of the World's Greatest Paintings, and they'd enlisted Athena and Dan as two of their ten or so pastiche painters. Athena had reassured her parents that pastiches were not forgeries but were good quality, legal copies of famous paintings, signed by the pastiche painter. Some of their pastiches sold for fifty thousand dollars, a steal if you considered the actual original by Cezanne or Monet sold in the tens of millions. Of course, the pastiche painters had to split the price with Martin and the other gallery owner.

Mick gave her a hearty thumbs up and walked away on her stilettos. After lunch, she had a modeling audition for another magazine that kept her on their speed dial. But at twenty-six, she was doing less modeling and more interior designing, which was her major at the Art Institute. Already, the writing was on the wall. Next stop, start her own modeling or interior design business. Mikayla had often spoken of doing one or the other but her main goal, Athena knew, was to land a guy. Hook, line and sinker.

Anyway, that night would be an all-out, let-down-her-hair blast. Athena and Dan would nurse their Moscow Mules and halfheartedly gyrate among the crowd on the dance floor as Mikayla played her nonchalant role with Barry. Max's was their favorite watering hole. The drinks were strong, the music throbbing and the dance floor, jamming. Best part, the club was in Georgetown, four blocks from their loft. Dan would drive over from Baltimore and spend the weekend with her, and the two would assess the attributes of yet another one of Mikayla's conquests.

The car sped off and she turned to Detective Ochoa, who shot her an apologetic but friendly smile. "I better be back in time, Detective. My shift at the Visions Gallery starts at two. I can't be late."

"No problem, Athena, I'll have you back. We have a one-hour window to get this done. Actually, a little less."

"Get what done?" she asked, tossing her hobo bag in the back seat. Ochoa was a good-looking man in his forties, a dedicated cop and investigator. Athena liked him better than his partner, the older dour Lieutenant Gino Palomino. Ochoa was easy to talk to, so even if she hadn't seen or spoken to him in over two years, they fell into an easy and cordial familiarity.

"Our Person of Interest is in Interrogation with his attorney, as we speak. We got a search warrant for his new residence. The older brother, I mean, not our prime suspect, the younger brother. He's still in the wind. I'm talking about that serial killer case, getting colder every year. Y'know, the two brothers. With the electrical business and the black vans. The older brother sold their house and literally moved into his shop. Our new warrant covers this new residence site. I know, it's a stretch, but it's all we got. We're hoping you can look around and tell us what you see. Anything you get, we're that hungry." He looked over at her and added, "You should consider becoming a cop. Do art on the side."

Athena had to laugh. "No, thanks. I love beauty, not blood and bullets. Does your captain know I'm doing this?" Palomino's and Ochoa's captain disapproved of their use of psychics as police consultants.

Noncommittal, Ochoa said nothing.

"Oh, I see," she said. "This must be on the QT. You're taking me to the search site." Ochoa nodded as he shot her a glance.

"Hope you don't mind, Athena. We wouldn't do this, but we're jammed. If this doesn't get solved in the next month, it goes into the basement archives. Cold case. End of story. A serial killer gets off."

The detective drove in silence while Athena's mind wandered into the past. She mused over her first encounter two and a half years earlier with Dan Grantham.

Athena's first job when she graduated the Art Institute was painting pastiches for Martin's business and its wealthy clientele. At thirty to fifty thousand a pop, she could do two a year and pay many of her bills. And still have time to paint her own original portraits and landscapes. The gallery work was part-time and available for all the pastiche painters in Martin's GPWGP group. Most had enough sales of their own work, however, to avoid selling in the gallery. But Athena needed the work to satisfy her work-visa. If she couldn't renew her visa, it was back to merry ol' England for her.

Something — or someone — was holding her in the States. It was a tug she didn't like to think about, so Martin's pastiche work was a good excuse to stay.

When she looked up at their surroundings, she realized how far they'd traveled in about twenty minutes. They'd gone south and then east on Ninety-five on the outer Beltway and had veered off on Massachusetts Avenue in the heart of the industrial section. Ochoa then bypassed Union Station on his way north towards New York Avenue. Down the street from the Greyhound Bus Station, Ochoa pulled into a side street that housed a small industrial park. The neighborhood wasn't that seedy, just full of tradesmen's businesses, most of which were well maintained and kept clean of street debris.

A green entrance door next to two large black metal garage doors led to his Person of Interest's electrician's shop. Ace Electrical was the shop name, she noted. Off East First Street. Ochoa had keys to the business' main door, but kept his hand resting on his hip holster, his sports jacket tucked aside to reveal both his badge and gun. According to the older brother, whose name Ochoa and Detective Palomino had never revealed, all the panel trucks were out on calls at this time of day, so Ochoa expected no interruptions to their search.

"Don't worry, Athena. The owner's not here. He's down at Headquarters."

Relaxing a little at the news, she followed him inside the small lobby or main reception room, which was painted steel gray and held just a scuffed wooden settee along one wall. One long corridor went west to both large garage bays, empty now but lined with counters and shelves filled with boxes, which she assumed contained electrical supplies. Her heart began to pound, nerve endings sparking. She watched Ochoa quickly check the rooms to their left. There was a subtle miasma of cold, heartless efficiency about the place. And something else that made her uneasy.

"Office, supply room, restroom, small staff room," he rattled off, sounding half bored. "We wondered why he sold off their house. It was in his and his younger brother's names. The older brother's claimed legal fees and such, but we think he's funneling money to our prime suspect, who's been on the run for over two years now. How, we don't know. We're checking his accounts, emails, phone calls. Nothing going abroad over wire or paper. Palomino thinks he's paying couriers to take the brother what he needs—new ID, passport, money. In exchange for a free ticket to Europe."

Athena listened to Ochoa's summary of their fugitive tracking attempts and nodded, then followed him into an office off the lobby, which he entered. There was a metal desk, a swivel chair along one wall, and four black metal file cabinets along the other. A print and fax machine sat on one table. This electrical company looked like a small but prosperous operation.

She touched one of the two metal desks. A wave of nausea assailed her, causing her to stare longer at the desk, chair and space around it. No vision came to her, however.

Ochoa began to exit the office. "We checked out the computer and phone lines, the files, everything. Nothing irregular here. The other three rooms on the east side of this lobby are new. He converted one into a bedroom, another into a sitting room, the third, a private bathroom. Come with me, you'll see." Ochoa rattled on, clearly nervous about this search. "Let's speed it up a bit. We're running out of time. He's ready to sue the precinct for harassment, so this is our last shot at him and any link to his younger brother. They're hoping we'll go away and this'll all blow over. We'll forget about them and pursue other leads. Except right now, there are no other leads. Let's concentrate on those three private rooms."

Ochoa stared at her. "You okay, Athena?" She frowned but nodded. He glanced at his watch. "You've got ten minutes."

Her ears throbbed. Something wasn't right, but she followed him to the rooms that served as an apartment for the owner.

They entered the bedroom, about twelve by twelve, bearing one window along what she assumed was the back alleyway. The stacked bunk beds struck her as odd, as did the double-wide dresser. The wood was newly painted, probably hardwood and appearing sturdily built. There was a large wide mirror over the dresser. Stuck along the frame were photos of the two brothers as children and teenagers; none of them as adults. Both brothers had dark hair, unsmiling faces, dimpled chins. Along one wall was one junior-size desk with a small swivel chair and a small bookcase stacked with children's books and games.

"Go ahead, Athena, touch, meditate. Do whatever you do."

Athena nodded reluctantly. "Strange, almost like the older brother's trying to recreate a childhood bedroom that the two brothers might've shared."

"Yeah, crazy, huh?"

Two years earlier, she'd heard from the detectives about the brothers' horribly abusive childhood, the death of their parents in a household fire one night. Their background had inspired the homicide detectives to focus on them from the start of their investigation, in part because the electrical business had a bay full of black panel trucks, a type of vehicle seen by a few witnesses at the scenes of the kidnappings.

However, no physical evidence was ever found in their panel trucks to link either brother to the murders of those schoolgirls. What she and her mother had seen clairvoyantly while touching the older brother's jacket was, of course, inadmissible evidence.

Overcoming her revulsion at the brothers' apparently dysfunctional relationship, Athena moved forward into the bedroom and began touching the bedspreads and opening the drawers of the dresser. The three large drawers on each side were full of clothes, neatly folded and stacked — top drawer, underwear; middle drawer, tee shirts; bottom drawer, folded jeans and knit workout suits. All the clothes in the left-hand drawers appeared newly bought and in sizes that would fit a medium-sized man.

Almost as if the older brother, the electrical company's owner, was taunting the cops. He was supposedly taller and heftier than his younger brother. *Try to get me on these clothes,* he was saying. *No law against buying clothes in a different size, is there?*

She studied the photos, the haunted eyes of both brothers fighting to survive their vicious parents. The younger boy's eyes burnt with fear, whereas the older boy's smiles were almost grimaces. Somewhere along the way, their fears must have morphed into rage and hatred. Ochoa suspected they got revenge on their parents in that fire and now their mission was, what? Get revenge on society? Kill, just like their parents tried to kill them? They'd picked poor girls, throwaway kids, kids with little chance of a normal life. What for? To put them out of their misery?

They'd both been traumatized, clearly. But who understood such a twisted outlook? Certainly not her.

Then she began to see . . .

Almost in a trance, she went to the sitting room next door, as if accompanying the older brother on his usual routine. She touched the TV, sat on the sofa, ran her fingers along the shelves filled with their childhood paraphernalia—toy cars and trains, action figures, comics. But the trappings of childhood were all newly bought. She stood there, absorbing the truth, suppressing a giant sob growing deep within her. Yes. The older brother had reconstructed their childhood. An idealized childhood. A safe childhood, one they had never experienced. But one thing was missing.

The man's younger brother. She felt his presence, however, in everything she touched.

"He's been here." She pointed around the small sitting room. "He's all over this room."

"How can this be? We've had hidden surveillance cameras on this shop for the past year. The younger brother has never turned up."

Athena shook her head. "I don't know, Detective. I just sense he's been here."

A quick tour of the bathroom showed her evidence of one man's use, but there were two soap dishes, two bottles of shampoo, two jars of aftershave lotion on the counter, two toothbrushes in the medicine cabinet, one still in its store box. "And in here, too. I feel him, his presence, his rage. But strangely, mostly his fear. He's trying to please his older brother. How, I don't know."

Ochoa watched her closely. "His fear? The younger brother's a killer and he's afraid?"

"Oh yes, fear is what makes him act, Detective. The fear goes away when he kills. But only for a while. Then it comes back." She couldn't help but shiver. So horrible, so sad, that kind of human motivation. The killer's psyche was destroyed as a child and he would never be normal again. Never.

Ochoa joined her as she walked back to the lobby in a kind

of daze. Her stomach was in turmoil, like a cauldron of hot acid. The place had become warm and stifling. She had a craving for fresh, cool air.

"I've got to get out of here, Detective." No sooner had she turned her back than the main door opened. Two men stood there, the taller of the two in a suit and lightweight coat, an older man with graying temples. The youngerf man was in a dark-blue windbreaker, plaid shirt and jeans and wearing a New York Yankees baseball cap. He had a cleft chin, just like the man she'd seen in the mirror when she'd handled that jacket over two years ago.

The older brother of the killer.

CHAPTER FIVE

"You finished, Detective?" The older man in the suit held up his cell phone and took a photo of Ochoa and Athena. "For our lawsuit, to verify the date and time you and Palomino's team encroached again upon my client's right to privacy. Now who is this? If she's a reporter and any of this winds up in print, we'll have your badge. We'll add defamation of character and libel to our list of rights violations."

Ochoa took a deep breath and glanced over at Athena, then swung hooded dark-eyed gaze back at their Person of Interest and his attorney.

"This is Sergeant Jane Wilkes. Internal Affairs, just making sure we're doing everything by the book. We're done here." Ochoa ushered Athena to the front door.

As the older brother and his attorney stood aside, both radiating looks of outrage and venom, Athena hastened by them. Her side look at the older brother was quick, but what she saw astonished her. He was smiling at her, as if telegraphing his arrogance and superiority. Their arms brushed accidentally. He was thinking *I'm too fucking smart for all you morons. You'll never get him.*

Outside, she hurried with Ochoa to his car parked along the side street. As they approached, Ochoa swore. Someone had keyed the side of his car. The man in front of the business next door, a mechanic shop, saluted them with a heavy dose of sarcasm.

Ochoa scowled, his hand automatically flying to his shoulder holster. The guy by the mechanics shop disappeared inside. "Sonuvabitch! Let's get outa here. Sorry about the run-in. Palomino said he'd try to keep them until one-thirty." He looked at his watch. "It's only one-twenty-five. Dammit, I should've gotten a heads-up call." He took out his cell phone, examined it and swore again. "Battery's dead. I'm so sorry, Athena."

They drove as far as the Beltway around D.C. before Ochoa finally asked her what she'd seen. Her silence thus far had seemed discouraging to him, she realized. How little he realized that she was rattled to her core. Her insides couldn't stop shaking. She couldn't trust her voice, so she kept silent.

Ochoa glanced over at her. "This was a bust, huh? Except you say the younger brother's been there?" A little distracted by the traffic, he steered them back onto the ring road.

Athena blew air dramatically out of her cheeks before she spoke, as if she'd been holding her breath underwater, like a freediving snorkeler. She supposed she'd been trying not to breathe the toxic air of those living spaces inside the electrical shop—as though the pathological air the two brothers breathed in and out might infect her as well, as if each molecule of oxygen contained a pathogen of madness.

Oh God, I'm going to lose my bloody mind if I keep helping the cops.

"The only words I can think of right now . . . sick, twisted, pathetic."

"That's all?" Ochoa shot her an ironic smile. "Didn't take a psychic to draw that conclusion."

"No, I saw him bringing his younger brother home. That's all he's been living for. He had a plan. The fake papers, ID, money—all part of his plan. I think his brother's back."

"Then we'll keep surveillance on the place, twenty-four-seven. We know what the sonuvabitch looks like. He makes a move on that shop, we'll get him."

Athena glanced at Ochoa, whose mouth had thinned with

frustration and anger. "I don't think you'll know him."

"What do you mean, we won't know him? We've got photos of the bastard, his life history. Even his fingerprints. If surveillance picks him up, we'll be on him like hawks."

"Detective, that bedroom, everything was all staged. The men's clothes, the two shaving lotions. The two of everything. I think the older brother is just taunting the police. Besides, I think the younger brother, the killer, looks very different. I couldn't see anything, but I think he's gotten plastic surgery. You won't know him from your . . ." She thought a moment. She'd seen something by that desk. A vision came through, then quickly evaporated like smoke. *Not possible.* " . . . from your pizza delivery guy. Or the waitress at your favorite diner."

Ochoa's knuckles turned white as his hands tightened on the steering wheel. "What're you telling me, Athena? You mean, the surgery to change his looks is that extreme?"

"Yes, extreme. I saw the back of a woman's head. Or what appeared to be a woman. Long hair, a flash of makeup. Red lipstick. He's in disguise but I couldn't see his . . . or her face. I'm so sorry."

Ochoa's jaw dropped. "You gotta be shitting me. He'd go to such a length?"

All Athena could do was shrug in wonderment and horror. Human beings . . . Would she ever understand them? Did she even want to? Doing this kind of criminal investigation work was totally out of her comfort zone. A wave of nausea rippled through her again. Her stomach was a mess. She wanted to vomit. Forget lunch today.

"I got just a flash. Her head was turned, but she had long, dark brown hair. Down past her shoulders in a low ponytail. I could be wrong, but regardless, Detective, your prime suspect won't look the same. His face, his total appearance will be different. Don't rely on those old photos."

"Well, if you're right, Athena, then so much for facial rec software. And our fugitive database." In front of the Visions Gallery, Ochoa stopped at the curb, his expression contorted in disbelief, muttering under his breath in Spanish. "If I can get permission, I'll keep the surveillance going. We might get lucky."

A minute later, the realization hit Athena. *Bloody hell!* The older brother now had a photo of her! How long before his attorney discovered who she really was?

Athena looked over at the detective. "They saw me. They'll find out who I really am, won't they? Could I be in danger?"

Ochoa said nothing. His grim expression said everything. "No, I told them you were a cop with Internal Affairs. That should satisfy them."

Athena clasped his shoulder. Ochoa was lying. He knew he'd made a mistake by taking her to the electrician's shop. A critical timing mistake. His captain was going to chew his ass, and Palomino wasn't going to defend Ochoa's decision. The search was tainted, and once the attorney had a meeting with the homicide captain, Ochoa would be removed from the case and he knew the captain would refuse to approve surveillance on the electrical shop. The case was as good as dead.

Deader than a door nail.

A heartbeat later Athena gasped. Oh God, what had she gotten herself into? Her mother had warned her. Stay away from the police. Don't help them anymore. It's too dangerous.

Yet her mother continued to work with the *carabiniere* in Milano. It was her calling, she said. That was why God gave her such a gift.

Some gift, all right.
Bollocks.

CHAPTER SIX

A thena's nerves hummed like electrical wires, more so even than during the attack on the British Embassy over two years before. Or the time the Embassy's security team had used her as bait outside of Martin's gallery in order to expose a terrorist cell plotting an attack during the Prime Minister's visit. Now, two weeks after her encounter with Detective Ochoa, she was sitting next to Dan Grantham in the Visions Gallery in Georgetown, watching intently as each pastiche was unveiled on its large tripod stand. There were four, ready to be viewed and either criticized or praised by the artists present today. She could barely concentrate on the unveiling even though the event used to be something she once enjoyed.

Dan held her hand and smiled at her encouragingly as Martin Larson and his partner approached the stand to the left of her painting. It held Dan's latest pastiche, Paul Gauguin's self-portrait in his old Breton clothes. An anonymous client had commissioned it and was willing to pay dearly for it. Athena had seen it during a private unveiling in Dan's apartment the day before. The painting's colors were bold, as were its brush strokes and daring outlines. And it was a magnificent copy.

Dan was a skilled and gifted painter. She was grateful to have him as her boyfriend but ... he wasn't Kas—no, don't even go there. In her mind, she scraped off all memory of Kas Skoros with her trowel, like a mistake in paint on one of her canvases.

She turned her attention instead to the unveiling. With a

flourish, Martin Larson unveiled the Gauguin pastiche and the assembled painters in the Visions Gallery's private backroom all murmured their approval. A few even gasped their admiration aloud. Everyone there applauded and approved it unanimously. If a copy didn't pass muster with Martin, his uncle and the other pastiche painters, it was rejected and the painter could either toss it or go back to the drawing board, so to speak, to improve it. The other painters always obliged with tips for improving a pastiche that didn't pass their scrutiny. Athena's first pastiche had been sent back twice.

Dan, grinning from ear to ear, clicked his crystal flute of champagne against Athena's glass. "Good," he said, "that took me two hundred hours of painstaking work."

"Perfection," she said to him. While everyone applauded, Dan stood and, a little embarrassed at the attention, modestly nodded and sat down.

Martin now approached Athena's pastiche. Three had passed inspection with Martin's pastiche group, but the GPWGP painters were not about to let down their standards.

"Let's look at Edouard Manet's *The Dead Toreador* by our youngest painter, Athena Butler. As you all know, the perspective of the toreador's body was unusual for its time. Avant-garde for even the French Impressionists."

Martin's brows rose in anticipation. He hadn't yet seen her painting, so Athena was bracing herself for criticism and a possible flat-out rejection. He might soften the blow with suggestions for how she could improve the masterwork copy, but she was pleased, herself, with the outcome. Several trips to study the original painting at the National Gallery of Art in D.C. had proved their worth in time and energy.

Martin turned around and carefully removed the cloth cover. Hums of surprise and approval followed as the entire painting came into view. She'd reworked the main background color several times, but her practice work with the chiaroscuro technique two years earlier had helped her duplicate what she thought Manet had intended. A dark, solemn portrayal of a Spanish hero's death. The world of *La Corrida* had transfixed Manet for some reason, and this was one of several paintings he'd done on the subject.

Dan leaned over. "Awesome," he whispered, "Just awesome."

"Studying the original close-up in person, helps," she said, "Next one, if I get the choice, will be *Plum Brandy*. That's also at the National Gallery."

Dan leaned over to whisper. "Do we ever get a choice? It's what the rich want, not what we want to do." He looked and sounded resentful. "We're paid little more than house painters."

Still, despite his sour look, Dan stood up and applauded along with the others. Athena couldn't help but beam at her peers' approval. She stood likewise, scanned the group, and smiled her thanks.

"What about taking on Manet's *Bar at the Folies-Bergere*?" Martin asked her when the applause had died down. Heads turned her way. "We've been offered a hundred and fifty thousand for anyone who can paint a reproduction of Manet's most famous barmaid."

Holy crap. Her cut would be seventy-five thousand! *A Bar at the Folies-Bergere* was considered Manet's masterpiece. It was a highly complex and skillfully executed painting with reflections in a large mirror behind the pretty blonde barmaid. Athena empathized with the master's subject, a young French girl stuck in a thankless, dead-end job. Like the girl, perhaps, Athena wanted to excel at something that she was passionate about. But was she ready to paint a copy of Manet's masterpiece?

Indeed, no.

"At some point, I'd like to tackle it," she confessed, "but not yet, Martin. I have a lot of learning to do before then. Has anyone put in an order for *Plum Brandy*? I think I can manage that one."

Martin smiled knowingly and nodded. "I'll have to check my stack of orders, Athena, and let you know. I know that painting. I've seen it in the National Gallery. The current value for the original, I believe, is fifty million. Maybe there's a collector who'd be willing to pay a hundred thousand for the pastiche. Maybe two hundred thousand if a perfect match."

That elicited a loud hum of murmurs in the backroom. The other painters, including her old painting instructor at the Art Institute, Professor White, nodded in agreement with Martin, as if expressing their grave doubts that an authentic copy of Manet's masterpiece could be made, but a minor work was indeed possible. Each pastiche painter had his or her own area of expertise and individual famous master artist. They knew there were different classes and qualities of paintings, even by the same artist.

Martin added his own doubts. "We all have the passion for great art, but the question is, do we have the skill to do an exact copy of a great painting?"

Everyone nodded soberly, including Athena.

Painting was her passion. Her clairvoyance she'd kept a secret from nearly everyone, including both Mikayla and Dan. That was all she needed to end another relationship, a young man freaking out and thinking she was crazy or, at best, delusional. She'd read him enough to know he liked her very much, even loved her a little in his own distracted, self-absorbed way. True intimacy and deep love set one up for heartbreak.

Was she willing to take that giant leap again . . . and fall madly and truly in love?

Bloody hell no!

No, that's over and done with. Ah well, what do the Americans say, if you can't be with the one you love, then love the one you're with. Good ol' practical American logic. That's probably how Dan feels, too.

"Another announcement," he said, "Meanwhile, the champagne's going flat."

Athena looked up at Martin and his partner, Mark, co-owners of GPWGP.

"I think we've reached a milestone in our business," Martin announced to the group. "In the three years of our existence, GPWGP has sold nearly one hundred pastiches and has made for its incredibly gifted painters collectively over three million dollars."

Applause and cheers followed. Not surprisingly, there were many very wealthy art lovers and collectors in the D.C. area. The cut to the painters had climbed to fifty percent, so when the average pastiche sold for fifty or sixty thousand, the painter's cut was half or up to thirty thousand. Of course, each one took time, talent and effort. Sometimes a pastiche would take a painter up to three, even six months to complete. Many had to be improved upon several times. Seldom did a painter get it exactly right the first time. It was painstaking work and required total concentration.

Yet each effort that passed inspection always sold, usually for Martin's listed price. The painter's cut was generous, she felt. All in all, Athena wasn't sure why Dan resented this. Was greed beginning to rear its ugly head?

"And we're expanding, so good news and bad news. The good news. A gallery in San Francisco has requested a least one painting from each of you who are specialists in the French Impressionists and French Romantics. The owners wish to stock their new gallery with at least twenty pastiches in a promotional campaign to attract high-end collectors on the West Coast." Martin paused dramatically for effect while his partner and lover, Mark, clapped him on the shoulder.

"The bad news?"

Martin sighed. "The bad news is, the owners want these twenty paintings in two months. Two months. August first, to be exact. However, they'll pay the airfare and hotel stays for the painters who would like to attend the showcase in person, and they've agreed to a twenty-five, twenty-five commission with us. That means a fifty percent split with the artists. And because it's San Francisco, land of the millionaire computer nerds, we'll be asking top dollar for our pastiches."

Something niggled at the back of Athena's mind. She raised her hand.

"What's the name of this gallery?"

"The Stargazer Gallery. It's located close to the George Moscone Convention Center, I believe, south of Market in the so-called SOMA district. The gallery is on the ground floor of a new residential tower. I'm planning to go ahead to arrange things, the displays and promotions. How many of you would like to take part in this? I need to let the owners know as soon as possible. I'll need your promo photos, too, your bio sheets and your painting credits. I sincerely hope we can get together a group of at least six or eight. The time commitment would be about three days, longer if we want to stay in San Francisco and sightsee."

Martin held up a clipboard and wrote down the names of those who raised their hands. Both Athena and Dan volunteered. "This is superb, divine. Come up and sign this commission contract. The Stargazer Gallery owners will let you decide which painting to do—"

As she and Dan picked their way to the front, Dan snickered. "Well, we finally get some perks from this outfit. I could do with a couple of days or even a week in California. All expenses paid, thank you. Let's go find a warm beach while we're there, lounge around and drink Margaritas."

Athena smiled. "We'd have to go to southern California to find that warm beach. San Francisco can be cold in the summer, from what my parents told me."

She hadn't told him that she'd fallen in love with a handsome Greek American sheriff's deputy in the Sierra foothills during her visit to California two and a half years earlier.

"Oh yeah," Dan said, "what did Mark Twain say about San Francisco?"

She smiled. "I don't know."

"The summer he spent there was the coldest winter he'd ever experienced," he supplied. "We'll have to bundle up."

She approached and shook Martin's hand and offered him congratulations on finding another venue for sales. Then she accepted his hug. When he let go, she saw in Martin's blue eyes and read in his mind his genuine admiration for her talent. That pleased her immensely.

"So which Manet?" Martin asked her.

"The *Plum Brandy*, or maybe *Olympia*," she said, waffling a little. It might be time to try one of Manet's most famous nudes. "Maybe both," she added.

"In two months?" Martin looked dubious. "You'd have to work nonstop."

Athena shrugged. "I have nothing else to do, do I?"

She printed her name on the contract, hesitated a moment, and then wrote the titles of Manet's paintings. *The Plum* and *Olympia*. One of Manet's most famous nudes would be her greatest challenge so far in contrasting light and texture. The other, a study of a young woman's mood as she sat in a Parisian café with her brandy-soaked plum, was not that different from several portraits she'd already painted—including the two portraits of the Skoros brothers, Alex and Kas. Flesh tones and facial expressions that tugged at one's heartstrings.

"I'll try to do both."

Martin's jaw dropped teasingly but his eyes twinkled. "Well, go for it, girl. People absolutely adore both paintings." To the room, he announced, "Athena's going to paint *Olympia* and *The Plum*."

She smiled to herself as she signed at the bottom of the contract page. No doubt about it, her confidence in herself as a painter had made a leap forward. But, omigod, over the next two months she and Dan were going to paint their asses off.

Distracted, she turned around to face the room full of fellow artists. She could tell they approved her choice of Manet's work. It was one thing she liked about this group, their support of and encouragement for each other. Her gaze around the room paused at Doctor White. Her painting professor at the Art Institute, the Cezanne specialist of the group, was beaming with pride. They nodded at each other. What could be more complete a triumph than this? Her heart burst with unfettered happiness. Then a healthy dose of self-doubt made her heart skip. She hadn't painted them yet. Two pastiches in two months meant all her work and free time would be devoted to creating near perfect duplications.

Yes, this is what I was born to do. I was born to paint beautiful art.

A few of her fellow artists approached and wished her well. When they had drifted away towards the refreshment table, anxiety seized her, leaving her breathless.

Olympia? One of Manet's best? Has all this approval gone to my head? Dear lord, what was I thinking?

Briskly, Dan appeared in front of her.

"After this I want to buy you dinner. French, in honor of Monsieurs Manet and Gauguin? Or steaks, to fit our appetite for hard work. Boy, are we gluttons for punishment?"

She laughed. Thank heavens he was nice and tall. And handsome. And not afraid to speak his mind. She liked him very much. He was a fellow artist who shared her passion, who understood what it took to fall in love with something and never let it go.

"Steaks. I'm famished. By the way, which Gauguin did you choose to do?"

"The Tahitian one, the one that starts with *Nafea*. The title of the painting translates to *when will you marry?*

"Hm, I don't think I know that one," she said.

"Yes, you do. I showed you a print of it. It sold earlier this year for three hundred million to a Qatari sheikh. The highest amount for an original French Impressionist painting, and it goes into his private collection. A Swiss collector sold it to the sheikh. Great colors and a sublime composition. And no one gets to see it except the sheikh and his pals." Dan held out a flute of champagne for her before taking a hearty swallow from his glass. "Hey, you're taking a leap of faith. I will, too. Guess it won't hurt to emphasize the fact that the original is the highest paid painting of all time."

They clicked glasses. "Good idea, Dan. Here's to our leap!" Then she added, "We have a lot on our plates, don't we?"

"Yes, mam'selle, that we do." Dan winked "But here's to taking leaps of faith in ourselves." They clicked glasses again and laughed together. Athena shook her head as the reality of their situation took hold. "What if we crash and burn?"

"Uh-uh, no talk like that," he said, "We can do it. We're just as talented as Gauguin and Manet. No one thought much of their paintings while they were alive. Hell, look at their legacy now. Three hundred million. Wow."

Athena grinned. "Well, maybe in a hundred and fifty years, someone will pay a couple million for one of our original works. Even so, it most certainly won't do us any good at that point." Her smile changed. "Meanwhile, while we're waiting for a hundred and fifty years to pass by, come back to my place and I'll show you my etchings. Might be our last chance in two months to, you know, fool around. Or as Mick says, last chance to get down and dirty."

She seductively pressed her breasts against his arm. Tempted to read his mind, she nevertheless closed off that channel. A part of her didn't want to know. Besides, knowing Dan, she already knew what images would spring to his mind.

Understanding lit his face. His hand stroked her shoulder as he leaned over and kissed her ear. "I'm all for that. After tonight, we're living like monks."

CHAPTER SEVEN

His bike parked at the curb, Dave — alias Shawna — sat on the apartment building's stoop across the street from the Visions Gallery. The same gallery in posh Georgetown where he'd followed that fucking cop after his search of Sam's shop the week before. That day last week he'd gotten a call to his burner cell phone — the one his brother said to carry and dispose of every week. The call told him the damned cop, Ochoa, was hot-trotting his way over to the shop with a search warrant. So Dave, disguised as his new persona Shawna in full leathers and black visor helmet, had followed the cop's unmarked car from the Metro Police Station to Georgetown. Almost three years after their investigation, Palomino and Ochoa were at it again. Sam already knew about the two not-so-hidden surveillance cameras watching his shop and his every move. He and his tradesmen neighbors had destroyed the cameras repeatedly, sneaking up on them with black masks and hoodies on in the dark of night. So far, the cameras had been replaced twice.

In Georgetown, Dave had quickly pulled over to the side of the street when the cop unexpectedly stopped to pick up a chick. Then, even more surprising, the blonde girl went with the homicide detective to his brother's place, Ace Electrical.

On his burner phone with Sam that day last week, Dave had given a running commentary on how long the detective and the girl had searched Sam's shop. Using the cover of a motorcycle shop down the street, he'd watched and waited.

Watched as Sam and his attorney braked to a stop in the lawyer's Cad. Watched as Sam glanced his way and nodded. Then made his move after they came out, Ochoa looking fit to be tied and the girl looking green around the gills. This time, very carefully, Dave stayed two car lengths behind and followed them back to Georgetown on his motorcycle. To the Visions Gallery.

Later, the photo Sam's attorney had taken of Ochoa and the girl cinched it. Didn't take much investigating of his own until the damned lawyer finally earned his keep. The girl turned out to be a stupid artist who did sketches for the cops. So what the hell had she sketched while Ochoa was pawing among Sam's things? She didn't even have a sketch pad with her.

A little more digging and bribing one of the police station custodians turned up something else for Sam's lawyer, something that Dave and Sam didn't expect. The blonde chick was thought to be a psychic, for chrissakes. That was what the guys in the homicide squad were saying, according to a night custodian who'd passed on the rumor to Sam's lawyer. She sometimes consulted with Palomino and Ochoa's team of detectives. Dave could've pissed his pants. A freakin' sideshow psycho.

Dude, how nuts can those fuckin' cops be?

"What do I do, Sam?" Dave had asked Sam several days later after their lawyer found out who the chick really was.

"Keep an eye on her," Sam had told him. "See if she meets up with the cops again. If she does, let me know. She might be a threat."

"How?" he'd asked. Sam always thought two steps ahead of him, Dave figured. He was one smart guy.

"The psychic chick might know more than we think. Why else would the cops use her?"

Dave inhaled from his worn-down cigarette, then crushed it underfoot with his boot. So far, nothing. Nothing but going from the girl's apartment to the gallery, back and forth. Sometimes to the grocery store, or a guy would come over and they'd walk to a restaurant on Wisconsin or M Street. Dullsville!

Now, across the street from the Visions Gallery, his girl disguise, Shawna, had taken up her own kind of stakeout. The biker crouched down, her elbow on her knee, her hand covering half her face. The helmet dangled by her side. She watched as the blonde chick and a tall, slim dude—same guy Shawna had seen before—left the gallery, walked down the street and turned the corner. Going back to her place, maybe, or into one of the many eating joints in this neighborhood.

The blonde was pretty, on the curvy side, but walked with a rod up her ass. Like she was worried about something. Right now, Dave couldn't help but wonder if the girl was the real deal, not that he believed in psychics. They were just scam artists, like every other fucking politician in this miserable, greedy town. Sam even said so, and Sam was always right about these things.

An hour later, Dave had parked the bike at the curb in front of a corner coffee and bagel shop. From his vantage point at the corner bagel 'n coffee shop, he could watch the girl's apartment building. Even had a sight on her loft apartment's front windows. For weeks, the girl did nothing but stay up in her loft and, as far as Dave could tell, paint pictures. The chick's boring routine was grating on his nerves. Another ten minutes and he'd take off. He had better things to do with his time, for pete's sake.

So what game was this blonde chick playing? And what did it have to do with Dave and Sam? Could she be a threat to them? If so, he would take care of it and make Sam proud. It was the least he could do to repay him for all he'd done for Dave. Dave was free because of Sam's sacrifices.

They were a team.

CHAPTER EIGHT

Athena smiled at the progress in her pastiche. Sighing aloud, she sat on a bar stool in her large corner of the loft, designated as her workspace, and studied the flesh of her nude. The shadows around the nude's breasts were not quite right, not the right color. Working from an oversized museum print of Edouard Manet's masterpiece, "Olympia", she could tell the burnt sienna she'd used was too vivid. Manet's sienna was muted, a lower intensity and much paler. The same tone, only darker, was used as an outline along the courtesan's body, from her left shoulder and breast down her slim body and along her legs and feet.

She slipped off the stool and arched her back. Trying to get this pastiche done in time for the San Francisco gallery's exhibition was costing her. Her daily routine was shot, meals forgotten or caught on the run, exercise erratic, and sleep troubled. She found herself sighing again, this time more loudly, making her laugh at herself.

Well, ninny, this is what you wanted. A steady painting gig. You happy now?

On her way to the open kitchen, downstairs in the middle of her and Mikayla's loft, Athena paused and lifted the cotton cloth covering Dan's pastiche-in-progress. His Gauguin's *Nafea* was barely begun, and they had only three weeks left. He'd said he wanted to paint with her to avoid the renovation mess and noise at his apartment building. After working for a week, he'd disappeared and hadn't returned for days. Numerous phone calls had kept them in touch with each other, but peering into his mind one night alerted her to his lies. Something was going on at his apartment that he didn't want her to know about. He was painting there but didn't want her to know what he was painting. Or why.

She wanted to know what was going on, but she had to be able to touch him to find out. Waiting for the kettle to boil water, she heard a motorcycle rev up outside. Curious, she went over to the tall, curtain-less windows to look out. The street below, narrow and clogged with parked cars, throbbed now with the engine of a motorcyclist's bike. It was parked across the street diagonally against the curb, squeezed between two sedans. What caught her eye were the bike's fenders and metal side saddlebags, painted an iridescent lime green. Athena didn't know what kind of bike it was, but it looked new.

A young woman in blue jeans, leather jacket and boots had taken off her helmet to shake her head from side to side, spilling out her hair. Her shoulder-length dark brown hair settled upon her back, and when the woman looked up at Athena's window, she looked surprised, even alarmed for a moment. The woman wore a blue bandana over her nose and the bottom half of her face, as though filtering out road smog. Athena smiled down at the young woman, wondering fleetingly if she should someday paint a woman posed on a motorcycle. What kind of statement would that make about their modern world? As opposed to Manet's nude courtesan reclining on her bed, waited on by an African servant?

Wasn't it time she devoted herself to her own creations? She longed for her own exhibit of paintings. A series of contemporary portraits — modern life in Georgetown — might be just the thing for Martin's Visions Gallery. Contemporary life deserved to be painted as much as nineteenth century life in France.

Quickly, the woman looked away and began trifling

through the contents of her bike's glove compartment, and Athena lost interest. She mustn't stare, she reminded herself. Although that was what figure artists often did — stare at people, study them and either paint them from memory or from a model or photograph.

The kettle whistled and Athena rushed over to pull it off the stove before Mikayla woke up. Her roomie had gotten in late from a weekend photo shoot on Long Island and was still sleeping. Nine o'clock in the morning, and Athena was bleary-eyed, having been at work at her easel for three hours.

She poured from the kettle into her cup, the bag of English black tea plumping out in the hot steamy water. The heady aroma began to fill her nostrils as she carried her cup to the kitchen counter. Exhausted, she sat on a stool and looked down at her cell phone. Her mother was supposed to call that day and let her know how her father was doing, having been bedridden for a week with pneumonia. How did one get pneumonia in Milan? In London, she could understand, but Milan, Italy? Of course, viruses and bacteria cropped up everywhere. No place or human was immune to disease. Her mother's powers of healing had alleviated some of her father's symptoms, but Anna Butler was getting worried. And so was Athena. Her father was only fifty-four. But then her English grandfather had died when he was young. Her English half seemed not as sturdy or as hardy as her Italian half.

More's the pity.

Her phone chirped the first few measures of *Ode to Joy* while she took a sip of tea. She picked it up.

"Hi, Athena. I'm downstairs. Buzz me in, I've brought a friend for you to meet."

Dan bounded up the stairs to the third floor loft apartment. She could hear him approach and saw him round the bend in the staircase landing while she held open her door. An older man in a tan trench coat followed him. Dan bussed her cheek and whispered, "A German friend from Turkey. Just got to town."

Clearly excited, Dan was panting a little as he paused at the door and introduced her to the older man.

"This is Klaus Schoenaerts, owns galleries in Munich, Berlin and Istanbul. My girlfriend, Athena Butler," said Dan.

She and Klaus shook hands, Athena leaving her clairvoyant channel open for information. The man appeared in his late forties, had thinning blond hair and a receding hairline. He was about six-feet tall, heavy of frame, a thick, graying mustache obscuring half of his mouth. What little German she knew, she translated immediately as his thoughts in his native language came through. *Ah, pretty girl, nice lay, I'll bet. Wonder if she will be interested in our enterprise . . .*

Now intrigued, Athena invited them both in and offered cups of tea, which they declined.

"Coffee, if you have it," Klaus asked while he shrugged out of his trench coat.

"Athena, I invited Klaus to look at some of our paintings, including our pastiches," Dan said, "Hope that's okay. For his galleries and private clients."

"Certainly," she said after a brief pause, then addressed her guest, "I'll make some coffee. Won't take a minute. French roast?"

"Delightful," Klaus said, distracted by the paintings lined against the window wall of her side of the loft. "Yes, please, Miss Butler. Just coffee. Dan and I have already eaten."

Since Mikayla had given up painting, she'd encouraged Athena and Dan to use the entire length of the wall to prop up their work. Eight paintings, some of them finished and varnished, adorned the wall and gave it color and context. Two of Athena's were standing on easels, the one incomplete pastiche by Dan on a third.

While making coffee, Athena wondered what kind of enterprise or business agreement Dan was involved in with Herr Schoenaerts. An uneasiness clutched her stomach.

Dan proudly showed the German their work. Two of Dan's unfinished Gauguin pastiches—the Tahitian period—caught the man's attention and he stood before the two for a long time while Dan leaned over and spoke softly to the man, his words out of Athena's earshot. When they arrived at Gauguin's, *Nafea*, barely begun, they paused and exchanged a few words before Dan laughed derisively. She overheard *three hundred million* mentioned.

"Do you take cream, Herr Schoenaerts?" she asked in German, keeping her gaze trained on the two men.

"Ah, you speak German? *Jawohl, bitte.*" He smiled at her broadly before stopping in front of her Manet pastiche, Olympia. "Very nice, very accurate rendering." He murmured something to himself before adding, "Flesh colors are a trifle off. Her skin needs to be lighter."

"Yes, I know." She came over to him with the cup of coffee and handed it to him. The slow hand-to-hand transfer was enough for Athena to glean a little more.

Again, she translated the rapid German thoughts. *Needs work but it could pass with one of my dilettante clients, a wealthy Turk who wouldn't know a Manet from a Monet.*

Pass? Was the German looking for pastiches which he could pass off as originals? In other words, forgeries? Scrape off the pastiche painter's real signature and use only the copied one of the master painters? Rather bold and foolhardy. She watched the man and Dan step from one painting to the next along the wall. They said nothing for several minutes. Finally, she felt compelled to speak up and set the man straight.

"Mr. Schoenaerts—"

"Klaus, please."

She smiled and nodded. "Klaus, Dan and I paint pastiches. Not forgeries." To emphasize her point to Dan, she added, "Passing off a pastiche as an original masterpiece will get you six to ten years in an American federal prison. Won't it, Dan?"

Dan's pale cheeks colored a little before he chuckled and slapped a hand on the German's shoulder. "Are you in the market for selling forgeries, Klaus?" he joked.

A rapid look passed between the two men before the German glanced over at her. His hand raised to his chest in outraged surprise.

"Miss Butler, I'm aware of the risks of selling forgeries. I'm a reputable art dealer with three galleries and looking to open another one, possibly in New York. My clients are vetted by Interpol and several private European security firms. I have no wish to run afoul of American, German or Turkish law, for that matter."

Dan shot her a fulminating look as he led the German art dealer over to the hallway wall which led to Athena's bedroom. There, stacked two deep on the floor against the wall, were more of their own originals that occasionally graced Martin's gallery walls but that no one seemed to like enough to buy. Dan said as much to the German.

"Both Manet and Gauguin had difficulty selling their work while they were alive," the art dealer reminded them bluntly, "In point of fact, most of the French Impressionists couldn't sell their pieces, apart from their portraits. People always like portraits of their loved ones."

Athena had to agree on that score. She left them alone to paw through her and Dan's latest originals while street noises drew her to the window again. Her artist's eye took in details.

The garish motorcycle was empty while the young slim brunette was now sitting outside the bagel and coffee shop across the street and two doors down. Her face was now visible, and she was texting on her cell phone. The woman looked up once but a second later went back to her phone. The woman's skin was light, slightly flushed, and her lips glared a bright red. She had high cheekbones and a rounded chin. A gold stud dotted the one ear that Athena could see. The blue bandana was now wrapped around her throat, the collar of her leather jacket raised.

Somewhat attractive, Athena concluded.

Maybe a contemporary series isn't such a bad idea. Modern-day Washington, D.C., not where you find the politicians. Just ordinary people going about their lives.

Athena looked back at Dan and the German. The art dealer looked a little disappointed. What was he hoping to find? Another Courbet, Van Gogh or Picasso in the making? Would he even know a potential masterpiece if he saw it?

She sighed—seemed to be doing a lot of that lately. Sighing, feeling tense and worried about her father, losing sleep over an overwhelming sense of disconnection, like love and life were passing her by. Her life was out of balance again. Every waking moment she spent on her paintings. There was nothing left over for family, friends, or love. Not much for Dan, either. Morose thoughts seemed to consume her these days, she realized with alarm.

Will I ever be happy again?

The German approached and she met him halfway. Dan was staring at her, shooting her looks of warning. *Be nice to the man.*

"Thank you for the opportunity to look at your work," said Klaus, passing his now empty cup of coffee to her. "I'd like to buy that one," he added, pointing to a contemporary street scene of their neighborhood in Georgetown. "How's two hundred?"

"Euros or dollars?" she asked, disappointed to hear only one of her originals had met his approval. Not even the portrait of Mikayla interested him.

"Whichever you prefer, Miss Butler." She nodded as he pressed two hundred-dollar bills into her hand. She gave him her unframed painting, which he took in both of his hands. He opened a portfolio case and stuffed it in along with one of Dan's original paintings. Athena realized his purchase was mainly for show, having read his thoughts a moment before.

What a pity she won't be joining us. Her Manets are very good, good enough to pass . . .

"I'll take my leave and catch a cab back to the hotel," the German said, nodding his farewell. To Dan, he smiled. "Shall we meet later this evening? I have another two artists to visit today."

After Dan saw the man off, he came back upstairs and closed the door behind him. He stood glaring at Athena, shaking his head. Then he appeared to shake off whatever was bothering him and joined her at the kitchen counter.

"I'll take a cup of coffee. Strong, no cream." He leaned in to kiss her, but she evaded him and jumped up to skirt around the counter.

"What's the problem? I thought we might sell a few of our paintings. Two hundred's nothing to sneeze at."

Busy at the coffee machine, she heard the lie and said nothing.

"C'mon, Athena, it won't hurt to sell a pastiche to the man. Martin's not the only game in town . . . or in the world. His business is moving at a snail's pace. We should broaden our market of collectors. Lots of rich guys over there in Europe and the Middle East, looking for good pastiches. Serious collectors who'll pay serious bucks."

She said nothing as she punched the button and watched the richly brewed coffee stream into Dan's mug. When the mug was filled, she took it over and placed it in front of him. Then her gaze leveled on his face. She stared into his blue eyes.

"Good pastiches, or do you mean good forgeries?"

His face turned livid. "What the fuck are you talking about? I'm not doing forgeries."

She leaned over the counter and clasped his arm with two hands. "Say that again."

He frowned as he stared down at her hands. "I said I'm not

doing forgeries."

She stood upright. "You're lying through your teeth, you bloody wanker."

"Don't swear at me in Brit," he hissed, "keep it American."

"Okay, you're lying through your teeth, you sonuvabitch. So, you've gone over to the dark side of the art world?"

Dan shook off her hands. "I have not. Just because I bring over a German art dealer, you think I'm doing shady business with him? Didn't you hear him? He said he wasn't in the market for forgeries. Just pastiches. What's with you Brits? You don't trust anyone who's German? Wasn't that war over like seventy years ago?"

Athena narrowed her eyes at him, knowing this was going to be the end of their relationship. "Then you're both bloody wankers. I can't take liars, Dan. You can get away with a lot, but not lying."

He thrust his chin at her, his mouth turning down into an ugly sneer. "What makes you think I'm lying to you?"

She hesitated. Only one man, besides her father, brother and the two homicide detectives Palomino and Ochoa, knew her secret. Oh, and one or two security men assigned to the British Embassy. One man. And even that one man had rejected her — though for different reasons.

Did she want her — whatever it was with Dan — to end like this?

She kept her gaze steady but inwardly caved. Maybe Dan was just trying to protect her. What did those police detectives call it? Plausible deniability. If she didn't know the truth — hadn't been told the truth — she couldn't become an accessory-after-the-fact to a felony.

Regardless, everything had changed. "I just know. I have a sixth sense about these things."

Dan laughed while brushing an escaped side tendril away from her face. He looked relieved.

"Yeah, well, I've got a sixth sense that you need to get out of here, get the cobwebs out of your head and take a break from these fuckin' paintings." He wrapped one arm around her waist and snaked a hand up to one breast. His other hand gripped one butt cheek. "Or let's screw for the first time in . . . weeks? Won't a little shagging spice us up?"

She let him kiss her mouth but then broke it off and gently squirmed her way out of his possessive hands.

A flash of anger crossed his face, but then was quickly schooled by his attempt at humor. "Or take a walk. C'mon, I'll treat you to a raisin bagel with strawberry cream cheese. And a hazelnut latte."

Something inside her fragmented and crumbled. Her self-respect?

She knew what her friend and lover, Dan Grantham, was going to do, and she wasn't going to stop him. Was she so lonely that she'd now willingly welcome a forger into her bed? The compromise of one's moral principles was an ugly thing. Ugly and pathetic. And here she was, tempted to do it. Compromise her moral principles.

She was pathetic.

Athena looked down at the tiled counter.

"All right. I do need a break."

CHAPTER NINE

While Dan cooled his heels in the living room, Athena changed her smock, all spotted and smeared with paint, shrugged an oversized V-neck tee shirt over her faded jeans, and slipped her bare feet into a pair of sandals.

"Hurry up," he called out.

Automatically, she took a deep breath, holding her temper as she rouged her lips with dark-red gloss and quickly redid her long ponytail. A moment's hesitation as she gazed at herself in her bathroom mirror. Her green eyes returned a haunted, accusatory look.

Be strong. Time to break it off.

Rejoining Dan in the living room, she avoided his eyes. His tense posture told her that he was wondering if he could convince her of his innocence. Or if he couldn't, whether she would keep quiet and not expose him.

They spoke little as they walked to the corner bagel and coffee shop. The girl with the motorcycle was still there, facing the street and punching into her cell phone between sips of coffee. Something about her was a little off, a little strange. But Athena couldn't pinpoint what, exactly. Probably because she and Mikayla knew very few young women who drove motorcycles. There were a couple at the Art Institute who had sported arm and neck tatts along with nose rings, spiked absurdly-colored hair, and their distinctively masculine bike apparel. One of them had been in her Western Civ class, but she had kept to herself. There were punk biker chicks in Britain, too, but it wasn't the way Athena had been brought up. Her parents were educated but conservative, middle class, and had traveled a lot. Her polyglot Italian-born mother, not only a gifted clairvoyant, translated bestselling novels from English into Italian and French. Her strait-laced English father was a diplomat in Her Majesty's Foreign Service. He'd loved Prime Minister Margaret Thatcher.

Athena tried to avoid labels on people. Everyone had a story and a rationale for their chosen look and behavior. Who was she to judge if someone chose to look punk instead of traditional? Athena's own mother would have called her daughter's sloppy casual dress *bohemian*. Not that Athena considered herself a bohemian or a hippie. She was just a hardworking artist who didn't care as much for fashion and makeup as Mikayla did.

About five-nine—Athena's height—and very slim, the biker chick was wearing a black turtleneck cotton tee tucked into her jeans, tall black boots covering half her legs. Her long dark brown hair draped down her back, and she wore blacked-out aviator shades. Bright red lipstick filled her sculptured lips. Her skin was creamy, her eyebrows dark and well-shaped.

Determined not to be a snob, Athena smiled at her as she passed the girl's table with Dan. The girl looked surprised but smiled back.

More woman than girl. On closer inspection, the girl looked to be in her mid-twenties. She pulled a pack of cigarettes out of her black leather vest pocket and proceeded to light up. She held her cigarette in the manner men did, between their thumb and forefinger. A tomboy affectation, perhaps.

Inside the store, Dan bought Athena a caramel macchiato and raisin-nut bagel stuffed with strawberry-flavored cream cheese and the same for himself. Her stomach growled, making her realize how hungry she was. For the past four hours, she'd ignored the grumblings of hunger in her drive to finish more of the Olympia pastiche. Blocking out the noise inside the shop, Athena focused on her inner thoughts.

Three more weeks! Would she ever finish the two Manets she'd committed to taking with her to that San Francisco gallery? She had to allow a week for the oil paint, then the varnish overlay, to dry completely. Wow, two more weeks. Holy crap!

And now this. To add to her tension and worry over her father's health, Dan was doing black-market forgeries. Had already lined up a shady art dealer. She was convinced the man's thoughts implied that he dealt in art forgeries as well as legitimate originals.

After emerging from the coffee shop, they settled into two wrought iron chairs at one of the sidewalk tables. Athena looked around. The sky was leaden, overcast, hinting of possible rain, but the air was warm and humid. Almost muggy. The street smelled of car exhaust and an overlay of tree blossoms. Thank heavens for the tree blossoms. A row of cherry trees lined her street, lending it a gentrified air, reminding her of Europe.

"Feels good to get out." She smiled at Dan, who nodded as he glanced about the sidewalk tables. "Thanks for reminding me there's another world out here."

He didn't smile back. "We're missing out on so much, Thena. We live like medieval monks, stashed away in some monastery, bent over our parchments and old before our time. Don't you miss the world out there?"

"Yes, of course. But this was what I trained myself to do. Paint." Having lived in a variety of cities her entire life, she wondered what it would feel like to live in the country. Or the mountains. To do what Edouard Manet and Claude Monet did and move to a small town or the country. Would the quiet and fresh air drive her to abstraction?

Not if I had someone to enjoy it with.

"Well, I did, too, but we're too young to spend every waking hour hunched over a canvas trying to produce great art that no one seems to care about. As you Brits say, bugger to that."

Athena had to grin. Droll, how Dan had picked up Brit-speak and she'd picked up American slang. Her parents would shake their heads.

On top of everything, she missed her parents, missed her brother Chris, and the smells of France and Italy. In Milan, at her parents' apartment in the city within the Consular General's small mansion, she'd be enjoying right now the wafting scent of croissants, fresh fontina cheese and fig jam. Two visits in the past few years had helped to alleviate some of her homesickness, but maybe it was time — after the visit to San Francisco — to go back. Check up on her father and his health.

Dan sipped his latte, then frowned and lowered his voice. "I'm so fuckin' tired of it all. Same-ol', same-ol'. Know what I mean? Everything else, all the fun in the world. It all takes money."

"I know, Dan, but this is what we chose to do. We can be art teachers, but this is what we chose to do." Athena said nothing more as she dove into her bagel and drank her coffee. The hot liquid she could only sip, but it helped soften the chunks of bagel she wolfed down. Her mother would be horrified by her lack of table manners. Couldn't be helped. She was a starving bohemian artist. Wouldn't Manet and Van Gogh be proud of her.

Dan's eyes grew hard and flinty. "We're spinning our wheels, getting nowhere fast. We're damned good, and what do we get? Martin's leftovers?" He slipped into silence as he attacked his own bagel. When he noticed the biker babe watching them, he nodded, obviously embarrassed that he'd been overheard.

"Those bagels are scrumptious, aren't they?" the biker

chick offered breathily. Her voice was deep and a little raspy, as though she was a longtime smoker.

"Hmm, yep," was all Dan could manage as he gave the girl a thumbs up. He slurped down his coffee before turning a cold, blue-eyed stare on Athena.

Soon to be ex-girlfriend and boyfriend. Avoiding their coming confrontation a moment longer, Athena shot a friendly smile at the biker chick.

"Do you live around here?" she asked the woman, "I think I've seen you a couple of times."

The woman looked a little surprised at Athena's question. There was a brief pause before she replied, "No, but I'd like to." The woman inhaled from her cigarette, her elbows resting on the metal table. She blew the smoke out gustily. "I come by every few days to check on apartments, to see if any are available, y'know. I work at Club Fiore, by the way. Come in some time."

"Club Fiore?" Athena asked. The name wasn't familiar to her.

"The drag queen club," Dan filled in. He leaned forward a bit, as if trying to determine the biker's gender. "Are you in the female impersonators' show?"

The biker chick laughed softly and tossed a business card with the club's logo on the front over at Dan. "Nope, can't sing or dance. I'm one of their servers." She smiled broadly, revealing a row of even, ultra-white teeth.

Caps or implants, Athena knew. They were too perfect, too white. Despite the woman's smooth, pale skin, she appeared to have lived a rough life. Athena could see it in her eyes. As if she'd spent time in drug rehab or on the streets. Athena watched Dan take up the card and glance at it. From his slight frown, he indicated his confusion. He glanced over at Athena, raising an eyebrow. Meaning, what gender was she? Male or female? A female impersonator? He wasn't sure. Neither was

Athena.

The woman's face was feminine, certainly, and her hair. She seemed to have a bosom, and her voice was low and breathy. Who knew?

What difference did it make? There were transgender people wherever one went. No big deal. Not anymore. But she sympathized with the woman ... or man. Life was tough enough without being confused about one's gender.

The biker chick squashed her cigarette under a thick-soled boot and stood up, collecting her keys and cigarette pack. Her hands looked unblemished, fingers long and slim to go with her skinny frame. The nails were trimmed and polished, better groomed than Athena's. Athena glanced down at her own hands, stained with paint caught in the lines of her palms and knuckles. No amount of scrubbing could get them perfectly clean. She sighed.

The biker chick moved from her table. "Well, gotta go. Come to the club some time," she said, "My name's Shawna. Ask for me."

Dan grunted and hiked up his head. "Sure, next time we go clubbing, we'll look you up. I'm Dan, this is Athena."

Athena smiled and said goodbye. Both she and Dan watched the woman walk down the sidewalk to her motorcycle.

"What do you think?" Dan asked her. "Male or female?"

"Would I be daft to guess?" Her mind lingered on a more vital dilemma. Should she reveal the truth to Dan and tell him how she knew he was doing forgeries and risking everything for a big payoff? She'd never told him about her clairvoyance. What would he think? At this point, did she really care?

Dan huffed out an impatient breath. "I swear, Athena, you're so closed up. I'm talking about her, the biker babe. Is she or isn't she? I mean, look at those hips. I've never seen a woman with hips that narrow. And I think there was an

Adam's apple under that turtleneck. Shawna is a Sean."

Dan cut a brief nod as the biker chick, her helmet and visor concealing her face, rode past the coffee shop and, turning right at the corner, sped off in a noisy rumble.

Athena shrugged. "I don't know, could be a chap. Or just a skinny woman with a smoker's voice. Hard to tell these days. The clothes and everything else are so unisex. I dare say, one day in our desperate attempts to be equal, we'll all look the same. That's what my father says, anyway." She sipped her coffee. "Anyway, what does it matter?"

Her mind flashed back to her hour with Detective Ochoa and their search of the older brother's electrical shop and attached apartment. Something she had picked up on then about the younger brother. But the thought fled her conscious mind as other matters intruded.

Dan hiked up one shoulder. "If she's a birth male, is she a transgender female or a female impersonator? If she works at Club Fiore, she's probably a female impersonator. I hear these guys pull in the bucks at that club. Most of them are straight, too. How's that for a weird, topsy-turvy existence? Paid big bucks to pass for the opposite sex? And yet you're a straight guy and all the hot-looking babes there are really men. Must be damned frustrating." Dan picked up the club's card and slipped it into the pocket of his black running suit. He shook his head and snorted. "Y'know, I've been working so hard, the only time I get out is when I run in the morning. We need to go out, Thena, and have some fun. You've been working too hard. That's why you're in such a black, pissy mood."

Athena shot him a quelling look, so Dan changed the subject. "Hey, did you read Martin's newsletter? Cezanne's *Card Players* just sold at auction in London for two hundred and fifty million bucks. White sold her *Card Players* pastiche for sixty thousand, got paid thirty. Enough to pay her DC property taxes for the year and some change left over for new supplies. What's the fairness in that? Her Cezanne was a perfect copy. In better condition than the original, in fact. Two hundred and fifty million, and all White got was thirty thousand. Where's the justice in that?"

Athena sighed. Back to his old loop of complaints. He was trying to convince her that forgeries were indeed what the smart, talented painter did these days if he or she wanted to make money. Real money, he meant.

"Authenticity, Dan, that's what it's all about. And provenance. You know that. If an original can be authenticated, and it's proven to be the work of a master painter, the price goes up. Let's face it. Society doesn't regard us as master painters. We know we are, but we need society's validation. The art world's validation. Sorry, but that's how the real world works."

Dan jammed his paper cup down so hard on the tabletop, coffee sloshed over the top. "Yeah, well, the real world sucks. I can paint a Gauguin better than Gauguin, himself. He's dead, I'm alive. I need the bucks, he doesn't. Where's the fucking justice in that?"

She'd laugh if the choice weren't so grave. One more attempt at showing Dan the dark side of the art world was not the way to go and she'd thereafter save her breath.

"The risks are so high, Dan. Everything you've worked so hard for, your condo in Baltimore, your new car — all for nothing if you end up in a federal prison. All your own paintings, your reputation as an artist down the loo."

He leaned his elbows on the table and hunched close to her, lowering his voice, his silky baritone quivering with anger.

"I told you, Athena, I'm not painting forgeries. Why do you think I'm lying?"

Because I'm clairvoyant and have been since the age of nine. I come from a long bloodline of psychic women. I can read your mind as easily as you can read Martin's sodding newsletter.

The words stuck in her throat. He would think her crazy, delusional at best. Or he just plain wouldn't believe her and would think she was grasping at straws. Still, she had to try.

"Call it my clairvoyance. I can tell when people are lying."

"Your sixth sense, yeah I know," he mocked. "And I'm Paul Gauguin's reincarnated spirit. An improved reincarnation. I paint better than he ever did! My reputation as an artist, *my* paintings. What a joke. I sold two landscapes last year for five hundred bucks each, only four of my abstract paintings so far this year, and only three of my minimalists. And what, for peanuts. Barely enough to pay for the canvas and paint. Those damned pastiches are the only things that keep me afloat. Besides, I read that up to forty percent of all famous art pieces are forgeries, anyway. Forty percent! Athena, it's a booming business. Even the experts can't tell half the time."

Athena, tired of the same old argument, stood up. "C'mon, let's go. I have to get back to work on Olympia."

Dan ignored her and remained sitting. "Collectors are paying millions for work they think has been touched and blessed by the hand of a famous painter. All along, it's Joe Schmoe from New Jersey who's painted it. Some art dealer or museum curator has determined its authenticity with his electronic microscope. Bullshit. There are so many ways to fool them." Dan paused and took a gulp of coffee, as if calming himself down. "The art world is saturated with forgeries. What's one or two more?"

Her chest heaving with anger by now, she stared him down. "You won't look good in black and white stripes, Dan. Won't go with your blue eyes."

He glanced up at her with hooded eyes, then added after a moment, "If I was considering doing forgeries, which I'm not. But I wouldn't be the first painter to consider going that route. Just saying."

He stood up and joined her on their short walk back to her

place.

"Just saying," he repeated, huffing out the phrase, his hand waving in the air for emphasis.

"I want no part of it," Athena murmured softly, "I won't turn you in, Dan, if you're worried about that. You've meant too much to me. I don't want to see you thrown in prison, but I want no part of it. It would be my luck to get caught, and my parents would go ballistic. I'd be deported to a British prison cell. I've got claustrophobia, so there's no way I can end up in one. My mother's and father's careers would go up in flames from such a scandal. No, I'd never risk it."

He looked at her, eyes narrowed with the unspoken question, before clasping her hand. "I needed to hear that, that your loyalty to me comes first."

She read his mind, needing to know.

Thank God. Athena never lies, she won't let on even if she finds proof. She better not — no, she won't tell anybody. Klaus' organization, god, what would they do? I don't want to see her hurt. I'd never want her hurt over this. What she doesn't know won't hurt her. I'll make sure she never knows the truth.

Swept by a wave of sorrow, Athena withdrew her hand. It was the end of their relationship, and there was nothing she could do about it. Again, the fickle weathervane of fate had turned, and everyone was affected whether they liked it or not.

Dan's a liar. And now a forger.

People always lie, and they always think they'll get away with it.

When Dan leaned over and kissed her, she let him. It would be one of their last kisses, she decided. Such a shame. She liked him so much. For two years, they'd been friends, lovers and nearly constant companions.

"Hey, let's go out Friday night," he suggested, "to this Club Fiore. We haven't had a blowout in a long time. Let our colors burst, as the song goes. What do you say, Thene?" He nuzzled her temple. "We haven't done the dirty deed in a while, too.

I've missed you. You know, there's no one else but you in my life."

At least, that seemed to be true. So far, anyway. Their dedication to their art had taken precedence even over their sex drive. Small thanks for big favors, she groused to herself. Eunuchs for art, they were. Both their lives were lopsided, out of balance. They were twenty-two and twenty-four and Dan was right. They lived like ascetic monks bent over their sheepskin scrolls.

"Okay," she told him. She kissed him back, but it was a dry, perfunctory kiss.

Another compromise, another fragment of her conscience chipped off. But there would be no sleepover. She had to draw the line somewhere. Their love affair was over. Friday night she'd make it very clear to him. She'd remain his friend, but their romance was over.

Tears sprang to her eyes, but she hastily wiped them away. She would be compromising her moral principles by not exposing him as a forger, but too bad. She wouldn't expose him. That was as far as she would go in her compromise.

It's your choice, girl. It's always your choice.

A heartbeat later.

Living with heartbreak should be getting easier. Why isn't it?

CHAPTER TEN

Club Fiore burst with colors, as befitting a nightclub named after flowers. The neon-lit abstract flowers in sculpted glass adorned the black walls and exploded in colors like a rotating kaleidoscope. It was like, Athena decided, being in a psychedelic field of throbbing colors, lit by gyrating stage lights in sync to the music. An exciting place, full of motion, lights and color.

Something was wrong, however. Her heart raced like a frightened prey sensing a predator lurking nearby but not seeing it. The fine hair on the back of her neck stood on end. She didn't know why. There was nothing to fear here, her rational mind told her. She hadn't yet confided in Dan the entire truth about her clairvoyance, nor her impending breakup with him. Would he believe her or accept her explanation for why she knew he was lying? Probably not.

"Not bad seats, huh?" Dan surveyed the area around their table in relation to the stage. The female impersonators show was due to begin in fifteen minutes. The performers, in full costume, wigs, makeup, would sing their renditions of Broadway showstoppers made memorable by iconic singers such as Judy Garland, Rosemary Clooney, Cher, Barbra Streisand and more contemporary stars like Alicia Keyes, Taylor Swift, Lady Gaga and Adele.

"Twelve songs, about an hour's worth," she informed Dan while scanning the program. "Intermission for thirty minutes, then another show. Do you really want to stay for two shows?"

"Sure, why not? I paid for both." His blue eyes met hers over the white tablecloth. He looked annoyed, as if sensing her tension. Or maybe even what was coming later that evening. She'd certainly given him enough hints over the past week that she was emotionally detaching herself from their relationship.

He turned accusatory eyes on her. "You don't have anything against female impersonators, do you? I think what they do is extraordinary. To make themselves look and sound like women. I mean, how does a guy do that?"

She smiled weakly. Dan was asserting his masculinity along with many other males in the audience around them. From the way they sat with their dates to their basso profundo voices, the men, including Dan, appeared both titillated and intimidated. Must be a guy thing. Maybe they were afraid of whatever they perceived was feminine inside themselves. Soft and vulnerable.

Shawna, she spied, was waiting on a table near them. Athena shrugged. "Lots of makeup, push-up bras and wigs, I imagine. Falsettos or naturally tenor voices help, too, especially for a singer. It's quite a feat to sing like a famous singer of the opposite sex," she agreed. "I certainly couldn't even look or sound like Adele, and she's my same sex."

Their acquaintance from the bagel and coffee shop appeared before them. This time, Shawna—according to the name pinned to her costume—was dressed not as a biker babe, but as a French maid, thigh-high black dress, flouncy-white petticoat, black fishnet stockings and all. She wore a wide black ribbon and lace choker around her neck and a bouffant, scarlet-red wig.

Their server beamed at them as she greeted them effusively. "My friends from the bagel shop—so awesome you came tonight. It's going to be a great show. You'll love it. Now, what can I get for you two lovebirds?"

Athena cringed inwardly and glanced over at Dan as he ordered. One diet soda and Jack, one Jack neat. Shawna flounced off, her hands aflutter like a parody of an eccentric gay man. She stared after the woman, then glanced around the club. Her heart was still racing. Something was wrong, her instincts told her. What was wrong, she didn't know. But her antennae were up and working. Swiveling around the club like a damn radar dish.

She and Dan talked about the showstoppers on the show's list of tunes.

"These were all in movies. Did you see any of these films, like *Funny Girl?*" Dan asked, keeping the topic neutral. She could tell he sensed what was coming later. The Big Breakup.

"Oh yes, most of these, I think. *Secondhand Rose* from *Funny Girl*. Should be funny." She shot him another wan smile. Sorrow consumed her. When people disappointed you, what could you do? Run away and start afresh? Or make compromises? What a slippery slope that was. But weren't compromises the basis of long-term relationships?

Not if the compromise went against your own basic morality.

The conversation was stilted, probably in part due to their unaccustomed dress. She was wearing her only cocktail dress, a clingy red sheath, and Dan, groomed to the hilt, wore a navy-blue suit over a French blue tee. As she learned more about Dan Grantham, she realized how strong the need to succeed was in him. But more than that, he had to be superior to everyone else. He had a great need for social validation, and with that validation, money was required. Lots of it.

She sympathized somewhat with him. For her, however, her own validation of her work was enough. But she could barely blame him for wanting to make a fortune from painting forgeries. Tempting. Doing forgeries was different, though. She respected the world of art too much to take advantage of the dilettantes who collected what they didn't truly understand or know but were only too happy to hang on their walls. Too many people ended up being cheated and losing money. Forgeries cast a bad light on the entire art world.

If it was true that the FBI considered at least forty percent of the masterpieces sold today were forgeries, then Athena was truly shocked. A lot of people who loved art were being scammed.

Shawna returned with her tall drink and Dan's short one. "Jack with Coke and a Jack neat, right?"

Dan took them both after slapping a fifty-dollar bill down on the table. He was proud to be able to afford to take her to such an expensive nightclub and buy twenty-dollar drinks.

"Keep the change," he told Shawna. In return, she favored him with a flirtatious wink, a hip swing and a pat on his shoulder.

"What a charmer." She fixed her narrowed eyes on Athena. "He's a keeper. Don't you dare let him go."

Athena smiled resignedly as the server flounced off to another table. Dan handed over her tall glass of soda and whiskey, condensation from the glass making her fingers wet and tingly. No, tingly for another reason. A vision strained to intrude into her mind.

An office with two desks. A familiar man's face glaring and angry. Ranting into a cell phone that he'd taken out of a wall safe. Keep your damned nose clean!

She frowned. What was that all about? There was no time frame for that vision. Had that already happened, or was it happening now?

"Cheers!" Dan clicked his glass with hers, jolting her out of her vision. She automatically echoed his toast with her own version, "Cheers, to your health," figuring he'd need it if he crossed the wrong person in the art forgery world. She sipped a bit from hers.

Strange, that snippet of a conversation. She had no idea whom the man was speaking to. The first speaker, she knew from recent experience.

The older brother, the one who owned the electricians' shop.

Bloody hell. She turned in her seat, scanning the night club. Table by table. The older brother wasn't in the audience area, and the bar alcove was too dark for her to see into.

Why would she overhear such a thing? Out of context, out of anything that made sense? She wasn't touching anybody. It was like her psychic antennae were reverberating out of control, like a spastic satellite dish, and picking up anything that reminded her of that horrible search with Detective Ochoa.

She glanced around the nightclub again. Other servers, like Shawna, appeared to be female impersonators like the men who performed on stage. A few might have been actual young women. Athena couldn't tell. Not until she touched one of them, and that wasn't going to happen, not tonight. She couldn't care less what gender these servers were. Not her business. She looked down and stared at her tall glass. There was a cherry and lime slice stuck through with an extra-long toothpick angled on top.

In her mind's eye, in place of the toothpick was an icepick jammed into someone's red heart. Lots of blood, red blood. A man or woman – she couldn't tell.

The flash of a vision made her shiver inside, a cold ripple rising to her head. She tried to shake it off, but that horrible vision from The Flow persisted.

Fuck it, how horrible! She looked over at Dan before scanning the crowd once again. No one around that she recognized from the Art Institute or Visions Gallery. None of Mikayla's friends.

"What's the matter?" Dan asked. He'd obviously noticed

her expressions change as fleetingly as a weathervane. She was getting bombarded with visions coming out of nowhere! What the bloody hell was going on?

"Nothing, nothing. Just all the noise."

In confusion, Athena leaned over and placed her hand on Dan's shoulder. His blue eyes slid in her direction and he smiled the old smile that used to warm her insides, that made her like him so much.

Another vision took its place. Inside Dan's head now, she witnessed a memory of his—a pretty brunette with short, curly hair pulling him into her flat, her mouth painted with bright coral lipstick and matching the coral, hip-length lounge robe she wore. Suddenly, the robe fell to the floor, revealing a naked young woman with open arms . . . and a broad smile. A surprised but pleased Dan enveloping her nude body. She even felt his thrill and rush of desire—

This had happened, she knew with awful insight and certainty, last night. She removed her hand as if burnt after touching a hot pan. When Dan said he was busy painting his Gauguin pastiche at his place, he'd cheated on her instead. Her rational mind assessed the situation, staving off the emotions that she knew would flood her in a matter of seconds.

If those visions were true—and she had no reason to suspect they weren't—she'd just received two shocking revelations. Someone inside this club was a killer, or was going to be killed, stabbed in the heart with an icepick. But who was he or she?

The other one—Dan was already hooking up with a new girlfriend. He'd already written Athena off and was moving on. Tonight would be their last date.

"Now what? You look angry."

"Nothing."

Athena sipped her drink, letting the whiskey seep into her blood. This helped to close off her clairvoyant channels. Alcohol always did that. She didn't know why and neither did her mother. It just happened that way. The Flow closed off.

She'd seen enough for the evening anyway. Tears collected behind her eyes and her heart seemed to tear a little. The pain of Dan's betrayal should have cut deeply, but it didn't, not as much as she expected. She must've known that his long absences of late had just as much to do with another woman as his sequestering inside his flat to work on his forgeries. Still, betrayals of any kind always kicked one in the gut.

She wanted to weep, but bloody hell, she remained dry-eyed.

"What's the matter?" Dan persisted. "Are you obsessing over that German art dealer? I swear, Athena, you've become so moody lately."

The stage lights flashed on and an emcee in a black tux walked to the standup microphone, stage right. The red velvet curtain opened to reveal a small, five-piece band. The drummer let loose a staccato of a drumroll.

"We'll talk later," she said. He wouldn't believe her when she told him about her clairvoyance, wouldn't believe that she'd seen his new girlfriend in all her naked glory, and he would deny everything. The art forgeries, the new girlfriend, the betrayal, everything. Dan was going to think she'd lost her marbles, or so he'd say. But deep down, he would finally realize what Athena Butler was capable of knowing.

It was going to be a long, painful night.

CHAPTER ELEVEN

After a sleepless night, Athena gathered her wits about her and joined Mikayla for breakfast. Her flat mate had insisted after seeing her friend pad out of her bedroom in a state of disrepair. Over a cup of French roast and a toasted English muffin, Athena explained it all. What had led up to her breakup with Dan. His cheating on her. Their general fatigue and disillusion with each other. She didn't mention his throwing in with a gang of art forgers.

"Oh, Mick," Athena sighed. "I wish I had your luck with men."

Mikayla looked so put together, neat and clean and shining with a good night's sleep. She slid off her counter stool and hugged Athena tightly.

"You take men too seriously, girlfriend. I don't. Lots of fish in that proverbial sea, y'know. You gotta learn to shrug off those—what do you Brits call them? Oh yeah, those wankers. Another one'll come along soon enough. You can't change 'em and you can't fix 'em."

Mikayla plied them both with enough black coffee to fill an SUV gas tank while they talked. "By the way, how did you find out Dan was cheating?"

Athena took a deep breath. She'd never told her one close American friend about her and her mother's clairvoyance. About Kas Skoros's mother and her precognition. About their psychic bloodline going all the way back to ancient Greece. Maybe now it was time.

She stared into her cup and said the damning words.

70

"I read minds. I'm clairvoyant."

Mick's reaction was explosive. "Shut the front door!"

Athena laughed. The tension in her dissolved immediately.

Then Mikayla's black eyebrows furrowed a little as she grew serious and canted her head. "Tell me more. I'm all ears."

And Athena continued. How her mental channel had opened when she was nine years old and allowed her to read the thoughts of others with just a touch. Then how other channels opened, including a channel to The Flow, that strange, collective, universal mind. What the Hindus called the Akashic Records. How she and her mother used mental telepathy to make nighttime visits with each other. How psychometry — touching things that gave them visions, sounds or smells — enabled them to help the police with criminal cases. How Kas's mother, a precog, could see into the future.

Athena had fully expected Mick to laugh at her in disbelief or back out of the room in fear. She fought the tears that welled up inside her but couldn't help herself. Losing her close American friend, as well as Dan, in the same week would be too much.

Mikayla stared at her for a long moment, and then did the unexpected. She narrowed her eyes and hopped off her stool. "I knew it! I knew there was something different. In art school, you always knew what I was painting before you saw my canvas. I know you slipped up a few times, tried to cover up." She snapped her fingers. "I just knew it."

Athena's mouth gaped open. "I knew you suspected something but . . ."

Mick hugged her again. "You were afraid to say anything, I know."

A single tear of relief slid down Athena's cheek. "Who's the psychic now?"

They laughed and talked. Then they decided to paint. Mick

wanted to paint a portrait of her newest boyfriend, the magazine photographer.

"I'm going to give it to him for his birthday next month."

"Alright," gushed Athena, scanning her own paintings. She felt an enormous weight had just lifted, felt lighter than air. *Let's just get these done. Time's running out.*

By six that evening, they'd finished their own separate projects. They stood back and assessed their own work, then each other's. This was the process Athena had found so rewarding when she and Mikayla used to paint together at art school. They'd been trained by the Art Institute to be honest to a fault when their own work was involved.

Mick studied Athena's self-portrait. "Okay, I like it. It's in the Itzhak Tarkay mode, bright colors and unusual, expressionistic lines, but I like it. Unique. Eye catching. You've caught your . . . your intensity of concentration despite the fly-away hair. You might end up an Abstract Expressionist after all, Athena. What do you say to that?"

She shrugged and smiled. "I doubt that. I'm a Romantic Realist at heart, but these two were fun to paint. I was experimenting with the style."

Mick's black brows furrowed as she stood before the other square original, the one featuring a young, dark-haired man holding a little, dark-haired boy. The warmth emanated between the two figures despite her expressionistic rendering of the two figures. Athena was pleased with it. She'd tried to show that even portraits could convey emotion, just as Picasso's abstract *Guernica* had conveyed the horror of German bombing on the populace of a Spanish town. How Manet's *Plum Brandy* conveyed the sorrowful contemplation of the young woman. And she felt she'd succeeded. Mick held her chin in her right hand and stepped back.

"This one's strange. You've never painted a child before. Who were your models? I mean, I can tell the man is Kas

Skoros. Your old flame."

"Just some dream I had," she said, staring at Kas's eyes in the painting. She'd captured them perfectly, at least in her mind. The dark, penetrating eyes of the man and the wistful gaze of the beautiful little boy as they looked at the starry night sky. The warmth and love shared by the two.

Athena turned to face Mick. "I used a kind of mental telepathy to enter the man's mind, and through him, I saw the child. I felt what he felt towards that child. His son."

When she'd told Dan days before about The Flow and how she could enter the minds of people even as she slept, he had turned away, his hands shaking in the air by his head. "Not that again. I'm telling you, New Age spiritualism and all that is just bunk. You're delusional, Athena. You're not getting enough sleep. No human can do that, no one can read minds and jump into another person's head."

She'd leveled a cold stare his way, her arms akimbo, her fists at her waist. "Oh, really? You think I'm delusional?"

"You're intuitive, insightful, I'll give you that. But what did you call it before—clairvoyant? You told me before that you and your mother were clairvoyant. I didn't believe you then, and I don't believe you now."

Sorry to say, Dan. Two years of friendship and lovemaking . . . over and done.

And then Athena had described in excruciating detail the image of Dan's new girlfriend in all her coral-colored robe and naked splendor. Speechless, Dan just gaped at her.

Now, Mick just nodded her head. "Yes, I can see that. You really captured the man's feelings for the child." Mick's gaze met Athena's. They smiled at each other, and then they moved over to Mick's portrait of her boyfriend. It was a work-in-progress. Athena could see her friend's strong feelings for the handsome African American man. Barry Lewis, a fashion photographer. "I can see how you feel about him. What a hottie."

Mick giggled and winked at Athena. "In all the ways that count."

Two hours later, after Barry picked up Mikayla, Athena watched through the front window as the two lovers walked together down the street. They crossed the street in front of the coffee and bagel shop but kept on going. Athena noted the biker chick at one of the outdoor tables, smoking her perennial cigarette and lost in her usual thousand-yard stare. Shawna. Still checking for vacancies in the neighborhood.

Her mind dwelling on all that had taken place over the last week—the work, the breakup with Dan, her gratitude to Mikayla for her endearing friendship—Athena turned away from the window. Listlessly, she took a shower and scrubbed all the paint off her hands and arms, eradicated all whiffs of paint thinner from her skin. Feeling clean, refreshed and in the first upbeat mood she'd felt in weeks, she climbed into bed. She tried to read the next chapter of a novel, but something plagued her.

She got out of bed, retrieved her cell phone from the kitchen counter and fished Detective Ochoa's card out of her purse. When he answered, she immediately regretted calling him. It was late at night, and he was home with his wife and kids. She could see the family watching a movie on their TV, the two oldest kids—young teens—stretched out on the carpet, Ochoa and his wife snuggled together on the couch.

Athena felt like kicking herself for such an intrusion, but now that he'd answered, she went ahead with her call.

"I'm so sorry to bother you at home, Detective Ochoa."

His voice sounded tense. "Thought this was the precinct. What's the problem, Athena?"

"No problem, not really." *Not yet.* "I was hoping you could advise me on something."

"Sure, shoot."

"All right, well, here goes. Tell me what you know about serial killers. What makes them do what they do, their motives, that type of thing."

"Athena, have you picked up something about the Missing Brother case?" That was how Ochoa had referred to the cold case that day of the search.

"I'm not sure. Tell me about serial killers, please."

She heard Ochoa clear his throat, heard a rustling sound and a muted voice. Ochoa was leaving the room where his family was relaxing with a movie. She couldn't blame him. Who wanted his kids to overhear something about serial killers? After a moment, he came back on.

"Serial killers tend to be males, by the way. One theory is that males have more fragile psyches than females. Or the testosterone compels them to be violent. Or both. Anyway, they usually fall into two broad groups. The psychotic killer or criminally insane one, the one who hears voices or sees visions that tell him or her to kill, maim, shoot someone, whatever. They're usually found because their behavior is so bizarre, people notice and send out an alarm. They're usually in the system young. I mean, the psychosis starts when they're young or in their teens."

"Okay. And the other group?"

"They're the pathological killers, the sociopaths. They're not considered insane by our legal standards, but they lack a conscience that most people have. They kill because they enjoy it, the power over other people, getting away with it, even the one-upmanship over cops. The high that murder gives them, like a drug. They're more difficult to find because they're usually very intelligent. They can behave somewhat normally on the surface, but underneath they're seething cauldrons of hate, anger, revenge. Or their needs and urges are so strong they become addicted to the thrill of it all. Doing the kill and getting away with it. They're compulsive, but some can control their urges when they must. Some can't. Some get more of a thrill from the planning of a kill than the actual kill, itself." He paused to let her digest what he'd said.

"Yes, I think the younger brother is this kind of killer."

Ochoa cleared his throat before continuing. "They're as sane as you and I, legally, anyway. And like I said, they tend to be clever, smart, cunning. We in law enforcement have a lower arrest rate with this type of serial killer. Unless they slip up and make a mistake. Like leave DNA behind, or their timing is off, they miscalculate, and they leave a witness behind."

"What do you mean, their timing is off? They miscalculate?"

"Well, a kill might take longer than usual, and a witness shows up. Or something happens that they haven't considered. Anything that disturbs their kill pattern or ritual could become a break for us."

Athena was silent. The moment stretched.

"Athena, tell me what you're seeing or sensing. Is it about the Missing Brother case?"

"I will tell you in time, but it's too soon. I'm not sure and I don't want to point a finger at someone who's innocent. I'll let you know as soon as I feel certain. Thank you for your insight, Detective Ochoa. I'm sorry to disturb you at home."

"How do you know I'm at home?" When she didn't answer, he added, "Oh, I see. Never mind."

"I'll call again if I get something more . . . concrete."

"Whatever you do, Athena, don't take on this person, yourself. He would have no qualms about killing you to eliminate a potential threat. Don't be foolish."

"I'll be careful, Detective. Remember, I do have an advantage over most people."

"Yeah, that's true, but don't you have to touch the person or something the person owns or wears to get a reading on

76

him? By then, if you're that close, you're already in grave danger."

"I promise you, I'll be very cautious."

They rang off and she went back to bed, but not before she checked their front door. The deadbolt was in place. She checked Mikayla's bedroom window, which she sometimes left open. It faced the east side of the building and led to a metal fire escape. Sure enough, the window was ajar, so Athena shut it and locked it. Mick liked fresh air in her bedroom most nights but tonight, since her flat mate was spending the night out, Athena wanted it locked.

After returning to bed, thoughts of serial killers churned around in her mind for a while. Sometime later, fatigue claimed her and she fell into a deep sleep.

Meanwhile, it was four o'clock in the afternoon in California. Athena slept and a channel opened onto The Flow.

CHAPTER TWELVE

K as watched the children in his parents' swimming pool. All seven of them were his nieces or nephews, including the youngest one, now officially two years old. Officially, his son; biologically, his nephew. Alexander Philip Skoros, named after his biological father, stood hesitantly on the highest step. A cookie-cutter image of his father, Alex, whom the Skoros family had lost in a car crash two and a half years ago, displayed his father's personality. Charming but impulsive. Leap first, think later.

Little Alex jumped into the water near the waiting arms of his cousin, Sophie, the oldest daughter of Kas's eldest brother, George. At fourteen, she and her sixteen-year-old brother, George Junior, held responsibility for the welfare of their younger cousins. When the little guy began flailing his arms and kicking up a storm, Sophie stepped back and covered her face instead of reaching out for him. A few seconds later, little Alex surfaced, red-faced and coughing out water. He began to wail.

Kas leaped to his feet from his Adirondack chair on the grass next to the pool. "That's it! Put the floaties on him, Sophie. I don't care if he screams he doesn't want them. He can't swim, can't even dogpaddle yet. I'm not taking any chances."

Sophie complied while Kas jumped into the pool feet first and comforted the two-year-old in his arms. He held the toddler still while his niece slipped the floatie contraption on the little boy.

"No! No!" little Alex screamed, crying like he'd just received the biggest insult of his life.

Kas spoke to him calmly. "Kick and scream all you want, Xander. You're wearing that friggin' floatie." He held his adopted son still against his chest, like a captive puppy, as Sophie fastened the strap that ran across Alex's back.

"Ahmm, Uncle Kas said a bad word," announced Leon's seven-year-old Cassie before adding loudly for all to hear, "Frigging. Uncle Kas said *frigging*."

Sixteen-year-old George Junior scoffed. "What a baby. That's not a bad word. The one it substitutes for *is* a bad word."

At water's edge, their legs hanging over the pool's edge, Kas's brothers George and Leon chuckled. George was forty and CEO of Skoros Enterprises, having taken over from their father after his last heart attack. Kas thought he was doing a super job. The next eldest, Leon, was thirty-six and now CFO after Alex's death. Kas had been told many times how the three brothers resembled each other, although Kas always knew that Alex had been the best looking of the four of them. According to his sisters-in-law, they carried well-built physiques. At six-three, Kas was the tallest of his brothers. Thick dark hair and dark eyes paid tribute to their Italian and Greek ancestry, but his mother had often remarked that Kas's facial features, chiseled and more angular, resembled her Northern Italian side of the family.

Leon turned to his older brother. "Poor Kas. He got the job no one else wanted, Chief of Operations. Dealing with architects and contractors on a day-to-day basis has ruined his sense of humor."

George laughed. "I don't think Kas minds. That's his forte, trouble-shooter and on-site supervisor. His military and deputy grunt work, his boots on the ground history — that's the kind of hands-on work he likes. I think we did him a favor."

Alex's child was still complaining loudly about his floatie restraints, but Kas turned him loose to paddle away. Having overheard his brothers, Kas looked over at them as they lounged poolside.

"Big favor, dudes. I'm stuck in the city five days a week."

Leon mocked a pout. "Oh, poor guy. He gets a high-rise condo for his troubles in one of the most gorgeous cities in the world. Tough luck."

Pointing to the rambunctious little Alex and referring to the boy's biological father, George smiled. "Reminds me of someone—and I don't mean you, Kas."

"Yup, the kid's a spitting image in looks and personality, even down to his stubbornness," said Leon, pausing to take a sip from his bottle of beer. Although wealthy thanks to their father's real estate development empire, the four brothers had been raised as down-to-earth middle-classers with a strong work ethic. Despite their growing influence in the world of real estate development, none of them had changed his ways. Now the surviving three carried on the family name, George and Leon doing their best to add another generation of Skoroses. And Kas doing his part as substitute father to the child of their dead brother, Alex.

Kas smiled and nodded. "Tell me about it. He's a real little pistol."

He left unsaid what he knew everyone in his family was thinking. *Too bad Alex the father's not here.* Instead, it was now Kas's job. Which he really didn't mind all that much. His mother, Lorena Skoros, loved babysitting on the weekends when the boy's mother, Nikki, wanted a break. Even his eighty-two-year-old father, Philip—retired but still Chairman of the Board—doted on the boy.

Little Alex paddled back to Kas. "Look, Daddy! I'm swimming!"

"Sophie, why don't you teach Xander how to dog-paddle?

Y'know, arms and legs both." He bent down, kissed little Alex's forehead and sent him off again. The chance to learn how to swim, like his older cousins could do, seemed to satisfy the boy and got him the attention of the other kids. It was apparent that the toddler was not going to shirk the challenge. For this child-style courage, Kas felt the warmth of paternal pride.

"Okay, Daddy." Then he turned to Sophie to await instructions. Soon the toddler was working hard to learn.

"Good, Xander, you're doing it!" he hollered to the little boy as the toddler imitated what his cousin Sophie was doing. Sixteen-year-old Alex chimed in with encouragement and a high five. Little Alex beamed. Soon the four other kids made a loose circle around him, cheering him on. The little tyke loved all the attention.

Leaving the kids to their pool games and swim practice, Kas stepped out of the pool, grabbed a beach towel, and wrapped it around his lower body to cover his skimpy Speedo. George's and Leon's wives threw him appreciative looks as they surveyed his body from head to foot. He noticed their eyes paused midway down his length, spurring George to yell out, "Hey, cover it up, pal. Don't give our wives heart palpitations."

"Where does it say we can't appreciate masculine pulchritude?"

"Yeah, rippling muscles and a six-pack of abs deserve at least a moment of appreciation."

It was Leon's turn to complain. "We have 'em, too, just hidden a bit."

"Too much time being desk jockeys," added George, patting what little flab he carried in his middle.

Kas ignored them all. Despite his injuries from the car crash over two years ago — his leg limp — the rest of him worked well enough. Workouts at the gym had helped. Women in general seemed to appreciate his looks, anyway. And one appendage, in particular.

"Look all you want, girls. In ten years, he'll be just as chunky as we are."

"I love all your chunks, George. You're the man."

"You can quit panting now," Leon called back, then clicked bottles with his brother George. The women giggled and toasted each other with their own bottles.

Embarrassed but accustomed to the ribbing, Kas took his seat on the grass.

George's wife turned her outsized sunglasses on him. "When're you going to bring home a girlfriend, Kas? I mean, now that you're nearly a free man again. Surely, there are plenty of babes in San Francisco."

"Been too busy to notice." Kas leaned back on his hands, waiting for the onslaught of questions about his personal life. They were sure to follow.

Leon's wife giggled. "I think his standards are too high. Gotta lower your standards, Kas, if you want to get lucky."

They were baiting him to reveal his latest conquest. "I'm lucky enough, thank you very much for your concern over my . . . uh, personal needs."

"Still carrying a torch for that girl, that artist?"

Leon lightly slapped his wife's thigh, clearly reminding her it was a forbidden topic. Kas clammed up and glanced over to where his mother sat watching her grandchildren. Under the shade of a large umbrella pine, his mother Lorena leaned over to hand him his bottle of beer that had tipped over on the grass.

At seventy, his mother looked pretty darn good. She kept her short hair dyed dark brown, wore the latest fashions befitting a woman her age, and read everything she could get her hands on. The fact that Lorena Skoros was one of the living descendants of a powerful bloodline of psychic women was the family's secret, guarded as zealously as the Vatican guarded Saint Peter's bones.

Lorena turned to her youngest son and smiled. "Why do you call little Alex *Xander?* I know it's part of the name, Alexander, but it sounds like a name for an older child."

"In part, to keep him separate from his cousin Alex," replied Kas.

His soon to be ex-wife Nikki called him Alex, and she did so with a special tone in her voice, as if she were remembering the relationship she once had with the boy's father. Despite his lack of admiration for or friendship with the boy's mother, Kas respected how affectionate she was to the child during the week, when she took care of him. Little Alex's weekends were at the Skoros compound in the Loomis hills, where Kas spent all his weekends.

When the latest Skoros Enterprises project, the Stargazer Tower, began over a year earlier, Kas had to be on site in San Francisco during the week. Occasionally he'd bunk over at Nikki's house during the week if she needed emergency childcare. Like the one night over a month before, when he swore Athena was in his head.

"Well," his mother said, patting Kas's arm, "I hope you don't mind if we continue calling him little Alex. He's too young, Kyri, to understand his connection to his biological father. In his eyes, you're his father. There's no need to keep from remembering Alex, my son, however painful it might be. It was never your fault." She paused and gazed at him with a look that told him she'd just read his mind. She knew he was still blaming himself for the car crash, an event that she'd warned them both about.

Damn. He'd let his guard down, forgetting his mother had touched him on purpose. Voyeuring, Kas called it. Loving curiosity, she called it.

"Ah, so you're going ahead with that art gallery opening,"

she asked, changing the painful subject. "Do you think people in San Francisco will buy those pastiches?"

"You tell me, Mom," Kas retorted gently, "you're the family's prescient."

Prescient was a nicer term, which his mother preferred. To Kas and his brothers, she was the family's precog. In addition to her clairvoyance, his mother had the extraordinary ability of precognition. The ability to see the future. This ability had helped to forge a path to prosperity for the family's real estate development business. She could see a farmer's fallow field and see a future Interstate with industrial parks and residential neighborhoods nearby. Philip or George would buy the field, and five years later, their shopping center or industrial park or high-rise would be in the middle of it all.

His mother's smile widened. "Oh Kyriakos, you're smarter than you realize. You have good business instincts. Yes, the young generation—what does the media call them, generation X—they'll love those pastiches. The ones who live in the city and work for high tech companies in Silicon Valley, they can afford it. They saw many of these famous paintings in their college Art Appreciation classes, and now they've learned those famous works of art are selling at auction for millions of dollars. They can't afford millions, but they can fifty thousand or so. That generation—your generation—always wants what is just out of reach. What they can't have, so they settle for the next best thing."

Her point struck home. He cast his clever mother an ironic expression. "Mom, are you trying to tell me I can't have what I want? That I'm settling for the next best thing? Because I'm not. Settling. If I can't have what I want, then I choose nothing. I won't settle."

His mother thought about that for a moment. "Kyri, do you think that she won't come back to you unless you entice her with a gallery show?"

Athena Butler, the woman he'd fallen in love with over two years ago and lost just months later when the family pressured him to marry Nikki Theopoulis, his dead brother Alex's pregnant fiancée. So that little Alex could be born with the Skoros name and the Skoros family could have custody rights.

"I'm not thinking of . . . her," he whispered. A glance over at Leon, George and their wives and their sudden silence indicated this was a topic that interested them—*poor Kas. Is he ever going to get over that girl?*

His mother cast him an expression of pity. "Yes, you are, Kyri. Don't deny it. You'll see her in a while."

"Define *a while*." He looked away. "Months? Years? I owe her friendship, so with reconciliation comes restitution. The rest is up to her."

"You can't buy her love, Kyri."

"It's not a bribe. Just an offer to advance her art career." He knew it probably wouldn't work, but he had to try at least. He couldn't stop thinking about her despite several casual relationships he'd tried in the intervening years. "I got the list of artists and she's on it. She's bringing two of her pastiches. I think she knows I'm behind it." He shrugged helplessly. Was she still in love with him? Probably not. Last thing he'd heard, she had a boyfriend who shared her love of painting.

His mother, apparently lost in thought, said nothing. Her silence meant only one thing, as he'd come to learn in his lifetime.

"Have you dreamed of her or her mother? Their family?"

His mother's precognitive dreams *always* came true. The good ones *and* the bad ones.

"Yes, a little. Her father will die young—in his mid fifties, which is young as far as I'm concerned. What a pity. Such a nice English gentleman. Anna Butler will remain in Milan where she is close to her family at Lake Como. But even sooner, I sense—I've seen a closer threat to Athena. All that police work she does, it's dangerous. I know her mother doesn't want Athena to get involved with the police, but she encourages it by setting the example herself. For the greater good and all that, but it's dangerous."

Kas put his bottle down on the grass, his full attention now riveted on his mother and her strange, prescient dreams. His heart was beating like a hummingbird's wings.

"Go on. Is Athena in danger?"

"A young man she's close to—a young man with dark blond hair, a painter like Athena. He's going to cause trouble for her, but I don't know how. I saw someone else, a man. Maybe a woman. I'm not sure about that one. But he or she is hovering close by, watching and waiting. Waiting to pounce . . ."

Kas swore under his breath. "I've got to get her away from D.C. Convince her to move out here. I can protect her."

Yeah, like I protected my brother Alex. Don't be a dumbass. You can't protect anyone.

Hell, I can try.

His mother seized his wrist and looked him square in the eye.

"Yes, Kyri, you should try. She's of the Delphi Bloodline, and she has no one to protect her in this country. Her powers are growing, but she is so young and naïve. She's led a very sheltered life. If she gives you a chance, you should try."

When his mother let go of his wrist, Kas rose to his feet. He looked around at his brothers and their wives, at his father dozing on his hammock in the shade of two Scotch pines at the perimeter of the pool-patio area. The children were hooting and hollering, having fun, splashing around in the pool. Xander—no, Little Alex—was dogpaddling in his floatie back and forth from Sophie to her teenage brother, Alex. Oblivious to his stand-in father's heartache.

As it should be. They were all good kids. What did any of them need to know about his disaster of a love life?

"Hey, everybody, want me to bring out a jug of ice water?"

To a chorus of *yays*, he nodded and gestured to his two brothers at poolside. *Keep an eye on little Alex.*

Kas went inside the mansion, passed the large, state-of-the-art kitchen where the cook and her helper were preparing dinner, and asked them to prepare a large jug of ice water. Then he headed straight to the dark-paneled family room. The mantel clock over the fireplace chimed four o'clock. He glanced at it for a moment, then swept his gaze around the room. On the only wall devoid of bookshelves, his portrait hung over a credenza bar next to the painted portrait of Alex. Over two years ago, Athena had painted that portrait of him in his sheriff's deputy uniform before he'd even met her. And yet, she'd managed to capture his very essence. His soul, for want of a better term. She had seen into him, had perceived one of his deepest needs, perhaps the most dominant trait of his life's force—his need to protect those he loved. How she managed that without meeting him first was not only a testament to her clairvoyance, but also to her special connection to him.

Like now.

He froze. His skull tingled and a shiver ran down the back of his neck all the way down his spine. In his head, like a couple of times before—the night of the car crash, sitting with little Alex and gazing at the stars—he felt her presence now as he stared at his portrait. A kind of low-level humming. He could even smell her perfume, a light citrusy scent that pervaded his senses whenever he thought of her. This time, the scent was pronounced and filled his nostrils. He inhaled deeply.

Why are you here, Athena? Tell me. Are you taunting me?

An overwhelming sense of sorrow filled him. Her voice whispered in his head.

Kas, you hurt me deeply. But I miss you. I always will.

Then nothing more. Her voice disappeared, but the tingling remained. Somehow, his sorrow lifted a little. Her words had conveyed more than perhaps she had intended. She missed him. She was still connected to him. She didn't hate him.

Athena. I'll see you soon. Let me protect you, be your friend. I can do that much . . .

He didn't dare think anything more. He held his breath and waited. No sign from her, no message. The humming and citrusy scent continued for another half-minute. He felt a light touch along his back, his neck, across his face. Like her fingers were skipping across him.

Crazy, but there it was. And then she was gone.

Still, he felt hopeful. She hadn't blasted him with anger or hatred. Her presence was . . . well, friendly. And her voice had been whispery soft with longing.

First, restitution. Then, maybe reconciliation. If I'm lucky.

CHAPTER THIRTEEN

Shawna Robinson, her cover name, stepped through the front door of the electrical company's business site. Her cover job, part-time secretary and bookkeeper for Ace Electrical. She had her own key, so there was no need to ring the doorbell or go around the corner of the building to the cargo bay, where the company's vans entered and exited. Instinctively, she paused to scan the tiny reception area. Empty.

The first thing she did was slip out of her high heels, for her long, narrow feet were aching. The box of freshly made donuts held in the crook of one arm, she went through to the office, which was adjacent to the storage and stock rooms. Beyond was the cargo hold. One black van was just now pulling into the garage for the driver to restock before going on his next call. Three vans had already restocked and were about to leave for a big commercial job, a new strip mall in east Georgetown. The fifth van was out on a short residential run. Sam had already filled him in on that morning's field calls.

Sam was sitting at one of the two metal desks in the office, fielding phone calls. He looked up and shot Shawna his usual superior, older guy smile.

"Took you long enough." He took the box from Shawna. "The guys expect these donuts first thing in the morning." He glanced down at his wrist. "Seven o'clock, not nine."

"You walk three long blocks in high heels," she snarled softly in her usual baritone. "Had to stay till fuckin' closing time last night. The place was packed." She looked over at the guys in the bays loading up the vans. Some of them snuck looks at her, sizing her up. "All these new guys?"

With a mouth full of donut, Sam threw back, "Yeah. The old guys, they all knew about . . . our troubles."

He left the office through the half-glass door and Shawna could see him opening the box on the table where the coffee urn steamed. Paper cups, napkins and other coffee condiments littered the table. The six men from the three vans, in blue jumpsuits with the company logo, Ace Electrical, paused to assemble around the scuffed metal table. A few of them glanced over at Shawna as if speculating about her, but then abruptly turned their attention back to their breakfast. At nine AM, two of the guys looked half asleep after reporting in at seven and completing their first job. Other drivers grabbed donuts and left for their appointments.

Shawna shrugged mentally. Not so difficult to get good electricians these days, but she knew Sam missed ol' Thomas. The guy was due for retirement, anyway, and had worked for the company thirty years or more, ever since Sam's father ran the business. Thomas had been through some tough times with Sam and his younger brother, as Sam's and Dave's abusive parents avoided run-ins with the law and family services numerous times, thanks in part to Thomas's testimony that hyperactive Sam and his brother had hurt themselves carrying electrical supplies, falling over table-size spools of cables, and on and on.

When Sam's home caught on fire—the fire marshal declared an electrical short in the master bedroom was the cause—and his parents were killed in the fire, ol' Thomas had said nothing to the cops. And said nothing to the cops about the sedatives he'd found in the back of one shelf in the stock room that same week. Making amends, Sam had figured, to his new boss. For that silence, Sam had kept ol' Thomas on until a new round of police investigations began two years ago. Then it became time for ol' Thomas to suffer a seizure and have a fatal accident. Falling off a forty-foot scissor-lift did the trick. It took years, but Sam and his brother finally got their revenge, first on their parents and then on ol' Thomas. Sam had liked the old guy, but he just knew too much. If he'd gotten a streak of conscience and talked to the cops, well, they couldn't let that happen.

The others had been let go. No point in provoking the cops into another investigation. Keeping cool and not panicking had kept Sam and his brother alive and out of prison. It was a strength of mind forged from the crucible of their horrendous childhood.

After Sam re-entered the office, he thrust a cup of coffee at Shawna, who was trying to focus on this month's bookkeeping.

"Here. Stay alert today. Who knows when we'll get another fucking cop visit." Sam was clearly upset at the cops' last search two months previous of the company's venue, including his personal apartment now situated on the site. Three personal rooms violated. "Two damned years, nothing. The business and me, we were raked over the coals two years ago, then nothing. I haven't seen their unmarked cop cars on the block lately, but stay alert . . . Shawna. They took down their cameras, too. We checked."

At the harsh tone of Sam's voice, Shawna changed hers. "Of course, Sam. Whatever you say, big boy." She turned around in her chair and batted her fake lashes at him.

"Y'know, you don't have to go overboard with the heels and tight clothes. This isn't that drag queen nightclub. Wear sneakers, for chrissakes, jeans, what normal girls wear out there."

A rush of anger flattened her seductive smile into a grimace. Her feet still felt on fire, and the padded, underwire bra she wore dug into her ribs and back.

"Hey, I know what I'm doing. I'm doing the best I can. We

want them to think I'm your girlfriend, right? Now get out of my way and let me do what I can. I know how girls act. I've studied them. When I get on my Harley, I wear jeans and boots, act like a girl being macho. A tomboy. It's a chance to let loose a little."

Shawna flipped her long straight ponytail over her shoulder. Opening her purse, she took out a lipstick holder with the attached mirror and studied her image. "I look good. I got the best surgeon in Amsterdam, the one who does all the transgender surgeries and never does background checks. You gotta pay him big-time, but, dude, I look good. New chin, no more cleft. Higher cheekbones, smaller nose — all that facial fem crap. He put me on hormones to smooth my skin and tone down the body hair. Did a damned good job."

Dave had said no to a boob job and hell no to sex reassignment surgery. He wasn't getting boobs and losing his dick for nobody. When the doc wanted to shave down his Adam's apple, he drew the line there, too. Didn't want anyone carving up his neck or cutting off his balls or dick. He just needed enough to pass for a chick or tranny and keep those cops off his back.

"Hell, I look so good, I might even get on stage at Club Fiore's. Y'know, backup dancer. Some of those drag queens can't dance. The ones who sing and dance make the big bucks."

She'd noticed a newspaper ad two months ago that the nightclub featuring a show of female impersonators was hiring. Pay was decent, and no one gave Shawna a second look. Some of the female impersonators who sang and danced in the show had work done. They looked better than most chicks she came across. Work at Club Fiore was fun, exciting. Better than this boring-ass bookkeeping job. She'd help Sam for a few hours during the day, but at night, she wanted to be where the action and the people were. The raucous noise and people helped her stay calm. Helped her calm her black moods and violent urges.

She refreshed her lipstick, mostly out of habit and because one of the vans hadn't pulled out yet. Jesus and Javier, cousins and two of the newly hired electricians, were taking extra-long at the coffee table. Sam grew quiet and went back to his logbook of supplies, his movements helping Shawna focus. She couldn't fault Sam. If it weren't for his loyalty and money, sent through a series of paid couriers, she never would've survived two years roaming around Europe, evading Interpol, always staying under the radar and living like a pig. Sam had to sell the house and refinance the business to pay for it all.

So, Shawna, sweetie, do your best and stay out of trouble.

Tracking those two damned detectives, Palomino and Ochoa, didn't count. Especially after their search warrant. They wouldn't have gotten it unless they'd put their dirty hands on new evidence. But now the cameras were gone and those cops hadn't been back, so maybe they could relax. Sam was satisfied that they'd discovered nothing, since nothing had come of it.

Staring at the pages of spreadsheets on the computer made her eyes cross. Shawna opened the bottom-right desk drawer and drew out a packet of digitized photos developed at the drugstore. The one on top showed the cop Ochoa—the same cop Shawna had followed on her motorcycle because Murphy, Sam's attorney, had alerted Sam the day before to the search warrant. From the downtown D.C. Metro PD station, she'd hung back a couple of cars and followed the homicide detective over to north Georgetown. She'd watched as Ochoa pulled over to the curb and called over a blond woman standing outside a building of loft apartments.

At their shop, Ochoa had produced the search warrant for Sam, and his lawyer and had introduced the blonde as a fellow cop, a Sergeant Jane Wilkes of Internal Affairs. But that blonde dame was not Sergeant Jane Wilkes. It took lawyer

Murphy two phone calls and a bribe of two Patriots tickets on the fifty-yard line to get the information they wanted from one of the Metro station's custodians. Shawna swiveled in her chair and faced her brother.

"I can't help it, Sam. Something's going on."

Sam didn't raise his eyes. "Nothing's going on. They found nothing 'cause there was nothing to find. I swept the place for bugs after the search. There weren't any. No more hidden cameras. And there it is. As far as anyone knows, you're my new girlfriend, I gave you a job, and when the time is right, I'll sell the business and we'll leave town. End of story. Don't stir up trouble. Just keep your nose clean and we'll get through this. We always get through shit, Davey. Just keep your nose clean this time."

Shawna glanced over at the half-glass door. The two cousins had restocked their van and were easing the paneled van out of the garage. She decided to be aggressive and press her case.

"Hey, so when Murphy said this blonde chick was a psychic consultant, I want to know what kind of psychic goes on a search warrant with a homicide detective?"

Sam looked up and grunted impatiently. "The forensic kind. Who gives a rat's ass? Maybe Murphy's contact made a mistake. The contact also said she might be a sketch artist. The girl always carried a big bag, y'know, for art things . . ."

Shawna resumed her natural voice and jabbed a forefinger at the photo. "Could be. I went back to that neighborhood, the one where Ochoa picked up that blonde. Asked a bunch of neighbors, passed myself off as an old friend who lost the address. Blah, blah. Guess what they told me? Just artists, they said, lived there in that building. It's full of lofts. Five stories of lofts. They like the space, the big windows. Painters, a couple of sculptors, one cartoonist. This blonde's a painter, they said. Name's Athena Butler. Talks with a bit of a British accent. I acted like I knew her—y'know, an acquaintance. She lives on the third floor, apartment E. The front one." In a heated flood of exasperation, Shawna held out the photo of Ochoa picking up the blonde. "What the fuck is a British painter doing with a cop tossing our place?"

Sam's dark-eyed stare drilled into her. "Don't know, don't care. Like Murphy said, she's probably a sketch artist working for Palomino's homicide team. Maybe she's fucking Ochoa. Leave it alone, Davey."

Shawna puffed up in haughty disdain. "Haven't you heard, Davey's dead. I'm Shawna now."

Snapping her lipstick case shut, she turned back around and looked at her hands. They used to be strong and rough from scrabbling for years on cargo ships, then on the hard-bitten streets of working-class toughs in Holland, Belgium, Denmark. Breaking the necks of little throwaways in D.C. was as easy as cracking a tree branch. His Dutch pal had taught him to use an icepick. He'd tried it on a couple of Amsterdam whores. Shawna's hands were soft and smooth, purposely so, but that was the sign of a weakling. A mouse that got kicked and beaten every week. Weak was bad. You could die if you were weak. He'd almost died as a kid. Many times. If Sam hadn't saved him . . .

Her new disguise was a matter of life or death, Shawna knew, but that didn't mean Dave's mind had gone soft. The old instincts of a predator ran strong, one of the reasons the killings had gone unsolved for so long. The killer in Dave was smart and cagey, didn't leave evidence behind. He had changed the van's fake signs and stolen license plates after each murder and disposed of any evidence linking him and Sam to those crimes. In his own radical way, he was doing society—and those throwaways—a favor. In this horrible, heartless world full of predators and killers, only the strong

95

and clever could survive. No one gave a damn about you anyway. It was all about survival on your own terms. Whatever the cost.

But the fact remained, the cops had searched their place two years ago and now again two months ago. Which meant someone knew about them, about Dave and his brother, Sam. How, Shawna had no clue, but she was determined to find out. It was time for Shawna to do some detecting on her own. For Sam's sake, for Dave's sake. Dave hadn't turned into a damned hermaphrodite for nothing.

She gazed down at the photo again before putting it into the stack of photos and stashing it into one of the pockets in her bright pink backpack. Yep, Dave would play it cool and stay out of trouble. That didn't mean Shawna had to sit with her thumb up her ass and do nothing. Shawna was the one who could check out why an artist would go and help Ochoa with his search warrant.

It was time to do some digging into that blond chick with a British accent.

CHAPTER FOURTEEN

Shawna clocked in at Club Fiore at five o'clock sharp. For the time being, she was getting four hours a day, from five to nine in the evening. Sometimes they needed her until the club closed at midnight. The server's job didn't pay much, but tips made up for it. The club provided her an additional cover where she could blend into the background as well as an opportunity to check out the club scene in all its variety of temptations. As Sam had warned her, Shawna was keeping her nose clean, but all the flesh—the real hot, sexy chicks who appealed to Dave's maleness and gave him hard-ons, the gay men and lezzes whom he found titillating, and the trans people in between—was exciting. The only ones he had to be wary of were the straight guys, the female impersonators. Some of these guys were married and fathers. They could transform themselves into soft, pretty women with gadgets, wigs and makeup, but they were strong men who could give him a bad time. Shawna/Dave had to be careful around them.

The transgenders Shawna studied in order to pull off her disguise, but his real self, Dave, fed off the hot, sexy chicks. They unknowingly fueled the masculine, predator side of Dave and made him want to dominate, control and make the ultimate decision. *Do I fuck her and let her live? Or do I make her die?*

To this possible end, she carried in her large handbag—a hobo type, which was never checked by the security team at the club—her usual tools. Duct tape, a bottle of chloroform and gauze, and a folded up, lightweight plastic sheet which, unfolded, made a six-by-nine, makeshift tarp. A portable body bag. This was highly practical, and she'd used it before as Dave Millhouse, killer of the little throwaways he used to prey upon. Now, courtesy of her experiences in the Red-Light Districts of Brussels and Amsterdam, he'd learned how to use another tool. An icepick. Turning a bound prey onto her stomach, Shawna could let Dave out, let him get his kicks and then eliminate the potential witness with a single thrust of the pick through the ribs and into the heart. The prey was usually dead within five minutes and, unconscious from the chloroform, didn't feel a thing. An easy, clean kill. Easy because bitches never expected another bitch to kill them. If they were conscious and face down, they thought she was using a dildo on them. Never saw it coming. Or the bitch liked screwing a transgender female who still had his wood.

It was a way to fulfill his darkest desires and achieve the dominance and ultimate control Dave needed to feel so he could stay sane. And *sane* the Shawna broad had to remain, in order to live with the only human being Dave ever loved, his brother Sam.

Smiling at one of the other newly arrived female servers, Shawna stuffed her purse into her small locker and turned to see what the costume of the night was. Costumes were hung on a rolling rack and you grabbed one that fit you.

One of the other servers, whose short, blondish-white and pink spiked hair made Shawna think of a dipsy circus clown, pulled the costume off the clothes rack and squealed.

"Oh, fucking A, like I always wanted to be a pirate." She held up the black short-shorts, frayed at the bottom, a see-through red, gauzy shirt, a black eyepatch and black tri-corned hat with a skull-and-crossbones on both sides. "Guess we wear this over our bra. That's why they said to wear a black bra tonight. You get the message, Shawna?"

"Yeah, I did. But I brought my own shorts. Their bottoms

never fit me—got too much ass," she said, adopting a low, breathy voice she used whenever she was in public. She needed her own shorts with the extra crotch room. In addition, she always wore a wide blingy choker encrusted with big, thick rhinestones on velvet and lace. It served to cover her slightly protuberant Adam's apple in her neck. And the long, curved scar on the left side where her crazy bitch of a mother had sliced one time. That was when he and his brother had started planning their liberation.

"Good idea," the spiky blonde said and began to disrobe in front of her own locker. Shawna watched her as she managed to stuff into her locker the Yoga tights and top she'd worn to work. He watched and studied every nuance of movement, the blonde's hands, her slight swing of hip as she slipped off her tights and clingy top, letting her plump breasts spring out. Her dark bush was visible through the transparent bikini panties she wore. When the spiky blonde slipped her panties off and Shawna could see her cleft, the temptation made his mouth water. The man inside Shawna had to look away to deal with the steel rod his dick had become.

Sitting on the bench in front of their lockers, Shawna pretended to look over the costume as she slid side glances over the blonde's slim body, now sporting only a black thong and bra. The girl's skin was creamy and smooth, the way Dave liked them, smooth enough to knead. No fatty rolls, no cottage cheesy thighs, no flabby arms, no underarm hair. The girl was perfection. Shawna couldn't help but wonder if his Daveself could manage to find a way to fuck her. Maybe Shawna could reveal to the girl that she was a straight transvestite, a male with a dick, and boy could he get that dick hard and do the deed! There were other transvestite servers, not just the female impersonators on stage—the *talent*, as they were called by management.

"Better get dressed. They're calling us out there," the spiky blonde admonished as Shawna watched her struggle into the pirate's tight tattered short-shorts.

"Oh yeah," Shawna replied, grabbed up her costume and the black shorts from her locker—she'd say that there were no short-shorts in her size—and went through a doorway to the adjoining female employees' bathroom. Shawna chose her stall, went inside and began dressing. Dave's dick and balls were too apparent to hide when down to his bikini briefs, so he had to be careful when dressing among the women. Big Bill didn't like the straight male transvestites to be in the women's dressing room.

"I can't believe how modest you are," the blonde called out, "Sure you're not a dude in disguise? A TV or a tranny? No skin off my nose, but if you are, better tell Bruiser Bill so you can get a locker in the men's locker room. He don't like the TV men getting freebies from us girls, y'know."

"Gotcha. Let me buy you a drink afterwards and I'll tell you all my secrets."

"Betcha you don't even know my name."

Shawna could hear the flirtation in the blonde's voice. "Uh, Joanie, Jeannie."

"Jeanine, and don't you forget it, Shawna. Or shall I call you Shawn?" The chick laughed shrilly. "You can't hide your balls, y'know, not in these skimpy outfits. I bet everyone knows you're male. At least, some of us women do. You're male where it really counts. But no one cares. Not in this crazy, mixed up crowd."

Shawna frowned and let his natural voice out. "I'm a TV, not a tranny. Not that I give a shit what you think, girlie."

"Oh, I'm glad you're just a TV. Most male TVs I know like women." She stood outside the stall, her voice playful. "Straights who just like dressing in drag. So you're one of them?"

"You want to find out?"

Still inside the bathroom stall, adjusting the see-through blouse over the padded black bra and cinching it with a black belt, Shawna decided to take a calculated risk. She smiled and opened the stall door, then beckoned Jeanine into it. After Dave gestured to her, she slipped a hand down the pirate's shorts. Almost in a dreamy trance, Jeanine ran her hand over Dave's dick and balls. His cock ached for release inside some smooth female flesh.

"Ooo, maybe. I might be talked into it." Her voice teased him, but he knew she was more than just curious. She released him and stepped out of the stall.

Could he get used to a more normal woman like Jeanine?

Hell yeah! He just wanted to fuck like a man. An angry, domineering man. Yeah, that was what it was all about. Domination. Control. Release. Letting go of some rage.

Strange, that switcheroo. The more female he became on the outside, the more male he felt on the inside. An aggressive, domineering male predator who was ready to take on a normal, flesh-and-blood woman. No more whores or prepubescent girls.

"You'll find out after I buy you a coupla drinks," he said as loudly as he could manage in his chick's voice. "What'd'ya say, Jeanine? We buy a bottle and go somewhere afterwards?"

"Ooh, we'll see," Jeanine called out again after giggling. Her high-pitched voice faded as she moved away. "See you out there, Shawna! Maybe check ya out later, Shawn!"

Yep, Shawna decided, you'll see all right, you crazy-ass slut. Maybe not tonight, but you will see me. Sooner or later.

What the hell? The club was already hopping at 5:15 on a Sunday evening.

"'Bout time, Shawna." Bill, the crew supervisor, was at least six-foot-five, husky with bulging biceps and massive shoulders. His black hair had a military cut and tatts went up and down his arms and neck. His job was to keep everybody in line. He snarled. "Your tables are filling up." He looked Shawna up and down and frowned. "Those ain't the pirate shorts."

Shawna simpered softly, "I know, I tried them on but none of them fit. Good thing I brought my own."

"Better lose that butt if you want to work here," Bill growled before turning away to trouble-shoot another problem.

Shawna grabbed her order pad and pen, thinking, *You're the first asshole I'm going to try that icepick on.* But she already knew that would be impossible. The asshole outweighed Dave by a hundred pounds and had just been promoted from bouncer to management. No, too dangerous. The cops would be all over this place in minutes.

She fitted the eyepatch over her left eye and straightened out the front knot of her blouse. Fucking management. This creepy costume was supposed to pass for sexy?

Two hours later, a familiar customer showed up, shooting up Shawna's pulse rate. She watched him and his date, a petite brunette, take one of the reserved tables. The date wasn't the dude's blonde girlfriend, the artist chick who worked for the cops. Disappointed, Shawna went over and took the drink order, acting friendly as usual. Minutes later, when the drinks were ready and placed on her tray, Shawna went back. The brunette had most likely taken a trip to the girls' room, since her little clutch purse was still on the table. It was a good opportunity.

"What happened to the pretty blonde I saw you with a week or two ago?" she asked as she smiled and set down their drinks. What was the dude's name . . . Dan. "Did you do the mean-man thing, Dan, and dump her?"

Dan cast his eyes down at his drink and squared his shoulders. "No, we kinda dumped each other. It was time."

Shawna lingered beside the table. "Aren't you two artists? Uh, painters? What happened—I mean, it seemed like you had a lot in common."

Dan looked up under a hooded gaze. "You might say we had professional differences of opinion." He shrugged. "Probably better this way."

Shawna, feigning sympathy, glanced over at Big Bill. Management encouraged the servers to chat up their customers but not dally too long at any one table.

"Sorry to hear about the breakup. What d'ya mean, better this way?"

Dan glanced to the left and right of him before bending forward and lowering his voice. The band on stage was warming up, so Shawna had to hunch over to hear what he said.

"I found out she's a little nuts. A girl I dated for two years. Shows you never really know someone, I guess. She said she could read minds by just touching a person." Dan snorted his derision and sipped his drink, a straight, three-fingers Jack on the rocks. "She said she read my mind and saw me with this new girlfriend. That's how she knew I'd cheated on her. Can you believe that?"

"Amazing." Shawna touched the choker fixed to her neck. "Is the blonde—this Athena—crazy? Delusional?"

"That's exactly what I called her, delusional. She tried to prove it. She grabbed me and told me to think of something I'd never told her, something far in my past. Just to shut her up and play along, I did just that. She fucking amazed me."

"No shit," replied Shawna. "You think she's the real deal? A real psychic?"

Dan proved readily forthcoming, like he was sharing the shock of that experience with someone he thought truly cared. The drink had loosened his tongue, Shawna was pleased to see.

"She told me she's clairvoyant. She said she works for the

cops sometimes. Y'know, helps them investigate cases they're stuck on. Like that serial killer case on the TV news a few years ago. The guy was killing those young girls. She gave the cops a lot of clues and set them off on the right direction. Told them who to go after. Just before he disappeared." Dan threw up his hands, complete bewilderment clouding his expression. "Go figure. I don't believe any of that crap. She's conning the cops, is what I think. Don't ask me why."

Shawna's blood ran cold, sending a chill up and down the back of her skull. So that was why the blonde went with Ochoa that day, why she'd turned up at his brother's shop and apartment with Ochoa and the search warrant over two months ago. She wasn't just a police sketch artist, drawing what a witness would tell her he'd seen. The bitch was playing mind games with the cops. But was she the real deal? And exactly how had she helped them zero in on Sam and Dave Millhouse? How would she know anything about them if she wasn't the real deal?

"I don't believe in that psychic nonsense," Shawna said, straightening but maintaining her fixed, friendly smile. The crew supervisor, Bill, was staring at Shawna. *Gotta get this over with fast.* "She still helping the cops?"

Dan sat back as if in a daze. "Don't know . . ."

His voice trailed off as Big Bill appeared at the table. The hulk hooked a thumb at Dan.

"You trying to date our guest, Shawna? C'mon, get a move on. You've got five other tables to wait on."

Shawna smiled a forlorn goodbye to Dan, wiggled her fingers and moved on. For the next few hours, she had no more opportunity to speak with Dan, whose date had returned to the table and now consumed all his attention. The show started, and while Shawna kept busy with her tables, she once caught Dan looking her way and frowning as though regretting he'd said so much to a near perfect stranger.

Too fuckin' bad, dude. But thanks all the same, asshole.

With everything this guy Dan had told her, Shawna did what she always did with shocking information. She took her time to digest it all. And after that, she would tell Sam about it. Then together they would decide whether to act on the information or not.

Like they always did.

Dave could always rely on big brother Sam to know what to do.

CHAPTER FIFTEEN

A thena's alarm went off at six. Weeks had passed while she painted all day in order to get her two pastiches done. She'd rush out at dusk to buy a few groceries and then rush back to work some more. There was an all-night market and deli two blocks away, thank goodness. All in all, the time and effort had paid off. The pastiches were done — and done well. That morning she had an early flight to catch with Martin Larsen and the rest of the pastiche painters going to the big gallery opening in San Francisco.

Bleary-eyed, she yawned and roused herself from a deep sleep, but she lay in bed for a minute longer. She kept returning to the mind-hop that one day with Kas Skoros as he'd stood in his parents' family room, gazing at the portrait she'd painted of him over two years ago. He'd grown aware of her presence right away and spoken to her via his thoughts.

Athena. I'll see you soon. Let me protect you, be your friend. I can do that much . . .

She couldn't answer him, for she didn't know what she was going to do, herself. Why was her subconscious, or The Flow that her subconscious connected with, allowing her to enter his mind? Not once, but repeatedly? What was that all about? She almost wished an entity from The Flow would appear or send an audio message — *you're there because . . .*

A simple explanation was all she wanted. So typical of Kas Skoros to want to do something to alleviate her sorrow. He'd caused her excruciating pain, and yet he wanted to help her. Why? Didn't he realize how impossible any relationship with him was? Never mind their psychic connection. The pain was too raw. She could never trust him again.

Even a phone call to Milan had revealed no answers. Her clairvoyant-healer of a mother could only suggest that their psychic bond with their ancient female bloodline in The Flow was in some way responsible for her special connection to Kas Skoros. But why Kas, her mother couldn't say. Athena didn't have that kind of psychic bond with any other male. Not her father, not her brother, not even her Italian uncle whose mother, her dear Nonna, was of the bloodline. Her mother did suggest that Kas's mother, one of the most powerful descendants of the bloodline, had somehow imbued her youngest son with an ability that the other males associated with their bloodline did not have. The last words her mother left her with, "Be kind to Kas. Forgive him," still rang in her mind.

Impatient with all the unanswered questions that crowded her mind, Athena swung her legs off the bed and got up. Fifteen minutes later, she was showered, dressed and groomed to go.

California, here I come.

The Stargazer Tower. Quite a fitting name for a thirty-story residential tower. The gallery, according to Martin Larsen, founder of GPWGP, or Great Pastiches of the World's Greatest Paintings, was on the ground floor of the tower. The eight painters who'd finished their pastiches in time would be staying in the boutique hotel on the first five floors of the Stargazer Tower. Supposedly, the other twenty-five floors consisted of million-dollar-plus condos, most of which were already sold, according to Martin. And Kas Skoros was the operations director of the building, overseeing every aspect of the tower's construction, interior decor and sales of its hotel rooms and condos. He was also in charge of ground floor retail shops. From sheriff's deputy and part-time businessman to full-time tycoon for Skoros Enterprises. In two short years. Why was she not surprised?

Martin and his lover, Mark, would be helping to organize the exhibit, along with the gallery's manager, a Miss Valerie Thornton.

Athena slipped into her loafers and gathered her rolling suitcase and hobo bag together at her feet. Yesterday, she'd escorted, via taxi, the box containing her two paintings, pastiches of Edouard Manet's *Plum Brandy* and *Olympia,* to Martin's Visions Gallery, where she worked on the weekends. Athena had worked tirelessly on the two paintings for a little over two months, day and night, until the result had satisfied her. Indeed, she realized she was a perfectionist in her art.

In addition to the Manet pastiches, her abstract self-portrait and the other square painting in that same time frame had exhausted her. Those two square paintings, her originals, she'd take separately on the plane, herself. Those had a special purpose.

In the meantime, she'd broken up with Dan Grantham and had worried herself into a dither over her father, who had since recovered completely from a bout of viral pneumonia. Her mother had nursed him back to health with the unique healing powers of the Delphi Bloodline. Thank God. Their powers weren't a total curse.

Still, mentally, emotionally and physically, Athena was wiped out.

Even so, things had to get done. Martin had taken on the task of shipping the twenty pastiches ahead of the eight painters, making certain there would be no last-minute snafus. Too much money rested on the paintings' safe arrival in San Francisco, the shipping itself costing a small fortune, Martin claimed. If all twenty pastiches sold for what Martin had appraised and tagged them for, the bulk profit would be one million dollars, minus the Stargazer Gallery's twenty percent commission and Martin's commission and shipping costs. If the pastiches sold above Martin's estimated market value, well . . . even better. The sky was the limit.

A glance around the loft reminded her of something. She went over to the kitchen counter and found the pad of note-paper that she and Mikayla kept handy for note passing. Her roomie, a magazine and occasional runway model, was on a photo shoot in Bermuda for a week. Her new boyfriend Barry was the magazine's fashion photographer and he was using his influence to set her up with a score of jobs. Lately, it seemed like she and Mikayla were passing ships in the night, communicating to each other in a kind of abbreviated code. Athena wrote her message. "Bck next Sun 8 PM, taxi. XOXO, A."

Her buzzer sounded. The cab had arrived. She could've walked the four long blocks to the Visions Gallery, where the painters and Martin were all meeting to take the shuttle van to Reagan International, but today she was too exhausted to try.

Having locked the door behind her, Athena turned around to see her floor mate, Kyle, close his door to apartment F. See-ing her suitcase, he offered to help roll it down the stairs. She was grateful that their meeting was so fortuitous, for the suit-case was heavy and so were the cardboard box and purse she was juggling in her arms.

"Where to this time, Athena?" he asked. A very tall, slim, pleasant looking man in his late thirties, Kyle worked as a bar-tender by night and sculptor by day.

"San Francisco this time. A gallery showing." She smiled at him as he rolled the suitcase down the three flights of stairs. Always polite and friendly, Kyle had once asked her out but she'd declined, citing her relationship with Dan. She hoisted both the cardboard box that contained the two square paint-ings and her satchel-styled purse, the bag thumping a rhythm on her back vertebrae.

"Pastiches?" he asked. Kyle had come to one of the Visions

Gallery's exhibits of Martin's GPWGP. Later, after making contact with Martin, he'd sold several of his better sculptures at Martin's gallery.

"Yes, it's a big West Coast showing. Eight of us pastiche painters are going with Martin and Mark."

"Well, good luck. Let me know how it turns out. I might have to move out there, but I hear the housing is through the roof."

"Thanks," she said, glancing at Kyle, "so much. It would've taken me at least two trips to move all of this."

At the sidewalk, the cabbie took her suitcase and cardboard box and stowed it in the trunk. He held the back-passenger door open for her.

"Visions Gallery on Fourth," she told the cabbie, then paused at the open door. The biker chick—what was her name?—was across the street on her motorcycle, just sitting there and smoking a cigarette. The woman waved at Kyle, who waved back.

Her presence reminded Athena of something she'd heard the other day.

"Hey there," she called to the biker chick. The woman smiled, her white, perfect teeth and too bright smile almost causing Athena to change her mind. Too late. To Kyle, she asked, "You've met Shawna?"

Before heading off to cross the street, he said, "I met Shawna the other day over coffee. I heard there's a vacancy over there"—he pointed to the all-red brick building two doors down across the street from their loft building—"Ten-twenty-four. Told her to check it out, since she likes the neighborhood. Guess she did. She's taking me for a ride."

The biker chick made a gesture towards Athena after Kyle joined her. "Where you off to?" she called out.

Rather impertinent question. Athena hesitated. Her British reserve kicked in, so she deflected the question.

"Business trip," Athena called out, then hurriedly waved and stepped into the cab. "Let's go, quickly," she instructed the cabbie. Then she recalled telling Kyle where she was going. Big city, though, and she hadn't told him the name of the gallery. Though why did she care?

The driver immediately put the cab in gear and pulled away from the curb. Athena didn't look back.

There was something about the biker chick that jangled her nerves. Her nerves were already on high alert, vibrating like a crazy, out-of-control tuning fork. And she knew why.

Her nerves had nothing to do with selling the pastiches, but everything to do with seeing Kas Skoros again.

She recalled that head-hopping night with Kas and his son, Alex. Father and son. The moonlight in their eyes. Gazing at the stars. Kas singing *Twinkle, Twinkle, Little Star* to the little boy. That night had inspired the name of the Skoroses' highrise building, The Stargazer Tower. At any rate, she liked to think so.

It didn't take a gifted mind-reader like herself or an extraordinary precog like Lorena Skoros to know what their exhibition in the Stargazer's gallery was all about. Or who the developer was and why he had invited Martin's GPWGP to exhibit in the Stargazer Tower's art gallery.

Kas had called it restitution and reconciliation. The former wasn't necessary, she felt. Two years of maturity had convinced her that Kas had done what he had to do for the sake of his family. There was nothing she wouldn't do for hers, that much was true.

But reconciliation? Not possible.

On an impulse, she glanced out the cab's rear window. Kyle had climbed on the back of Shawna's motorcycle and the two were taking off down the road in the opposite direction. A moment passed before her mind pivoted back inexorably to thoughts of Kas Skoros.

Oh Kas, what am I going to do when I see you again?

A heartbeat later — *Just don't make a sodding fool of yourself.*

CHAPTER SIXTEEN

The airport shuttle van arrived in the heart of San Francisco, took a series of turns off Interstate Eighty south of Market and then pulled up at the curb on Mission Street. The North Entrance of the Stargazer Tower was as impressive as the gleaming black and ivory tinted glass façade of the tower itself. Huge black terra cotta urns sprouting queen and sago palms greeted them as they disembarked from the van under the marquee-lit *porte cochere.*

Their group of ten—eight pastiche painters and Martin Larsen and his assistant-partner, Mark—stood for a long moment in awe at the tower's splendor. Its size, taking up an entire block on each side, reminded Athena of a sleek Gothic cathedral. The vertical lines compelled one to gaze upward, the tower's upper reaches seemingly disappearing into the clouds. Bell hops from the boutique hotel on the first five floors rushed forward to help them with their bags. Soon carts filled with suitcases and carry-ons wheeled through massive sliding doors past uniformed private security guards and vanished up burnished service elevators. Check-in went smoothly and quickly in the black granite-floored lobby. Chandeliers of multi-colored, customized blown glass in the shapes of stars and planets seemed to float above their heads. Everywhere she looked, glass and granite glittered and gleamed.

The Skoros Group and their partners had built a modern wonder, a tribute to the city by the Golden Gate. Athena, reminding herself that Kas was Director of Operations for the

Skoros Group—her computer search had revealed that—found herself scanning the lobby, wondering if she'd catch a glimpse of him. No, why would he stick around? It was enough that he'd arranged the gallery exhibit of their pastiches. Was that what he meant by *reconciliation and restitution*? He wanted to make it up to her and be friends again?

But is that even possible?

Within minutes, the hotel's assistant manager ushered them through onyx-walled elevators and showed them their rooms on the fifth floor. He reminded everyone that a reception, organized by gallery manager Valerie Thornton, would be held that evening in the Ocean Bar and Grill, located on the ground floor adjacent to the lobby. Athena had noticed a coffee shop, a few upscale shops and a Spa on the ground floor, also. According to the Tower Directory in the lobby, the Stargazer Gallery was located on the Third Street side of the tower, facing east towards the Embarcadero and the Bay Bridge. They had three hours to kill before the reception, but several of the painters looked haggard after their cross-continental flight, declaring that a nap and shower awaited them.

With everyone ensconced in their rooms, and after unpacking the few things she'd brought, Athena took her card key and slipped downstairs. The assistant manager, Robert, looked surprised to see her so soon.

"May I assist you, Miss?" he asked solicitously.

"The Stargazer Gallery? Can I go there from inside the building? I'd like to see it." Robert indicated a hallway behind the elevators, a right turn and then a left one.

She followed his directions and located the back entrance into the gallery from inside the hotel. An older woman in her fifties, impeccably groomed in a black suit and maroon blouse, her dark brown hair coiffed in a severe comb-back and bun, sat behind a high, black granite counter on a metal-backed stool. Miss Thornton, obviously. She was already decked out for their business reception.

"Hello, you must be Valerie Thornton," said Athena, extending her hand. "I'm Athena Butler, one of the pastiche painters. I'm so keyed up, I just had to come down and see the gallery. May I look around?"

The older woman smiled politely. "Of course, help yourself. We've been exhibiting a local artist who paints the Wine Country. Tomorrow, Martin will help me hang the pastiches so that they're highlighted when people come in. We want to show them off to advantage, of course. The private grand reopening will be tomorrow evening and then the public will be invited in the following day. But I'm sure Martin has gone over the agenda with all of you."

Athena moved to the first wall of the nearest cubicle. The entire gallery length and width were divided into small cubicles, each the size of a tiny living room. Track lighting hung above each cubicle, but the overall impression was not appealing in the least. A customer had to move into the boxy cubicle to see the art hanging on the four small walls. If the painting was large and needed to be viewed at a distance for maximum effect, such a thing was impossible with the configuration of small cubicles. It looked as if the gallery was attempting to hide the art instead of display it.

"Actually, Martin hasn't kept us informed. We've all been so busy trying to get our pastiches done in time." She looked over at the woman and smiled in a friendly fashion. "We're all excited to be included in this event. Martin does his gallery events with a lot of panache and hoopla."

A moment later, she realized that perhaps the woman would interpret her words as a critique or warning. She remembered telling Kas about the first time she'd seen the pastiches unveiled at Martin's Visions Gallery — the champagne and hors d'oeuvres, the framed promo posters, the publicity and representatives of the press, the well-heeled clientele especially invited to see the exhibit, even the gold and black balloons. Martin, his uncle and Mark and all the servers wore black tuxes. Athena had bought an evening gown just for their last event and she'd brought it with her.

"Ah yes, I've heard of Martin's events. Mr. Skoros wants this re-opening to be just as exciting, just as sophisticated. I've publicized it all over the city, especially among the city's upper-crust and the Tower's residents. Did you say your name is Athena Butler?"

Pleased that Kas would remember her words, she was momentarily distracted by the paintings of vineyards that surrounded her. Very poorly done, she concluded. Impressionistic attempts, but gaudy and too heavy with impasto, their palettes too garish. This gallery manager might have a head for business, but she didn't have an eye for good art.

"Yes," she said, stepping out of the first cubicle.

Valerie Thornton held up a square-shaped envelope. "This is for you, Miss Butler. Mr. Skoros left it for you. I was to give it to you at tonight's reception, but I suppose he wouldn't mind if I gave it to you now. He said you were old friends."

Athena nodded and took the envelope. Her hands trembling slightly, she scuttled into another small cubicle and sat in the only chair available. Her pulse flared, like a struck match bursting into flame. She tried to calm herself but couldn't. The card inside was a cream-colored card stock embossed in gold with the Stargazer Tower logo. Kas had written a few lines in black ink. Strange, but she'd never seen his handwriting. He'd texted her and left phone messages the first few months after their breakup—which she'd never returned. This cursive note was his first ever handwritten note to her. Maybe she was old-fashioned, but this was formal and more personal. What did that mean?

Athena,
Welcome to San Francisco. Please accept my personal invitation

to have a nightcap with me on the Stargazer's Rooftop Terrace. Tonight, nine o'clock. You alone.

Kas Skoros

She sniffed the card. His cologne, a mixture of musk and lime, drifted into her nostrils. Was this her imagination going wild? She sniffed again, but the scent was gone. Her next question to herself. *How can I hate a man who's so kind to a little boy? A little boy who'll never know his true, fun-loving father? How can I refuse just one drink with such a man? Even though he broke my heart?*

A man who made this special exhibit possible for Martin's pastiche painters. Indeed, she could not refuse such a man one drink.

It would be so rude.

The reception for the painters turned out to be more than what any of them had expected. The bounty included a full meal from the bar and grill's menu and an open bar, of which ninety percent of the pastiche artists were happy to avail themselves. She knew that all eight painters, herself included, had worked day and night to get their pastiches ready for this event. The chance to sell another piece of art had motivated all of them, but the icing on the cake was the free vacation in San Francisco. Everyone was animated, although most of them complained about the cold and the fog.

Athena spent the two hours nursing one drink—well, maybe two or three. Moscow Mules were made of vodka, ginger beer and lime juice, and Athena found them irresistible. The tart of the lime and kick of the ginger added another dimension to the effects of the vodka. *Oh God, I'm cracking up with anxiety.*

Getting blinkered was not my plan.

"We're all clichés," she told Martin, who was sitting next

to her at the long dinner table set for twelve. Kas Skoros was a no-show, but Valerie Thornton had brought her friend, Naomi, to the happy affair. Soon Naomi had invited everyone to the Gay Pride Parade that was to take place in the city the following Sunday. Unfortunately—or fortunately, depending on one's point of view—they were all returning to D.C. on Saturday morning and would miss what Naomi declared would be the wildest Street Fair in the USA.

Halfway in his cups, Martin bobbed his head in her direction. "How so, clichés?"

"I mean, aren't all painters and writers supposed to be half-starved lushes? Look at Van Gogh, Gauguin . . . so many others. Toulouse-Lautrec, Corot . . ." She found it challenging to focus on any snippet of conversation when she kept glancing at her wristwatch. Nine o'clock, he'd said. "And the writers, look at James Joyce, Oscar Wilde, Hemingway, Fitzgerald, O'Neill . . ."

"We're not lushes, Athena," Martin retorted, "we're just celebrating and working off nerves. You artists, especially. You've worked hard, so now indulge yourselves. Tomorrow night's a big night. The *savoir-faire* of Silicon Valley and the Bay Area will be here, their tech-stock portfolios bulging with unspent profits and bonuses. Surely, they'll throw us some bones."

Sitting on Martin's other side, Mark waved a hand in front of his partner's face. "You're mixing your metaphors, bud. You mean *small change*. And while we're on the subject of lushes, I think we should stay for the parade. Don't you agree, Athena?"

She smiled and glanced at her watch. "I hear it's going to be outrageous."

Mark laughed and playfully slapped Martin's arm. "That is guaranteed. C'mon, you ol'fuddy-duddy, let's stay. I hear the going costume this year will be rainbow-colored tutus . . .

and nothing else. Can you imagine, our ding-dongs flapping in the breeze under some tutus? Doesn't that sound divinely decadent? Only in San Francisco." He sighed heavily and rolled his eyes.

Martin looked dubious. "We're here on business. What would the others think?" He glanced around the table at the assembled artists, most of them over forty.

The younger half of the M and M team, Mark turned away, showing his exasperation with his older, much more conservative lover. "Oh, brother, what a party killer."

Martin sat back and sipped from his martini. "What about you, Athena? You're the youngest of the bunch, but you're a Brit. You wouldn't want to stay, I bet."

She shrugged. "I don't know. Depends on what happens." She squinted at her watch for the twentieth time in as many minutes. "I once watched a Gay Pride Parade from the front window of The Texas Embassy Cantina. That's a Western themed restaurant and bar in London. It was fun. I sketched some of the participants and even thought about doing a painting. Never got around to it," she concluded, shrugging.

Martin looked across the table at Valerie and Naomi in a close tete-a-tete and lowered his voice to a whisper, his head close to Athena's.

"What do you think? I took a look at the gallery — simply ghastly, the arrangement of the art. All those walls. Closed up and dark. Ugh, simply ghastly. Wonder what she'll do when Mark and I start moving those walls around?"

"I don't know," she mused, "guess that's why you get the big bucks, isn't it?"

Martin snorted and chuckled as she, noting the time, scooted back her chair.

"By the way, dear, you look especially fetching tonight. Who're you meeting? Don't deny it, I know you're meeting someone. You've got a glow about you, and it's not just the liquor."

She patted her overly warm cheek. "I'm not glowing. Just an old friend of mine invited me up to the Rooftop Terrace for a nightcap."

"Oh, just a nightcap, she says." Martin threw her an exaggerated lusty look. "And you're wearing *that* for just a nightcap with a friend?"

She grinned appreciatively. Sprucing up a jot had made even Martin notice. She wore black velvet leggings and a low-cut black and white Zebra-patterned silky top with silver studs on the black stripes. Three-inch black heels seemed to slim her legs, and she'd swept her long ponytail down into a glittery red barrette off her left shoulder, which she kept twisting from an attack of nerves. Silver hooped earrings and a little makeup helped finish the look, but she still felt like a little girl dressing up in her mother's clothes to play house. Rather, to play seductress.

God, no, scrub that out of your mind, you daft ninny.

Compelled by curiosity, Mark had rejoined the conversation. "Rooftop Terrace? My dear, it's closed tonight. The hotel manager told me."

"Evidently, not closed to this chap," she said. She stood up shakily and grabbed her black clutch bag. "Wish me good luck, Martin, Mark."

"Just a private nightcap on a closed rooftop?" teased Mark, "how divine."

"Ah, *that* chap." Martin held up his martini glass in a kind of salute.

"We're just . . . well, I'm not at all certain what we are."

Enemies about to declare a truce? More likely than not.

CHAPTER SEVENTEEN

What immediately struck Athena as the elevator doors hissed open was the dense fog swirling around in front of her. She stepped gingerly out of the elevator, hesitant in the face of such a shroud of heavy mists. Nothing was visible except a couple of nearby lampposts on the perimeter of the roof line. She couldn't discern any outlines, no bar, no tables or chairs. The air was chilling, and she instinctively grasped her arms. She should've worn a ski parka. Brrr.

All of a sudden, a bearded and mustachioed man appeared in front of her, emerging like a phantom from the depths of the gray fog. She instinctively backed up a few steps. It took a moment before she realized she was staring into Kas's face.

"Amazing, isn't it? Fog this thick in the middle of summer."

His voice and his head seemed to float in the air. He smiled, and a hand emerged from the fog. She took it and let him guide her through the cold miasma and over to a bar stool. Too surprised and nervous, she forgot to open her clairvoyant channel. With all the alcohol soaking her brain cells, she was sure it wouldn't have worked, anyway.

Soon he was shedding his gray-and-black tweed sports jacket and wrapping it around her shoulders, all the while calling over the bartender. A tuxedoed man appeared out of the gray cottony swirl and set down a glass votive, the light from the tiny fire mesmerizing her briefly. He took her order — another Moscow Mule — and disappeared. Only then did Athena turn in her seat and look over the man to whom she'd once given her heart, body and soul.

Kas returned her silent gaze, taking her in as thoroughly as she was studying him.

He wore a black turtleneck over gray slacks, a big watch with a diamond-beveled face the size of a small saucer. There was a ring on the middle finger of his right hand; as far as she could tell, it was some kind of a signet ring. His ring finger was bare, she noted. Slight worry lines bracketed his dark penetrating eyes, and his tanned face was half hidden by a mask of dark brown hair. When he finally smiled, he allowed her a glimpse of teeth.

"You look wonderful," he said softly.

Oddly enough, she found his voice soothing. Her nerves had calmed, and the sudden surprise was gone. As if the time warp she'd always felt with Kas had vanished, along with some wisps of the fog that clung to the Rooftop Terrace. Two and a half years seemed to have disappeared in the swirl of tattered fog. The old emotions surged inside her, the anger and pain gone. Maybe she'd just grown up a little, had gotten wiser, had become more comfortable with the mysteries of men. And life in general.

"It does that," he said. "The fog. When the elevator opens, the warm air causes the cool fog to whip around a bit, and then it settles and blows away with the ocean breeze. You look like you've seen a ghost." He covered her left hand with his right. "I'm real, and so are you. You look great, Athena."

She removed her hand on the pretense of switching her bag from her lap to the bar's black granite countertop. Residual distrust instantly enveloped her, and she definitely did not want to read his mind. She already knew what he wanted, and she was not prepared to deliver it. Not yet.

What does he think I'm going to do? Jump in his lap like a desperate, simpering fool?

"Thank you, you look . . . well, different. The beard . . ."

Although neatly trimmed, it still covered half of his handsome face. Just as well, she hated facial hair on men. A memory of dark chest hair sprang to her mind, the light smattering arrowing down his belly, as if inviting her to gaze further. She liked his back and shoulders hairless. She'd liked that very much . . .

"Yes, well . . . it's easier to take care of. I'm on the go a lot, weekends in Loomis with my son and my folks, weekdays here for the past two years." Kas eyed her left arm as he took a swig from his beer. "Your arm has healed completely? No lingering effects from the bullet?"

"That ricocheted gunshot?" That was something she wanted to forget. She shook her head. "And you? Your leg and neck?"

He grinned mirthlessly at their comparisons of injuries. "Look at us, comparing war wounds. I'm fine, leg's okay, occasional twinges and weakness. Neck, healed. No more Search and Rescue, though. No more downhill skiing. I jog when I can. The piers are a good place here to jog, and they're close by."

He left that idea dangling for her to consider. They had jogged together once when he'd come to visit her in DC. Despite their friendly overtures, they were conversing like acquaintances who had once shared similar experiences but now felt awkward with each other. But there was a layer of emotion over all their words. Still, she'd learned that men with no wedding bands on their ring fingers didn't necessarily mean they were single.

"Are you still married?" she blurted out.

"The divorce will be final the end of this month."

She saw in his expression that he knew they were now slogging in emotional mud as he turned back to his beer. "Lasted longer than I thought it would. At Nikki's and her father's insistence, I might add. For Xander's sake and to keep peace among the business partners, I stuck around longer than I wanted to. Helped Nikki out with babysitting, that sort of thing."

"Yes, I saw you with him . . . that night. Xander? My mother said the little boy is named after your brother, Alex."

"Yeah, he is. I-I just have a hard time calling him Alex." Kas looked at her as though recalling the day of his brother's funeral, when he and Athena had held each other in a grief-stricken rictus of pain.

She was careful not to touch him as she drank the remainder of her Moscow Mule, her third, she reminded herself. Or was it her fourth? She'd lost track. The mists began to spin in front of her eyes like a whirling Dervish. She held onto the edge of the counter and looked back at him. Was he disappointed with her, with the way she looked or sounded. Was he just being polite to an old friend?

"It was kind of you to do this for us."

"Do what? The pastiche exhibition? Part business, part pleasure. An excuse to see you again." His voice had grown a little hoarse. His dark eyes seemed to swim with emotion.

Fear clutched her heart. No, she couldn't let him hurt her again. She slipped off the side of her stool and stood, her balance wheeling, her mind spinning. Blimey, she was plastered to the wall. Why had she drunk so much?

"You okay, Athena?" He was at her side, holding her shoulders, moving in close enough for her to whiff his musky lime cologne. Inexplicably, the barrier between their minds dissolved and she glimpsed images that made her heart skip a few beats.

"Fine, fine, just a little tipsy." Like a veil slipping off her tongue, she suddenly lost the ability to check her impulses and curb her mouth. "You're still wearing the same cologne, I see. I'm glad you have a beard. I dislike them so."

"Aha," he said, chuckling. "Still need an excuse to dislike

me? I guess I've given you enough reasons. Well, I better see you back to your room." His voice sounded like it drifted her way through a tunnel filling with water.

"No need, really. I'm sure I can manage."

"Right," he drawled drily, seizing her arm at the elbow. She felt an arm enclose and support her. "Let me help you, Athena. No harm in that, is there? I'm not going to jump your bones."

"Y-you're not?" She seized her clutch and stuffed it into the pocket of his lent sports jacket. She took a few cautious steps away from the bar. "S-see, I-I can make it on my own."

"Yeah, you've still got that disconnect between your mind and your emotions, don't you? One stubborn woman."

"So? You know, Kas Skoros, you're safe 'cause I don't like beards. M-mustaches, okay if it's a French sort of m-mustache. Not the skinny British kind . . . and the Italian m-mustache is, uh, is . . ." She lost track of what she was blurting out. Good grief, she had diarrhea of the mouth. *Say anything. Just don't say what you really feel.* "Your m-mustache is too . . . wild. Yes, too wild. Just like you."

Kas barked a short laugh. "Wild? I only wish. Those days are over, 'Thena. Thanks to you. It's all your fault. You've ruined me for other women."

"I'm sure I haven't." Athena leaned into him as he supported and guided her into the elevator. Amazed that she had so suddenly lost control of her balance—her legs felt rubbery and wobbly—she let him prop her up. Her mouth was on auto-pilot, more the pity. In addition to that, her thoughts were not connecting well. "I don't know what you mean, but I want—want you to know . . ."

"Know what?"

"Once burned and all that. Still, it's nice of you . . . to . . . for us, e-everything . . . the exhibit, the flight, the hotel rooms. V-very nice. Just d-don't expect anything from me."

"Ah, you see my ulterior motive. Selfish bastard that I am."

"You're raising Alex's son," she muttered, "M-maybe . . . not that selfish."

Unbidden, images and emotions flowed from his mind into hers. Some were welcomed, most of them not. They frightened her. He wanted her to meet the child, love him. Oh my God, he wanted so much more . . .

"Having a child changes you," he murmured against her hair, "The stakes are raised, and failure is not an option. Makes you a better person. Or should."

"Are you a better person?"

His silence left her question unanswered, but his thoughts said *God help me, I hope so.*

"Are you still with that guy, that painter?" he asked. He had his arm around her waist, leaning her into him like a support post. She flung her head back and looked up at his face. The black stare he returned was impenetrable, but the feelings he let loose into her mind were not. "I've kept tabs, you know."

"W-we broke up."

"Why?"

She hung onto his back with one hand, clinging to his shirt, liking the solid feel of him. His back muscles rippled through the shirt's fabric. She recalled how solid he'd felt on top of her, how safe she'd felt. She'd always felt safe with him. And yet, the thrills and excitement of Kas loving her, showing her extreme pleasure, had filled her body, mind and soul.

They were walking down a corridor, or rather, he was walking her.

"W-why? Why what?"

"Why did you two break up?"

"Ah, let me count the reasons." Shakespeare popped into her booze-sodden mind. "To thine own self be true . . . and, and as surely . . . uh, as surely as . . . something, something . . .

thou . . . uh, thou canst be false with any man." She giggled, happy she could still quote Shakespeare even though her mind was mush. "I-I'm the product of the British education system, w-what can I say?"

"Apparently, quite a lot, considering the circumstances." He looked down at her, frowning. "So what're you trying to tell me, 'Thena? He was false to you?"

Vaguely aware of their stopping in front of her hotel room, she pulled away and propped herself against the door. Her stomach felt on fire and her heart raced like a sprinter's. She was having more difficulty stringing words together, her thoughts like a stream of sludge. "He, uh . . ."

Kas interrupted her, an edge to his voice. "He cheated on you?"

She grimaced and nodded. "Among his other false . . . falseness." Was that even a word? No matter. She squinted into her evening bag, fishing for her card key. Where was it? "I-I was false to him. J-just not in the-the same way."

"Still can't hold your liquor, can you? Here, let me help you." He sighed audibly, as if he was annoyed with her and at the evening's outcome. Hadn't he told her once that the eight years' difference in their ages was like a lifetime?

But wasn't that part of the plan? Act like a ninny to drive him away? *Don't go back for another broken heart.*

A heartbeat later as he rummaged through her evening purse, she heard him sigh with exasperation. He found the card key, then used it while grabbing her around the waist when the door fell open behind her. Her arm wrapped around his back for support.

Guess this plan's working, you daft girl.

"I'm behaving like a d-drunk teenager. S-sorry."

"No apologies. Sometimes booze helps block out the pain. And fear."

She found herself lifted into his arms, decided to relax and cling to his neck. He was too strong, and the vodka had turned her arms and legs into rubber. She still trusted him completely, knew he wouldn't take advantage of her inebriated state. *Odd.* She feared him and what he could do to her heart but otherwise trusted him completely.

"Sorry, Kas." Why she was apologizing, she wasn't certain. She normally didn't behave in such undignified a manner. She'd dressed up like a sophisticate but couldn't carry it off. Not with Kas. Pain? She wasn't feeling any pain. Just a pleasant loss of self-control.

Fear? Oh yes.

When he let her down, she wavered on her feet for a moment and then — those damned three-inch heels — she toppled onto the carpet. Folded like a puppet with its strings cut. She hoped, with one sliver of her mind still lucid, that at the very least, she'd folded with grace. She lay on the carpet in a bundle, her face snug against the carpet, unable to make her muscles move like she wanted them to. Her eyes closed, she felt her fanny sticking up in the air but couldn't move even if she wanted to. All of a sudden, she didn't want to move. Falling asleep huddled on the carpet suited her just dandy.

The rest happened in a blur. Strong arms lifting her, her head falling back. Her barrette coming off, along with her shoes and her top. A blur of motion and color. Her entire body coming to rest upon her hotel bed. She was naked except for her black bra and black leggings. She half wished he'd undress her completely and himself, then climb on top of her. She'd feel warm and snug . . . like a bug in a rug.

His mind intruded. *It's been too long. I've missed you so much.*

She felt the same. She longed to tell him that but couldn't.

"I'm s-so, so b-bonkers," she muttered as she rolled onto her side and closed her eyes. A warm cover fell over her bare shoulders and she felt a weight beside her on the bed. Dimly, she realized a fully clothed Kas was lying next to her. She managed to roll over and cuddle up against him. A fuzzy, blissful cocoon enclosed her, and her mind went blank.

I must be dreaming. He's here, beside me.

Finally.

CHAPTER EIGHTEEN

A waking took forever, it seemed. Like a gradual floating up to the surface, the substance in which she floated sticking to her like viscous jello. Her mind experienced several layers of thought transference, telepathic visits in which she entered his mind, exited and then re-entered.

Right now, in her dreamlike state of Theta brain waves, her mind watched him. Kas was in his room. He looked in the mirror as he shaved off his beard and mustache. She watched him slip out of his slacks and underwear and enter his shower in his bare feet. The shower stall walls were a mottled brown granite, very masculine, the nozzle a brushed nickel. She knew his mind was preoccupied and a little troubled. He turned on the faucet and shuddered as the blast of cold water hit him square in the chest. The cold water sluiced off his body in rivulets and, as he looked down, shrank the hard erection he'd returned to his room with.

Minutes later, she caught his reflection in the narrow tinted glass window that ran along one of the shower walls, a floor-to-ceiling one filled with the steady lights of the city surrounding the tower. His whole body had tensed and stilled.

He paused as he eased open the hot water handle. Sensed something, a voyeur.

What're you doing, Athena? When I left you, you were zonked out. How can you be in my mind now of all times?

I don't know, Kas. I do like you better without facial hair. And naked.

She watched him grin and roll his eyes in the window's reflection.

130

Happy now? Go back to sleep and leave me alone. I've got troubles.

I am asleep. My subconscious mind has tuned you in. What troubles, Kas?

You, you're my trouble.

Why?

I was half hoping you'd leave me cold. Or at least numb. No such luck.

Why do we keep fighting this? The Flow's telling me it's fate. We can't fight fate, can we? Should we?

You tell me. You're the psychic.

You're angry because I came to you blinkered. You don't like me blinkered and immature? Like a rag doll?

Not really. But I understand why. Your fears got the best of you, Thena.

Sorry about that, I was so nervous.

What's to be nervous about? You know me. A heartbeat and a chuckle later. *Well, maybe you had good reason.*

Of course I did. Suddenly, blue sky appeared outside the tinted window next to his shower.

Look at this view. Awesome, isn't it? Worth every hour of work I've put into this place.

I'm really proud, and . . . dumbstruck by it all. What you've built.

Come see me when you're awake and sober. Coffee. I left one of my keys for you. Come and see me. I'm crashing, going to bed. It's only two o'clock. Go mind-hop somewhere else. Let me have some privacy. Or wake up and join me. Condo ten-ten. Tenth floor, number ten.

Go away or join me.

Stubbornly, she stayed in his head and looked down at his body. She knew he still sensed her presence. He stood straighter and sucked in his belly. His erection had resisted the cold water and sprung to life, even as he began to lather himself. He soaped his upper body, then worked his way down, taking his time, letting her gaze at his naked body.

I have to crash. I can't relax if you stay and keep looking.

Okay, I'll go. Good night, Kas.

Sleep well, my strange, pretty girl.

With whatever little control she still had over her lucid dreams, she withdrew from his head and fell quickly into a deep sleep.

At nine the next morning, she showered and dressed in a pair of black jeans, a scooped-neck metallic gold top and her sneakers. She'd promised to help Martin and Mark move around the portable walls that formed the Stargazer Gallery's god-awful cubicles, beginning at ten o'clock. She already knew what Martin had in mind for the pastiche exhibit. Several times, pertaining to her duties as a part-time gallery assistant, she'd helped him on weekends prepare for a special exhibit. She knew his gallery arrangements always displayed the artwork to best advantage and he would insist on enhancing the pastiche paintings in the same way.

But first, she had to get rid of her headache. The dull ache all over her skull was nothing compared to the humiliation she felt over her behavior the night before. Fortunately, she hadn't vomited or lost control of her other body functions. But what a crashing bore she'd been. Giving in to such an attack of nerves by getting potty was so . . . so juvenile. And then doing a Peeping Tom while he was in the shower. Indeed, she recalled that distinctly. What must he think of her?

A damp ponytail in place, she rubbed a coral gloss over her lips and then grabbed up the card key Kas had left on her nightstand. There was no note, and the card was unmarked with a room number — what had he told her? She fingered the card key until a number came to her. Tenth floor, ten-ten. The million-dollar-plus condos occupied floors six to thirty, she knew, and according to Valerie Thornton were eighty percent sold already. Apparently, a thousand dollars per square foot was the going rate these days for residential property in the city by the Golden Gate. Using that figure as a multiplier, a thousand square feet of condo space would cost a million, two thousand square feet of condo, two million, and so forth.

Holy crap.

Her and Mikayla's sizeable loft apartment, by contrast, at fifteen hundred square feet, would sell in San Francisco for one million, five hundred thousand dollars. Blimey. This was an over-the-moon, expensive city to live in, wasn't it?

She had to use Kas's card key to access the bank of elevators to the condo floors, which she thought was a good security device. The only security her loft apartment had was a locked front entrance door, so that she and Mikayla had to buzz people in. However, their own door lock had been broken by a former irate boyfriend of Mikayla's, and their super had never fixed it. A sturdy chain lock was the only obstacle keeping out a burglar or an intruder. Not that they had such valuable things to steal, but lately she'd been sensing danger. Though from where or who, she couldn't see. Like a sense of amorphous dread creeping up the back of her mind.

Something she didn't want to think about.

Nevertheless, by the time Athena arrived at Kas's condo door, she had decided to talk Mikayla into installing a dead bolt door lock. And she'd buy extra canisters of pepper spray to hide around the apartment.

She stood erect and smoothed aside her bangs. Instead of using Kas's card key for his door, however, she knocked. He hadn't appreciated her invading his privacy when he was showering. She knocked twice. When Kas flung the door open, a freshly scrubbed and fully dressed and groomed man smiled confidently back at her. His now clean-shaven face was still chafed from the shave, but he smelled of cologne and soap.

"I knew you'd come," he said with a deep-throated chortle, "especially after last night's debacle. Determined to redeem your pride?"

She smiled. "Again, I apologize. I don't always behave in such an immature fashion."

"I understand completely. I had some liquid courage, myself. I just hold it better. But what was the head visit about? While I was in my bathroom? The shower?"

"Oh, that." She sighed as she entered and looked around his condo. "Sorry but you know my mind has little control over my head-hopping visits. Guess I was more than a little curious."

"No need to explain. I found it a real turn-on."

Averting her eyes, she breezed past him, drawn to the floor-to-ceiling windows, similar to the bathroom window he'd been gazing out of last night. His living room held cozy comfortable furniture in warm earth tones—taupe, browns, muted pale greens—although the overall look was modern and minimalistic, the walls stark white and floors black tile.

"Nice, truly nice." She turned to smile at him then, aware that he could see her feelings for him when she looked at him. How could she hide them? What was the point? She just had to remain strong and resolute.

His wry expression conveyed acceptance of her intrusion. It was part of her, who she was. Came with the territory.

His dark eyes studied her. "It's just . . . It's unnerving sometimes. When it happens and I don't expect it. I don't want you to catch me at my worst."

"Yes, sorry about that. I wouldn't want you to catch me at my worst, either."

He shrugged and came up to her. "I have nothing to hide from you. Couldn't if I wanted to, anyway. Would've been more fun if you had joined me in person. The turn-on would've become something else."

He wore a white Oxford shirt tucked inside tan khakis, the collar open to a smooth shaven neck. His dark brown hair was combed back and long enough to hook a curl over the back of his white collar. Dressed for his work day? His close presence nearly overwhelmed her. Surely he could see how she felt when she looked at him. She trembled inside, couldn't hide it any longer.

When she spun around to take in the windows' views, his arms went around her waist, his hands lacing in front. She felt her soft behind cradled by his hard thighs.

"Ask me anything," he murmured against her hair, "I know you're full of questions."

With every touch, he was crumbling her wall of resolve. She held herself in check as she formulated her thoughts. Stay friendly, she told herself, but don't melt in his arms.

God, don't make it easy for him.

"Okay. Why isn't there fog this morning? Like last night's?" There were huge cranes like giant dinosaurs perched on top of nearby buildings. In the near distance, she spied the Giants' ballpark. A tall, round coliseum. Orange and black flags flew from its spires. A sliver of navy-blue bay water could be seen between two towers under construction. In the distance to her left, the Bay Bridge curved over the water.

"The fog usually burns off by mid-morning. We're facing south-east, so what you see out there is boom town building in what we call the SOMA district, South of Market. The techies want to live in the city where all the action is. They shuttle down to Silicon Valley to their jobs at Google, Apple, Facebook, Oracle. You name it, they're all down there. And they all pay well. Very well. These tech geeks—some of them in their mid-twenties—plunk down cash for a one-point-five million-dollar condo."

"Really? And you? You live here, too?"

"Weekdays. Instead of my share of the sales profits, I got this condo. Two bedrooms, two baths. Roomy, great location, great view. I like the city. You never get bored. But it's god-awful expensive to live here."

Her determination to remain neutral flew out the window. She turned on her clairvoyant channel as she finally asked., "Okay, I have to ask this. Did you ever sleep with Nikki? Did you ever want to? You stayed at her house a lot, didn't you? While Alex was a baby? I saw you there once, in the middle of the night. You were singing to the baby. The moonlight reflected in both your eyes."

Kas stiffened a little but then relaxed. She could see his mind registering the fact that lying or avoidance was pointless. Most men's instincts would be to lie about such matters. But she also knew Kas's choice, knowing her clairvoyance, was to tell her the truth and the consequences be damned. She'd always liked that about him. That instinct of his made her trust him even more.

But, hell's bells, he was also human. And Nikki was beautiful. One reason why his brother Alex had been so smitten with her.

"Ah, so I wasn't crazy that night. You were in my head. I felt it. I just wondered . . ." He cleared his throat. "Well, about Nikki. Yes, I was tempted. Maybe I just wanted to know what she had, what feminine wiles had trapped Alex into getting her pregnant. She came to me in a skimpy negligee, and I thought *why the hell not*. But then she opened her mouth and said something to the effect of *Well, now that Alex is gone, you might as well stand in for him in bed*."

"Oooh," Athena muttered. That was cruel. Not just that Kas had a healthy dose of male pride, but he'd loved his brother deeply. What Nikki said was cruel and callous.

"That worked better on a boner than a cold shower. I had to accept the fact that—the baby aside—I can't stand the woman and she can't stand me. She has no power over me. Around the boy, we're barely cordial, but to my everlasting surprise, our joint custody is working out. Weekdays Nikki has him with help from her mother and a licensed nanny. Weekends, she takes him to my folks' place in Loomis and I join them there. The little guy-" Kas chuckled with genuine humor. "The little guy's quite a character. He's got my brother's personality and looks. He's an Alex clone."

He nuzzled her smooth cheek with his own. "You know I'm telling the truth, Thena."

She inhaled his cologne. Musk and lime, an intoxicating combo. Her heart tripped with the happy sensation his words and interior feelings brought her. Very little had changed between them after two years. She even had to admit that the hatred she thought she once felt for him was just a turmoil of love denied and the pain of loss. "Yes, you are."

"I feel another question coming on," he teased.

"Okay, I don't want to pry but," —she shrugged within his warm, comforting embrace—"well, yes I do. Kas, you know about Dan and me. And I know you haven't been a monk these past two years."

"No, I haven't," he bussed her neck, making her shiver with pleasure, "and let's just leave it at that. Okay? I won't ask you for details and you don't ask me. Agreed?"

Tamping down the jealousy that spiked within her, Athena quashed it and slammed the mental door on those straying thoughts.

"Agreed. Now please give me some coffee. All those Moscow Mules have kicked me in the head."

"Okay, coffee coming up. But only if we're friends again."

She grinned. "Yes, we're friends again."

He kissed her cheek, then let her go and went behind the kitchen counter. The open floorplan of the condo made the living and dining areas accessible to the modern kitchen, a bare twenty feet away. A tray of sourdough pretzels, scones and muffins rested beside the Keurig machine on top of the black granite countertop.

"What'll it be? French Roast or Dark Verona? I remember you take hazelnut flavored creamer, no sugar. I don't cook much, but I can scramble an egg or two. The kitchens fully stocked, and the coffee shop downstairs sends up breakfast every morning."

"Not too shabby, ol' chap. Room service and a great view. What's not to like?"

She followed him out of the modern sitting room into the kitchen area, where two counter stools awaited them. His city pad was so different from his bachelor apartment over his parents' garage in the Loomis hills. Here, he was a busy businessman. There, in his mountain-friendly pad, he could escape the stress.

Still, she was surprised at her own lack of resolve. She'd caved so quickly. But why deny their friendship? Wasn't this a sign of her growing maturity?

"I see. Very nice, too. No eggs, thanks, just the coffee and a scone. Kas . . ." Athena stopped as he perched on one black leather cushioned stool and poured her a cup. He flicked a look of contentment over her way.

"What?"

"How's Spartacus?"

"Fine. More than fine, now that he has a female companion. Another German Shepherd. I named her Cassandra. The two trot around the Loomis property like they own the place."

He handed her the cup, the little bottle of creamer and a spoon. Dark eyes settled on her face. "You look . . . I don't know, like you've lost weight."

"I've been working so hard, haven't stopped to eat very much."

"You mean, the two pastiches you brought?" He looked puzzled. "I told Martin almost three months ago."

She had to laugh. "Do you know how much work goes into painting an exact replica of a masterpiece? We had a little over two months to do the pastiches. That's day-and-night work, so I hope you appreciate the prices we're asking."

"I do, I do. I just don't know anything about the kind of work you do. You're so gifted, you make it look so easy. Now I feel guilty that the gallery's asking a twenty percent commission."

She sipped the hot liquid, the caffeine already flowing through her veins like a magical restorative.

"That's low, believe me. I just wanted to let you know how hard we've all worked to be here. We appreciate the free airfare and hotel rooms, of course." She smiled gently. "Kas . . ."

"Yes?" His dark eyes sparked with amusement as his gaze roamed her face and hair in much the same way and with the same intensity as when she studied a subject before sketching it.

"I'm glad we're friends again."

Kas stroked a forefinger along her forearm. "I'm hoping we can be more than friends. Like before. You think that's possible? Be honest with me, Thena."

Her face heated up. She knew exactly what he meant. Was she ready to take the plunge again? And risk him breaking her heart again?

The very thought made her shudder. "I don't know. My heart's still cracked and bleeding from last time. I'm not the kind of woman that bounces back."

"I know, and I get it. I know I'm rushing things." He thrust his chin toward his laptop computer at the other end of the counter. "I was going over figures. The finishing contractor has raised his costs, so I've got to raise the prices of the remaining condos to keep our profit margins up. And that's what our investment partners expect us to do, keep our margins up. I'm hoping the big gallery re-opening tonight will attract some new buyers — for the condos, as well as the paintings. So like I said, part business, part pleasure. Wanting to see you again and . . . well, bringing in the bucks."

She sipped the heavenly coffee, reveled in the salty sweetness, and felt the headache dissipate. Good thing, she thought as she checked her watch. There was work to do in the gallery.

"Speaking of which, Kas, I have to help Martin and Mark rearrange the gallery display walls. Miss Thornton has it all wrong. I mean, she's not doing what she needs to do to show the art pieces in their best way. Martin knows how to do that. We have a lot of moving around and hanging to do before the gala tonight."

Her message sobered him and got his full attention. "Really? Y'know, I hired her six months ago, and her sales have been low and stagnant. Of course, Athena, you know this pastiche thing was a ploy to get you here and talking to me again. But"—he huffed out a breath of air—"my job is to get that gallery to make money, or the partners will boot it. There're plenty of other boutique stores and restaurants that could fill that spot. I want to save it if possible. Give me your honest appraisal of the gallery. I know you've been working at Martin's Visions Gallery in Georgetown."

"Is there anything you don't know about me?"

He grinned knowingly. "Like I said, I've been keeping tabs. Your mother, my mother. But I don't know how badly you feel about your breakup with that painter. Or if there's a chance you'll get back together with him."

She looked down at her coffee for a moment, then met his eyes.

"I was sad at first, but no, there's no chance we'll get back together."

He nodded solemnly. But in his eyes, there was a sparkle.

She went on. "About the gallery downstairs, all I can say after looking it over yesterday is this. Miss Thornton doesn't really know art, doesn't have a skilled eye for what is good and what just passes for good in the eyes of the unschooled public. And the mediocre art she does have down there is so poorly displayed, even an earnest art collector would be turned off."

"That bad, huh?"

She nodded, smiling at his worried, boyishly handsome face. "I think Martin and Mark, and all of us, can put on for you and your partners a jolly good party and maybe even turn things around for the gallery."

"Great. I want to help today. What can I do?"

"Okay. We'll need a lot of muscle to put things to right." The thought of the two personal paintings she'd brought to give him sprang to mind. "And when it's over, and we all make a bundle of money for ourselves and your gallery, I have two gifts for you. As a sort of thank you for doing this for all of us."

He shot her a sly, lopsided grin. "Only one gift I want."

She laughed as she slid down off the stool and patted his arm. A lascivious image from him almost made her stumble. Her heart threatened to race out of control, but she slammed shut the image.

"Oh, rubbish. Let's go save the gallery."

CHAPTER NINETEEN

To that aim, while the other artists went sightseeing, Kas, Athena, Martin and Mark set about to transform the Stargazer Gallery. The first task was to take down all the dubious art — even Martin and Mark made faces at several paintings — Miss Thornton had collected and put it into the storage room while the current manager sat behind her counter, fuming silently. However, with one of the tower owners helping, she kept her opinions to herself.

Next came the rearranging of the portable walls. The cubicles disappeared and instead, under Martin's direction, they staggered diagonally placed easels, which opened the flow of traffic. Most of the twenty pastiches, one for each easel, could be seen during a sweeping look from the extreme left wall of the gallery to the rear wall and over to the extreme right wall. Spectators could stand back and view the artwork or step in for a closer look. They were no longer boxed into a small square. Overhead lighting was also enhanced, and spotlights attached to ceiling tracks focused on each painting.

By the time they finished at four o'clock, they were all pleased. The large picture windows afforded views of all the art at a glance, and to further the accessibility, a smaller easel was placed beside each pastiche, sporting enlarged posters of the originals and of the master painters. On the three main walls, next to each pastiche photo, Martin had hung a photo of the pastiche painter with his or her name and art background. Catalogues of all the available pastiches covered all tables and the manager's counter. Guest hostesses had been hired by the hotel's concierge, whose job it was to smile and hand out these glossy catalogues, pointing out the listed prices on the back cover. Flutes for the chilled champagne waited on silver trays for the attending servers to pass out to guests as soon as the event began.

Kas personally greeted and positioned the two uniformed police officers outside the entrance door and the two bulky, private security men inside. The presence of security was meant to reassure the wealthy clientele that this private event would remain just that, private and secure.

Two hours later, as condo owners, their friends, invited collectors and other prominent guests milled around with glasses of champagne, each easel paid homage to the original artist and his work in addition to the walls of posters giving credit to each pastiche painter.

Kas Skoros, dressed in a black tux, was more than impressed with the final display and the turnout. The gallery filled with murmurs of approval and exclamations over how exacting the replicas were. He watched Athena as she stood between her two Manet pastiches and spoke to two of the guests. The man wore a suit and tie, but Kas knew him as a software engineer who usually dressed in jeans and tee shirt. Another man had joined them, another techie from one of the sold condos, and he, too, was dressed formally. Martin had indicated the dress code on the invitations he'd mailed to Kas to be sent out, and even these young geeks had risen to the occasion. Martin knew his stuff.

Athena looked so . . . well, he had to admit to himself, grown up. No longer the twenty-year-old nerdy art student, she'd come of age. Tonight she appeared as radiant as the Stargazer's lobby. She shone and glimmered in her green floor-length gown. The low-cut bodice was encrusted with sparkly glass jewels, as was the belt that cinched in her small waist. The gown flared with the shape of her hips, and when she turned to speak to someone, the folds moved with her.

Kas recalled every inch of her body from their rendezvous in that D.C. hotel two and a half years before. She was slimmer now, the contours of her face and body appearing a little more angular. Her thick, variegated blond hair spilled down over one breast, held to the side by a jeweled clip. To him, the young woman was as appealing as she'd been two years earlier. Just as pretty, mysterious, remarkable. Just as innately kind and honest. His feelings hadn't diminished at all, and that itself astonished him. For an easily bored man with a history of loving 'em and leaving 'em, this was a new revelation.

The revelation both pleased and troubled him.

And something else about Athena was new. She bore a confidence that she'd lacked before. Now she knew the effect she had on men, the second or third look they gave her, the flirtatious attentions they showered on her. Athena appeared to enjoy the attention, but he noticed she always drew their focus back to her pastiches. She had no trouble staying on task, and that task was not only to inform the public about Manet and his masterpieces, but to sell her pastiches.

All pros, the other painters were doing the same. Martin and his friend Mark were circulating and glad-handing anyone in their immediate sphere of contact. Occasionally, Martin would nudge someone over to a pastiche to make further comments. Guests were nodding as if agreeing to his assessment of the artwork. People were consulting the catalogues and then taking out their wallets, checkbooks, credit cards.

Kas smiled a greeting as the Stargazer's general contractor, Bill Swinburn, as he and his wife strolled up. He shook hands with them.

"I'm amazed," said Swinburn, "how authentic they look. I really like the Gauguin. What're they called?"

"Pastiches, Bill. Original pastiches. I love the Manet, the Plum one," gushed the wife, her diamond bracelet swinging on one wrist as she held up the catalogue, "but the price. Fifty thousand!"

Her husband was quick to interject, "But dear, the painter said the original sold for over fifteen million at Sotheby's two years ago. Wouldn't it be fun to have a copy in our living room, so when people come over, they'll think it's the real one? A conversation piece."

Kas smiled. "That would be a great icebreaker for a party. You know, they're taking the exhibit to New York next — what they don't sell tonight. The New Yorkers'll love this stuff. Grab it up for twice what they're asking here."

He knew what kind of money his general contractor made from the residential towers his company built all over the San Francisco Bay Area, knew the Swinburns could afford the real Manet if it ever came to market. They'd have to cut back on their diamond jewelry purchases and the amenities on their next yacht, maybe, but a brilliantly done pastiche wouldn't be a stretch for them.

"C'mon, Bill," Kas urged good-naturedly, "buy your wife a celebratory gift of a good-as-the-original Manet painting. The Stargazer's done, and when we're ready to start our next tower, you'll be first on my speed dial. The gallery could use it, and it's a tax-deductible business expense."

Bill laughed and looked at his wife. "You really like that Manet? Should I get the Gauguin, too? What about the Cezanne, the *Card Players?*"

His wife shook her red curls vehemently. "Oh no, too dark. You get the Gauguin, and I'll get the Manet. The girl in the painting, the *Plum Brandy* one, looks like our daughter. She looks so . . . young and wistful."

Kas shook hands with them again and wished them well as they marched over to Martin with the news and their check. Martin ushered them over to share the joy with Athena, and when they looked around for the Gauguin painter, Kas

---

watched Athena explain something about the painter's absence. Dan Grantham. Her boyfriend of two years. Did he not show up because of their breakup? What was really behind their calling it quits? Not that he minded in the least. He was overjoyed that Athena was now free.

But free for what? What was Kas prepared to do to win her back? Marry her?

God, no. He was still legally entangled to a woman he despised, although that would soon end. Was he going to offer Athena a cross-continental relationship, a once- or twice-a-month assignation? Hell no. Besides, he knew Athena wouldn't stand for it.

His eyes fell on the nude she'd painted, a copy of Manet's "Olympia." The portrait of a man's mistress, a courtesan attended to by a black-as-midnight maid and a little African boy. What was Manet trying to say with that? Damned if he knew. One thing he did know, he didn't want just a mistress, not from Athena. What then did he want from her? With her? What did Athena want from him?

Just like having little Alex — the stakes were high, and failure was not an option.

As the couple and Martin walked away to conduct business, Athena looked over at him and smiled. How could he deserve her if he offered her nothing more than an occasional hookup? He toasted her with a raised champagne flute. *Good for her.*

Her artistic talent left him awestruck. Her clairvoyance gift made him spellbound with wonder. The bloodline that he'd grown up with transfixed him, like The Sirens to wandering Odysseus, drawing him in, making him want to commit to a relationship that both intrigued and frightened him. Him, frightened? Hell, yes. Giving a woman all that power over him was friggin' frightening. At the same time, the woman that she was also made him humble and happy to be alive.

Her bloodline, that mind-boggling ability to read the

146

minds of others — well, that made her vulnerable. Got her into trouble. And that made him anxious. Too many scumbags would want to exploit that or eliminate it. She needed him but didn't know it.

And then as he gazed around the gallery, at the ebb and flow of the crowd, the bright lights over the paintings, Kas Skoros had an idea.

At eleven that evening, the last guest departed, and Martin gathered all eight painters together. He held open his catalogue and began to read. Her attention diverted, Athena watched Kas give checks to the security men, bid them thanks and farewell and locked up.

"All right, here's the tally," Martin told them. "Eighteen of the twenty pastiches are sold. Ten of these for fifty thousand, six for sixty thousand and two — Edith's *Card Players* and Athena's *Olympia* — went for a whopping seventy thousand each. The grand total is one effing million. Minus the Stargazer Gallery's commission of fifteen percent — yes, Mr. Skoros lowered his commission rate due to our stunning success. My commission — I lowered it, also, to twenty percent this time to make sure you all get your well-deserved sixty-five percent. So, minus the commissions, the average payout per painter is around sixty thousand."

Athena did a few mental calculations, followed by a roller coaster of emotions. Athough she personally had netted over one hundred thousand, a few of the painters with only one pastiche would walk away with a not so measly thirty to sixty thousand. Not bad. Certainly enough to write home about for two to three months' worth of sixty-hour weeks.

Kas had rejoined the group. He looked pleased as he shook Martin's hand.

"Well done, Martin, Mark, all of you. You've made more

for the gallery in one evening than it's done the past twelve months. The event that Martin and Mark put together was incredible, but the quality of your pastiches is what sold them for such high numbers. You're all a remarkable, awesome bunch of artists. If any of you would like to exhibit your own originals in my gallery, I'd be happy to oblige and at the same low fifteen percent commission rate."

The painters all murmured their approval. Athena glanced over at Martin's reaction to Kas's generosity. Her fellow artists looked more than impressed and several promised to send photos of their original artwork so that the gallery manager could look at them and possibly arrange future exhibitions. Kas passed out his business cards, ignoring those of the gallery manager, who had slipped out some time during the gala.

"If you're hungry or thirsty, go to the Ocean Bar and Grill. The tab's on me, personally. I'll call and let them know. They're open until one. Thanks again, all of you. And you, Martin, Mark." Kas shook hands all around, gave a few high fives.

Martin and Mark drifted off to collect the pastiches and box them for shipment once the checks had cleared. The Stargazer Gallery would provide the customized framing for each pastiche as well as collect their commission. Tonight had been a win-win situation for all concerned. Kas looked at Athena and smiled after the others moved away.

"You're invited to my place for a late-night snack, nightcap . . . whatever." When she remained silent, he went on. "You're happy with the way things went tonight? Everyone sold at least one of their paintings, right?"

"Oh yes, very happy. It's good to see this niche market open on the West Coast. I hope you invite us back."

His face fell. He'd misunderstood, had only heard a personal rejection.

"Kas, those two gifts I have for you, I'd like to give them to you tonight."

Disappointment morphed to surprise, then wariness. "Okay. Thirty minutes. I have to lock up and turn security on. Make it fifteen if you can." He gave her one of his cardkeys.

She nodded.

She made it in twenty. Wearing a loose black and silver sweater tunic over black leggings and low-heeled sandals, she carried a wrapped, square-shaped canvas in each hand. He opened the door, dressed in his tuxedo shirt and trousers. With a flourish, she set the two paintings against the backs of two kitchen stools and pivoted them around so that the paintings faced outward. Kas poured two glasses of champagne while Athena unwrapped the canvases. Both rendered in the romantic expressionistic style she loved to paint, her self-portrait garnered his attention first.

"Wow, that's beautiful. Your hair—whitened and flying about—what's that about? I mean, it's stunning."

Athena sipped some champagne. *How can one explain the impulse of the moment? The need to look more beautiful and carefree than I really am?*

"Difficult to say. It captures my inner me. Like how I feel now, the way I'd like to feel most of the time. Cinderella in the prince's castle." Maybe a lame reply, but the explanation suited.

Kas grinned. "I love it. Is it mine to keep?"

"Of course." She accepted his chaste kiss on her lips. *A prolonged but chaste kiss.*

A casual touch told her that Kas's thoughts were not so chaste, and her own emotions raged against her resolve to hold him at arm's length.

What's the point? I want him, pure and simple. Why pretend otherwise?

Athena looked at her portrait. The young woman in the portrait looked like her but appeared to have a strength

Athena didn't always feel.

She's not afraid. She's never afraid. Why can't I be like her? My alter ego? I can't. I'm still afraid. I just don't want to be hurt again.

She finished unwrapping the second one. His attention turned to it, the painting of a father holding his toddler son, both looking happy and proud as they gazed out of a window at a star-filled night sky. Both dark-haired subjects were reasonable likenesses of Kas and little Alex.

"I based the child on what I saw that night, when you were singing to him and the moonlight was in your eyes and in the child's."

It took a few moments before she realized that Kas was silent because he was choked up with emotion. He tried to speak but couldn't. With a rush of sympathy, she draped an arm around his back. They held each other, standing in front of the painting of father and adopted son. Kas fought to maintain control, but soon a tear escaped and rolled down one clean-shaven cheek. He sniffed and cleared his throat.

"Does it have a name? The painting?"

"I call it The Stargazers. I know how you feel about him. I felt it that night."

Kas moved over to the counter, put down his champagne and wiped his eyes on a nearby cloth napkin, his back to her. When he turned around, he was smiling.

"I'll treasure it the rest of my life. I promise you."

It was the catch in his voice that did her in. That catch turned the tables for her. Her common sense vanished. Not her fear of being hurt again, which she ignored. In four steps, she thrust herself against his body and wrapped her arms around his neck. His responding embrace nearly crushed her. Their kisses were long and deep and didn't stop.

They began to shed their clothes. Her tunic and his shirt came off next. His dress trousers. Then her leggings and sandals, his shoes.

On the faux cheetah-fur rug in front of a gas lit fireplace, they shimmied off the remaining obstacles to their merging of naked, throbbing bodies. She thought to tell him she was on the Pill, thought to ask him about his protection, a whole second before all thoughts fled. Nothing mattered. Even her clairvoyance channel closed. Drowning in sensual pleasure, she knew nothing else was needed. Nothing else was important. Desire surpassed all.

All their complications could wait until morning.

CHAPTER TWENTY

The warmth of his body next to hers drew her attention as soon as the first waking thoughts began to crystallize. Ah yes, she'd surrendered to both their needs. All her resolve to remain pleasant but aloof had melted like so much wax over a flame.

Indeed. Crikey.

Athena had to smile to herself. What a surrender it was. The heights of pleasure she hadn't experienced in a very long time. She could tell every now and then that Kas had fought it, too. At first. Enough of his thoughts and feelings had channeled through after their first coupling to let her know that genuine fear had nearly kept him from opening the door to her last night.

Well, so much for his fear of intimacy and her own fear of pain.

She rolled onto her side and stared at his profile as he slept on his back. Now that he was clean-shaven, his fine, masculine features could be seen and appreciated. He'd told her he'd grown the mustache and beard out of boyish spite, because Nikki had hated them. And he'd shaved finally because she, Athena, disliked facial hair. Well, so much for male logic. It seemed like men were always fighting for their little sphere of control. Always afraid of being weak and giving in to their need for love.

Athena was a perfectionist and had her own control needs.

But she loved him even more for this perceived fear and most of all for his need of her. That pleased her more than she could have imagined.

Did he really love her? She hadn't channeled that word through his emotional flood of thoughts last night. Desire and the need for release came through all right. The rest was all sensual pleasure, satisfaction, even the need for control and approval.

His black lashes were long and much darker than his head of thick, wavy hair. His looks and complexion were a pleasant blend of Greek, Italian and maybe a hint of Viking conqueror in there with his ruddy cheeks, especially rosy during exertion. And he'd certainly exerted himself bloody well last night. He was beautiful in a strong, masculine way, not pretty like Alex, but Kas had the kind of strength that made her feel safe.

His eyes fluttered open and he turned his head her way. He cleared his throat before speaking.

"I was just dreaming about you. Could you tell?"

"No, I turned it off. There are times I just like to experience you as a normal woman would. What I see . . . and hear . . . and touch . . . and smell."

"There's nothing abnormal about you, baby."

She bent down and kissed his big, brawny shoulder. "You know what I mean."

He grinned. "Like my new cologne?"

The mixture of cedarwood, pine and citrus carried a masculine, heady scent. "I approve," she said.

"Good. The salesgirl said it was popular. I mean, what do I know? I've been using Pop's old cologne for years. I was hoping . . . Anyway, I'm glad you spent the night. I've wanted to wake up with you next to me for . . ." He left unsaid what they both knew. Their two and a half-year separation. "I couldn't get enough of you last night . . . this morning. When I crashed, I really crashed. Must be getting old."

She rested her head on his chest. "Don't be silly. You're

only thirty."

"Thirty-one next month."

"September sixteenth, I know. We must get together . . . although . . ." It was her turn to leave unsaid one of many barriers to their relationship. She stroked his chest and traced a line down his rib cage to his navel. Her touches made him stir.

"Okay, let's talk about this." He seized her hand, drew it up to his mouth and pressed his lips to her knuckles.

"About what?" She propped her upper body on him, her bare breasts mashing down upon one side of his chest, swept her long hair out of the way and gave him her full attention.

"You know very well what. What we couldn't do two years ago but what we can do now. Move in together. Live together. See how we like being together every day." He grinned. "Maybe we'll drive each other nuts, maybe not. I mean, why not give it a try?"

His teasing reservations sent up a red flag. All the reasons why not flooded her mind.

"Kas, I don't know. You're a father now. You've changed. I've changed, too. I'm not such an ingénue about men, am I?"

He frowned and his jealous thoughts pierced her mind. "No, you're not. But I swore I wouldn't go there."

She knew what he meant. He pretended not to be jealous of her relationship with Dan Grantham, but she knew he was.

"Yes, don't go there. And I won't interrogate you about the women you've been with these past two years."

"Okay, fine. Getting back to my question. How do people learn about each other? By living together, finding out if personalities mesh, if we can get along when things get dull or tense. Do we chill or get mean and ugly? That sort of thing. You're the first woman I've wanted to live with. About the boy, if you're worried about that, my having a child, he already has a mother. Such as she is."

"Of course, I expect you to spend time with the boy, it's not that. Remember, I saw him those two times I entered your mind. He's a darling little boy, looks just like your brother, Alex. I get on with kids. I think, anyway. I haven't been around any lately. Everyone in my family is older than eighteen. Even my brother Chris."

"Little Alex is a spitfire, very stubborn, willful. But he's also affectionate." His words trailed off as his voice grew husky with emotion. He cleared his throat. "I hear Chris wants to come out west to Stanford. Rather than Cambridge or Oxford, where your father went."

Athena lowered her head and planted a kiss on his shoulder. "By golly, you actually have been keeping tabs." For that remark, she received a playful slap on her bare behind. "Kas, it's just . . . I have another life in Georgetown. I work part-time for Martin and his uncle's Visions Gallery. I must work to keep my temporary visa, you know. My H-1b visa. I paint, it seems like, all the time. You'd get so tired of that, wouldn't you? And I'm a cluttered mess when I'm working. I don't even comb my hair."

He snorted with humor. "While I'm working, I'm all military, strict and organized. But we'd be together in the evenings. We'd chill and hang out. What's wrong with that?"

She bent her head and this time kissed him on the mouth. Apparently, he wasn't in the mood for anything except to persuade her to his point of view.

"Nothing wrong, it sounds divine. I'd have some balance in my life, which I definitely do not have now."

He hoisted her fully on top of him and his eyes seductively slid to half-mast. "Okay, so what's the problem?" Same message, only now he was changing tactics.

Already, she felt herself weakening before she'd made all her arguments against the idea. She pushed on.

"I assume you mean my moving here. Leaving

Georgetown and moving across the North American continent. For starters, luv, I promised Martin a four-piece ensemble of the modern D.C. scene, done in a post-modern, expressionistic style. He'll launch the vignettes at a special gala, spotlighting me and two other artists. I have two months to get them done. We've already signed commission contracts."

"C'mon, Thena, that's not a reason. You can paint them here and ship them to Martin. Fly out there for the showing."

She considered that. "Another reason, I would have to give my roommate at least a month's notice before vacating. Mikayla counts on me to help pay the expenses on our loft. Oh yes, and above all the rest, my student visa expired. My temporary work-visa expires in one month, so I need to find a full-time job to renew my H-1b visa. Another thing, how can I afford to live here in San Francisco? I heard a one-bedroom apartment costs three thousand a month."

His look was piercing as he frowned. "You're on an H-1b visa? I just assumed you were a permanent resident."

"No, I don't have what you call a green card."

His hands roamed over her back and down to her bum. He squeezed both cheeks playfully, gently. "You'd live here with me, baby, in this condo. It's a two-bedroom, so you can move into the other bedroom for privacy if you want. Create your own space. You have floor-to-ceiling windows, great for painting, I imagine. A great view. Maybe you could teach at the Art Institute of San Francisco. There's one just blocks away on Market Street. You wouldn't have to worry about money. I make plenty."

His suggestion made her bristle. "Very kind of you, I'm sure. Being a kept woman won't qualify as a full-time job, the way the INS sees it. If I don't get my visa renewed, it's back to England, then maybe Italy. In Italy, painting full-time qualifies for a permanent work-visa if you can show income. They revere artists there."

They frowned at each other, stymied by their individual viewpoints and stubborn stances. Their relationship appeared to run into snafus every step of the way. Athena shrugged and smiled. Why ruin a very pleasant reunion with reality talk?

"I suspect we'll see each other now and then."

He scowled. "Not good enough. Look, I want you to stay longer so we can work things out."

"Sorry, I can't. We go back on Saturday."

Kas huffed out his displeasure, his dark brown brows curving downward. Even when disgruntled, he was handsome to her. She could almost see the wheels turning round and round. He wasn't going to let go of this problem until he'd solved it. Probably why he made a good Operations Officer for the Skoros Group.

"I have meetings all day and one over cocktails. Interviewing a framing contractor for our next project. The one who built the Stargazer is so good, he's booked for the next three years, and George and Leon want to break ground on our next tower a year from now. Can you meet me for cocktails in the Grill and we'll have dinner together afterwards? I'll take tomorrow off and show you the sights. Okay with that?"

She began to slide off his body as soon as he began to talk about that day's work. Kas held her fast against him and nuzzled her neck.

"I've got a little time before my first round of meetings."

Her head began to swim with desire.

"Okay, I've got plans for today. I'll go with the others on something called the Duck Boat. Whatever that is."

He chuckled against her temple, his face rubbing her hair. "It's an amphibious vehicle, starts out on land and converts to a boat. You'll get a turn around the bay."

"Oh, and I want to see Alcatraz. Can we go there? And

some tower called Coit Tower? It has frescoes inside that depict the history of the city. And the MOMA." She couldn't leave the city without seeing the Museum of Modern Art. Maybe the exhibits would inspire her four vignettes of D.C. street life.

"Anywhere you want to go . . ."

Her mind shut down finally. Their mouths met and their hands wandered as sweet oblivion awaited them.

CHAPTER TWENTY-ONE

At six o'clock, Athena joined Kas and another man at the Grill's bar. The two men were seated at a bistro table, but both arose when she walked up. Kas's face lit up as she approached.

She'd come home after the group's wet and riotous ride aboard the Duck Boat, showered, and made up for her dinner with Kas. She'd thought all day about his invitation for her to move to San Francisco and live with him. Such a notion was a serious one, and she knew Kas wouldn't have suggested lightly. He'd given it a lot of thought, maybe two and a half years' worth of thought. The idea never left the back of her mind all day, and every view the group had of the city from the bay water's perspective was one she savored. This life could be hers. Life in a prosperous, thriving city — a breathtakingly beautiful city with its hills, distinctive skyscrapers, expansive bridges and vast bay waters — could be hers if she packed up everything and moved out West. Living with a man she adored and was crazy in love with would be the frosting on the cake. Her mind ran to two columns, the pro side and the con side.

High on the con side, she'd be three thousand miles farther from England, Italy, her family. Leaving D.C. was not the issue. She'd always found the U.S. capital a strange contradiction. It was a city that held the richest and poorest, the government elitists and the nobodies, a city that boasted the strictest gun-control laws and one of the highest homicide rates by guns in the country. A city where it seemed only the few treasured its museums and art galleries. Power reigned supreme over culture. In addition, there was an omnipresent under-layer of violence that frightened her. She felt it, especially lately, every time she stepped outside her loft apartment. Her parents had never embraced D.C. and had been overjoyed to return to Europe. They had felt the danger there, too. That realization gave her pause.

Yes, maybe it was time to leave Washington.

Seeing Kas, all spruced up in a dark-blue suit and gray and blue tie, made her heart flop over to the pro side, the San Francisco side. He greeted her with a hug and brief kiss. His look as he ran his gaze up and down showed her he approved of her choice of outfit. She wore a black dress with a crossover bodice that clung to her body, and the kind of black stilettos that Mikayla wore when she wanted action on a given night out on the town. Her goddess Athena pendant hung above the V of her neckline, and gold hoop earrings completed the ensemble. She'd even taken extra care with her hair and had clipped one side over her shoulder.

"I'd like you to meet Jim Henderson. He's a general contractor, specializing in residential towers. Like the Stargazer."

Henderson was a middle-aged man with sandy hair receding from a broad forehead, blue eyes that missed very little, and a pleasant enough smile. They shook hands, during which Athena picked up only a few words. *Lucky guy, this Skoros fellow.*

Perching herself on the one vacant barstool, she smiled inwardly. *Good, at least I'm making an impression.* She dismissed her initial overactive sense of modesty. After all, she was young only once. Might as well make the most of it. If these men—especially Kas—could see her when she was up to her elbows in oil paint and mineral spirits, they'd see a hardworking artist, not a *femme fatale*. What would Kas think if he saw her as she really appeared on most days, and not on holiday in San Francisco.

Time passed as she nursed her glass of white wine—no more Moscow Mules for her—while the two men talked about the Skoroses' next project. She listened halfheartedly, enjoying most of all Kas's enthusiastic summary of his family's vision of a residential tower across the bay in Berkeley. It would have twenty floors of condos and be located within blocks of the BART station—Bay Area Rapid Transit—and trains, which transported people around the Bay Area but also under the bay water to a station in the city. *The City* was local lingo for San Francisco, she'd learned.

Kas had indeed undergone a change, from deputy sheriff and part-time skirt-chaser to full-time businessman. His injuries from the car crash which killed his brother, Alex, had curtailed his more gregarious physical pursuits and had caused him to develop other strengths and skills. He seemed genuinely happy with his current situation as COO of the Skoros Group. He had a no-nonsense way of speaking with people involved in the construction trades.

"One thing that's paramount to my brothers and me is having access to U.S. made steel. We don't want imported junk or any type of metal that might compromise our building. This is earthquake country, so our structural framing has to be the best, the strongest. If you can assure that, with the project estimate you've given me, then I'll recommend you to my brothers."

Henderson nodded and shot Kas a toothy smile. "Of course, I understand your concerns. We buy from Philadelphia Steel, the finest American made with a tensile strength superseding all other American steel companies. When you get the okay, we can sign the contract tomorrow. I want to act on this immediately. As soon as your architect gives me the word and I get a check from your company, I'll start ordering from Philadelphia Steel."

While Kas took a thoughtful sip from his whiskey sour,

Athena heard Henderson's thoughts loudly and clearly. *Listen, bud, you'll get Chinese steel and make do. My guy at Philadelphia will make me up fake invoices and I'll rake in the cash on the difference. Tough shit. You and your brothers are a fucking bunch of spoiled rich brats. So make do with fuckin' Chinese steel.*

She looked over at the man and frowned. Despite her not touching the man, she knew with all certainty that he was a liar and a cheat. Kas had no way of knowing this.

Henderson suddenly looked her way. *You, you little slut, what put a bug up your ass?*

"I'm very encouraged by your numbers, Jim." Kas kept talking even though he had now noticed Athena's discomfort. "At first, I couldn't believe how low your bid was . . . but if you use the materials we request, I can't see any obstacle to our doing business together."

The contractor turned his attention back to Kas and pulled a sheaf of papers out of his sport coat's inner pocket. "Here's a preliminary contract, pending approval by your CEO and CFO. And my pen. We can sign and seal the deal tonight." He held up a gold pen and placed the papers in front of Kas.

It was time to speak up before Kas made a terrible mistake. She glanced down at her wine goblet and began to slide off the barstool.

"Kas, I'm feeling ill. Can you walk me to the elevators?"

Distracted by the papers on the bistro table and Athena's cry for assistance, he blinked a few times, and then came to her side.

"Sorry, Athena, of course." He escorted her to the elevators and then turned to her, looking concerned. "How are you feeling? Too much fun in the sun today? Do you want to take my card key and go up to my condo? We can order in if you don't feel well."

They were out of earshot and sight of the contractor. She tugged on his sleeve and pulled him aside. "No, I feel fine. I'm just pretending to be ill to warn you. Get rid of this guy,

Kas. I'm serious. He's planning to substitute good quality steel with Chinese steel, inferior stuff that's cheap . . .and has bad welding. He's planning to cheat you. He's a liar and a fraud. I couldn't let you sign that contract with such a man."

Kas gave her a quizzical look. "Athena, are you sure? This is business. How could you read his thoughts? You weren't even touching him."

That fact struck her. She hadn't touched the man, except for their brief handshake, but still the man's thoughts had come through. There was no mistake in her mind, however. The man was a liar and fully prepared to put people's lives in peril.

"I know, I know. I could read his thoughts, Kas, no mistake about that. How did you learn about him?"

Kas straightened and looked away as he considered her question.

Emboldened, Athena went on, "Whoever it was knows about him. It's a sense I have. I can't explain how I know this or how I heard his thoughts, just that he was lying to you. He's not a nice man."

Kas's dark brown eyes met hers again. "The gallery manager. She knows him from somewhere. She recommended him."

"Well, well, birds of a feather. Don't trust her, either, Kas. You should have your accountant double-check her invoices and receipts."

"I had them both checked out. Vetted."

Athena shrugged. "False documents? It happens. Remember two years ago? My father's assistant at the Embassy turned out to be corrupt. He sold out his own country."

Kas took her hands in both of his. "If you're right . . . and I don't doubt you, 'Thena. You, your mother, my mother—you all have this amazing power. But you know this means that your clairvoyance is expanding. You're reading a mind without touching that person. Your powers are growing."

Something to consider. *This could be true, but what does it all mean?*

His hands rose to her shoulders and he bent down to kiss her cheek. "If you're right — and there's no reason why you shouldn't be — you've just saved me from a very bad decision. And potentially millions in lawsuits. Look, I'll get rid of the guy and I'll come and get you. I'll take you out, somewhere fancy, somewhere special."

She stared at his face, flush with gratitude — overcome with gratitude that he believed her. "You don't have to."

"Are you kidding?" he said, handing her his card key. "You may have just saved the Skoros Group a multi-million-dollar lawsuit. Our financial backers are expecting the finest quality of materials and craftsmanship. The last thing I want to do is disappoint them — and risk the destruction and death toll near two intersecting fault lines, the San Andreas and Hayward. Good God." He raked one hand through his hair and shook his head. An awful moment passed as he envisioned the collapse of the new high-rise building and the numerous lives at stake.

Athena acutely felt his anguish. She stroked his cheek with one hand.

His dark eyes burnt with intensity as he looked at her. A tentative smile tugged one side of his sensual mouth.

"I'll be up as soon as I can rid of the sonuvabitch. Then we'll decide where to go. Sky's the limit."

She smiled back, heartened to the point of joy that Kas believed her and welcomed her input. There was no doubt in her mind that she'd read the man's mind without having to touch him. But how? Why? Was Kas right? Were her clairvoyant powers expanding?

It dawned on her just then as she turned to enter the elevator. She would wait for him in his condo with a room service meal and wearing nothing—not a stitch—under his bathrobe except her goddess Athena pendant and—oh yes, those silly stilettos.

All I want is you, Kas Skoros. Only you.

CHAPTER TWENTY-TWO

Friday came all too soon. The pastiche painters' group along with Martin and Mark would be leaving the next day and returning to D.C. The group had a variety of places-to-see on its agenda, including the Presidio and Fort Point, the Marina, Ghiradelli Square, and something called *the crookedest street in America*. She and Kas were going to get some exercise and take a long all-day walk around the city, taking in Coit Tower, North Beach, Fisherman's Wharf and the Embarcadero.

Waiting for Kas, Athena was taking one last look at the Stargazer's street-floor art gallery, strolling around and noting the current pieces of artwork. Unfortunately, the gallery manager, Valerie Thornton, had returned the small, dim cubicles with their fabric partitions to the gallery floor and the same, uninspiring and mediocre paintings to the cubicle walls. There was a lot of foot traffic outside the two picture windows, but no traffic inside. Ms. Thorton sat behind her counter, poring over art catalogues and occasionally answering the telephone, which seldom rang. When it did and she answered it, her tone of voice was bored and distracted, as if she'd been interrupted from her favorite TV soap opera.

Athena's visit to the MOMA had been inspirational, and she was looking forward to getting back to work on her four vignettes of D.C. street life. One of them would be an expressionistic portrayal of the girl on the motorcycle, even though there was something about the young woman that set her teeth on edge. However, a lot of things about D.C. street life set her teeth on edge—the noise, the traffic, the dangerous

166

neighborhoods. What bothered her about the biker chick was more than that. Something else that she couldn't define. She'd never touched the woman or gotten close to her, apart from that one day at the corner coffee and bagel shop. That one time, when Dan had sworn that the woman was a man. That observation of Dan's kept circling in and out of her head over the past month. But so what? She'd encountered several transvestites and transgender individuals around D.C., Alexandria and Georgetown over the past several years. They were in London, too. No big deal in this day and age.

Her attention flashed to the present as she came across a twenty-nine by thirty-eight acrylic painting of a young Asian woman sitting alone in a café. The colors were vibrant, the composition reminding her of a Cezanne or Manet. The painter was obviously skilled and schooled in figure painting. The autograph showed the artist to be a Ian Chen; the title of the work, *Wondering*.

"Miss Thornton, this painting by Ian Chen, it's really quite good. You should display it in the window. Maybe instead of one or two of those dreadful retro vases."

Valerie Thornton appeared around the corner of the cubicle, her mouth pinched in anger, her posture haughty and indignant.

"Really, Miss . . ."

"Butler, Athena Butler."

"Oh yes, Mr. Skoros's girlfriend. Well, let me put this tactfully, then. I realize you're a figure painter and you sold both of your Manet knockoffs. But you know nothing about running a gallery. So fuck—" She turned to glimpse Kas Skoros in the hotel-to-gallery side doorway " —well, maybe I'll take your suggestion under advisement."

Athena sighed. "Please do, for Vince Chou's sake. He's very talented. Instead of letting his work languish in some cubicle, it should be front and center. Well, I've said my piece."

Kas was dressed like Athena, in warmup clothes and sneakers. He looked from one woman to the other, clasped his hands together and said, "Well, Thena, you ready for a long walk?"

"Absolutely," Athena said, "I need the exercise. Let's go."

They were halfway down the block on Market Street, heading towards the Embarcadero. The old but renovated Ferry Building loomed ahead, and sunlight glittered off the bay water. They'd just slowed from a jog to a walk when Kas finally spoke.

"What was that all about? In the gallery?"

"Artistic difference of opinion. Valerie Thornton wouldn't know real talent if it came up and bit her on the ass. Shame, isn't it? The city has all this local talent, and she can't see it. Instead, she shows off her sculptor friend's tired, drippy vases that are so 1970's handicrafts. Not the quality of your gallery, Kas, or what it should be."

He did something she didn't expect. He laughed. The cool breezes off the bay caught his laugh and snatched it away. The sun made dazzling flashes on the Bay as they approached the long Embarcadero walkway. Sea gulls cawed loudly and wheeled above the piers and bay water. Over the entrance of the Ferry Building, the façade showed a huge etched sign, *1915*, carved into its archway.

"Renovated a couple of years ago," Kas said, pointing at the Ferry Building, "the whole Embarcadero, too. All the piers have undergone reconstruction and cosmetics. I come here to walk, think, check the texts on my cell phone. You never once answered any of my emails or texts. I kept looking and hoping . . ."

Athena took his hand as they stood by a railing, facing east, and stared at the newly rebuilt Bay Bridge, much of it damaged in the 1987 earthquake. Its stark white support cables gave it the appearance of a gigantic sailing vessel. She thought of her own heartbreak during their years of separation and, God help her, tears sprang to her eyes.

"I was trying to forget you. I thought you'd fall for Nikki and that would be the end of it. Indeed, you *were* married to her." She turned to face him, her hair coming loose from its ponytail clip and scattering in the wind. "I think I misjudged you, Kas Skoros. Your heart runs true and deep. I know that now. You're not like most other men."

He smiled and stroked her face. "But you're still afraid? You know, there's no such thing as a safe love. When you love someone, you take a huge leap. You give that person the power to hurt you. Cut you to the core. I gave you that power two years ago."

She gazed at his eyes. They exuded fear and vulnerability. Her resolve to remain detached was already shot to bloody hell. What was the point in denying it? "And I gave you that power, too."

Joy lit up his face. "You can see it when I look at you. Thena. We can't hide it." Kas smiled broadly. "So neither of us is safe." He sidestepped around her back and wrapped his arms around her waist. "God help us. Do we give in to our fears? Or do we find the courage inside ourselves to take that leap? It takes guts. You feeling gutsy today, pretty girl?"

She said nothing. Together, they stared at the longest bridge in the country for a protracted moment. Finally, she said, "I don't know, Kas. I'm brave with my work. With lots of things, I guess, but loving you scares the bloody hell out of me. It's a beastly fear."

She heard him expel a deep breath. "Look, Thena, I think I have a solution. You need a full-time job to get your work-visa—your H-1b visa, right? I need a good gallery manager. You have experience with Martin's gallery and you know art. Why not give it a go? Move here into my condo, or if you can't stand living with me, if you need your own space, then move into one of the hotel suites. Or one of the smaller condos. There's a one bedroom that hasn't sold yet. I'd give you a discounted sales price or cut-rate rent if you don't want to commit to buying. Work at the Stargazer Gallery, do your thing — which will be far better than Valerie Thornton's thing. Make us both happy."

A bubble of hope rose within her. She hadn't expected an offer of employment, since she'd never picked up on his thinking of this before. "You surprise me."

"Good to know I can still do that. It just came to me. Why not? I can hire whoever I please. It solves your problem and two of mine."

She swiveled her head and smiled at him. "Oh really? I know the gallery problem. What's your other problem?"

"Besides making money off that prime commercial space, I'll have my favorite gal to make love to every night."

She heard the backtracking in his tone of voice.

"Or as often as you like, Miss Butler." He shot her a wry grin.

A rush of joy made her tease him. "Favorite gal? There are others?"

"Not what I meant, and you know it, babe. Look, I'm not presuming anything, I swear. Live with me or not, it's up to you. We'll be in the same city. It's a chance to get to know each other better. See if this is as real as I think it is. You'll get your H-1b visa and all will be right with the world."

She rotated around in his arms. Everything inside her was screaming one word. *Yes! Yes! Yes!*

"Oh my God, I want to say yes but . . ." She threw her arms around his neck and kissed his lips. " . . . I need to give this offer some thought. Moving here, a whole continent away — it's a huge step. Okay?"

He kissed her back, but she could feel his deep disappointment. "Sure, think about it. Your brother Chris will be just forty minutes away. Have you thought of that?"

"Yes." She paused as she thought of her younger brother, whom she hadn't seen since her last visit to Milan at Christmastime. He'd be coming to the West Coast to go to Stanford University, so-called Harvard of the West. "Would we be crazy to do this?" she asked him.

"Yeah, crazy in love."

"And if little Alex doesn't like me?"

"What—he's a two-year-old. He loves anybody who gives him a gummy worm."

Athena laughed along with Kas. "I do need a little time to wrap things up in D.C. With Martin, with Mikayla. I should make a visit back to Milan to see my parents, too. Can you wait a month? Maybe two at the most?"

His arms tightened around her. "Fine with me. Well, not fine, but I understand what you have to do. My mother says you're in danger, so the sooner you leave Washington, the better."

That stopped her cold. "What?"

"Okay, so part of me wants to protect you. I don't know if my mother is right or not about this threat. Mainly I want you here for my own selfish reasons, but I can also keep you safe."

She didn't tell him about Detectives Ochoa's sideline, his ongoing, off-the-books investigation of a cold case. What more could she do than what she and her mother had already done to help point them in the right direction? Finding that serial killer was not *her* job. Nor *her* moral obligation.

"What did your mother say?" Lorena Skoros was seldom wrong. Even Athena's own mother didn't have that kind of gift. Nor Athena's grandmother in Como.

"That someone—a man's been stalking you and means you harm. Who is this, Athena? Your ex-boyfriend?"

She shook her head. "No, not Dan. He wouldn't—no, not him." Her insides plummeted at the thought of a danger that she couldn't detect. Not now. Not when she and Kas had re-connected. It wasn't fair. She shook her head again. "I-I don't know who it could be. But now I'm forewarned, I'll be fore-armed."

"What do you mean by that?" he asked her. He slipped his arm around her waist as they continued walking down the Embarcadero. His body was stiff with tension as they passed one pier after another.

"I'll take precautions, Kas," she replied somberly, "I prom-ise, and I'll ask my cop friends for help."

"Ahh, I see. You're doing what your mother does, huh? Helping the cops again?" His voice was laced with disap-proval. "You have to stop doing that, Thena. It's too danger-ous."

"Well, just one time a few months ago. It's something I got involved with a couple of years ago. Now one of their cases might be coming back to haunt me."

Her thoughts flashed back to that search warrant and the hour she'd spent in that electrician's shop and his adjacent apartment. The older brother had returned with his attorney and had seen her and Detective Ochoa together. It wouldn't have taken much for them to find out who she really was. The younger brother's presence — the suspected killer — was eve-rywhere in that place. Like a toxic miasma, the smell of him had permeated everything.

He was there.

She recalled how the sick feeling had stayed with her for days. And then she'd forgotten about it as work piled up.

Kas halted on the wide promenade and he looked straight at her but did not let go of her. Reflexively, she held on to the back of his running suit jacket as the waves of passion and indignation rolled off him. She knew what was coming.

"Ask me and I'll be on the first plane out of here. I swear, just say the word and I'll get you packed up and back with me before the week's out. Fuck Martin's gallery and fuck that commission. Take photographs of your subjects. I've seen what you can do from a photo. You can paint here and send him the finished work. You don't need to stay there to do the paintings. I mean it."

"I know," she said, shooting him an appreciative smile. His argument was compelling. Still, turning her life upside down for a man who couldn't commit — could she do that? Was she really that blinkered over love? Maybe she was more like her cautious, conservative English father than she cared to admit.

They resumed walking. She heard him huff and sigh. Huff and sigh.

"I swear, sweetheart, knowing you is going to turn me gray before my time."

His humor eased her pain a little At least he could laugh about their star-crossed love affair. But could she? "Please don't worry about me — "

"Yeah, I know, you can take care of yourself." He looked away and suppressed another torrent. She read his mind, felt his emotions.

Kas loved her and wanted to be her protector. Unshed tears filled her eyes.

She needed him to love her, but did she really need him to protect her?

If so, assuming the worst, from what or whom?

She needed to find out.

CHAPTER TWENTY-THREE

Shawna thrust into Jeanine with all his might. With his climax, he had the urge to scream, but he suppressed it and just groaned loudly. The woman under him let out a screech, her face turning red, then purplish blue. His hands, as strong and lethal as they ever were, were frozen around her throat, but because his eyes were shut tightly, he didn't care. He was busy snapping his mother's neck, a long-held fantasy that gripped him in its awful power every time he had another victim in his grasp.

The woman gasped, "Let go — "

He opened his eyes then, jolting him back to the present. The woman's eyes bulged from the pressure and pain. He saw the fear in them, so he was able to finish his climax with a shudder. There was little pleasure, just release. Slowly, feeling drained, he let go of her neck. Instantly, the woman scooted to the opposite side of her bed, her hands clawing at her neck as she gasped.

"Are — are you fuckin' crazy?" Her cough was hoarse, breathless. "Y-you're c-crazy!"

His gaze swiveled over to her face. The welts around her neck were purplish, bruises on her shoulders, neck and face still bluish and swollen. He had forgotten how strong his hands were. How much his needs controlled him, even after Dave's warnings.

The girls he'd killed before — and then the whores in Amsterdam — they'd all lain still after he'd screwed and strangled them. This one — Jeanine — was still alive, still squirming around. Why? What was going on?

Reason returned to his fogged mind. He stared down at his hands while rising to his knees on the bed. His hands were strong, didn't let him down. But the one time he'd tried to strangle the one woman he hated the most—his mother—they'd turned soft and weak. Dave was only ten at the time, and his fifteen-year-old brother was off somewhere, not there to protect him. His father—Mr. Gerald Millhouse, Ph.D., a title he liked to intimidate his sons with—came home and thrashed him. Beat him with his belt and fists within an inch of his life—the belt he kept hanging over a dining chair. Sam would stare at it, wondering if he hid or destroyed the belt, would his father suddenly turn weak and helpless. He'd never had the courage to find out.

All bloody and weepy soft like a girl, he'd run to his and Sam's bedroom, lock the door and grab the only weapon he could find, an umbrella. His father had locked away all their baseball bats, anything that he and his brother could use to defend themselves from their violent parents. The knives were kept hidden. He could never find them. They could never find his father's pistol, which he often taunted them with.

Then Sam would show up, get whacked too for nothing, but end up saying it wasn't his younger brother's fault, that he was too young to solve their problem. "I got a plan," his older brother whispered to him one day. Two years later, they put their plan into action.

Good riddance, motherfuckers.

Shawna blinked a couple of times as he shrank from the horrified woman on the bed. He should have snuffed the life out of her, the bitch, the whore. But calm washed over him and he began to think more clearly. No, his DNA—cops used that—was all over, and his fingerprints were on the glass of whiskey she'd given him. Her neighbors downstairs had seen them come upstairs less than an hour ago. Sam had warned him not to get into trouble. Not to botch up things. His smart-as-hell brother had another plan in the works. They couldn't afford the cops coming and sniffing around again.

"I liked it at first, don't get me wrong, Shawna—Shawn." The bitch was talking to him, gently this time, trying to calm him down. "I mean, fuck, it was weird, but good weird, y'know. Like doin' a dude and chick at the same time. Weird but nice. A chick on top and a dude down under. A helluva rush—"

"Shut up," he snarled, "shut the fuck up." His heart rate slowing down, he remembered her name now. Jeanine. He worked with her at Club Fiore. She was a server like him on the same five-to-nine shift. This was Jeanine's apartment, and she said her live-in boyfriend was coming home at midnight. He looked at his watch. He had an hour, time enough to strangle the life out of the bitch and ditch her body somewhere.

He must've growled something under his breath.

"Hey, don't be that way. We had fun. I always wondered what you'd be like, y'know, getting screwed by a tranny. Y'know, a transgender person. That's what you are, right? A tranny but bi, huh?"

Studying her for a long moment, he grunted something that sounded like, "Uh-huh."

It'd take him too long to clean up, burn the sheets in the sink, wipe his fingerprints, sneak out with her body—there weren't any suitcases or trunks he could hide her body in to get past the neighbors and out of the apartment building. Too many people had seen Shawna with her. He worked with her at Club Fiore. When they found her body, the pigs'd come around and interrogate everyone who worked there.

He wasn't ready to leave Club Fiore, not yet. A couple more weeks, Sam had said. Then they'd leave this shitty town.

With effort, he quashed his violent train of thought but consoled himself with its future possibility. *Ah, some night after her shift, after I've left that job, after I'm all ready to leave with*

Sam. Then this bitch's all mine. Now, gotta think of Sam. The guys at the shop think I'm his bitch, but we'll have the last laugh. We'll fool them all. Only thing that matters in this stinking world, we're together again. And safe.

"So are you going to go all the way and become a chick? Y'know, get your dick taken off?" Jeanine was already up and stripping the bed, removing the evidence so her boyfriend wouldn't get wise.

Dave got dressed, his black mood making every move of his deliberate and slow. "I dunno," he growled. He pulled up the outfit that Shawna wore most of the time, jeans, padded bra and cotton shirt. Then socks, and finally he grabbed the boots with the secret compartment for his icepick. His jacket pockets contained money, keys and fake ID. He raked his hands through his long hair and re-rubber banded his low ponytail as he sat back down on the bed, preparing to put on his tall boots.

Jeanine held the wadded-up sheets in her arms. "If you got urges to do a girl every now and then, I mean, why not keep your dick? Don't go all the way and get it cut off. Being a girl is not all it's cracked up to be, y'know. I mean, like it's hard."

Taking a tube of lipstick out of his jacket, Dave remembered to dash on a bit of it before leaving.

"What d'ya mean, hard?" Now anxious to leave before the urge to snap her neck swamped him again, he bent over and touched one of his knee-high boots. Inside one, taped to the side, a modified icepick rested; inside the other, a small pistol sat in a customized holster. Customized boots for the biker prepared for anything. Carefully, he slid his stockinged feet into the boots.

"Just is. I have two kids, but their father, my ex, has them. He took 'em away from me, said I was unfit. I was doing meth, dealin' some, too. You know how it is. Got caught, did some hard time. Now I'm older, wiser as they say. Gotta keep my job goin' so I can get 'em back."

Now, made up and reverting to his female role, Shawna looked up, made his voice sound sympathetic. "Yeah, that's a bitch." *Her, with two kids. Don't make me laugh.*

"Yah, one more year of parole and I'm gonna go to court and get 'em back."

His motorcycle helmet lay on the floor, so he grabbed it and stood up. Jeanine was now in the bathroom, getting the shower going. Washing him away, washing away the evidence of her cheating. Evidence was key. He had his weapons—his hands, an icepick, a gun. It would be so simple, so easy to do the deed. Get it done. Eliminate from the world another piece of scum. Another unfit mother. The cops should've done their job and put his unfit, crazy-ass parents out of their misery. Instead, Dave and Sam had to do the job. Dope their drinks and trick out the electrical wires. An accidental fire, they said. Ha! No evidence left, the fire was so hot, they said.

Him and Sam, they were too smart for all those motherfuckers. They watched enough CSI shows on TV for him to know that eliminating Jeanine then and there would be a messy crime scene, one that would put him behind bars for life. He'd never get to live again with his brother.

The woman was in the shower now, couldn't hear him leave.

Another time. Scum.

The evening was still new. He was restless, a walking powder keg ready to explode. His mind churned around in a vortex. *Gotta eliminate all threats. Can't let anything or anyone stand in our way. Sam's depending on me. Can't let him down.*

Shawna rode for miles, taking care to obey all the traffic lights, stay within the speed limit, not even run the lanes. When Dave looked up and focused, there it was—the corner coffee and bagel shop. Down the street lived an artist who helped the cops with her supposed psychic visions. She'd been there in Sam's apartment with that homicide cop, sniffing around like fucking bloodhounds. Did she know anything? So far, the cops had left them alone. Just as he thought, they were shooting darts in the dark. The girl was a fake.

But what if she wasn't? What if the blonde chick knew something? What if she could cause trouble for him? She was away, and as far as he could tell, so was her roommate, the black chick. He'd scoped out the place every day for two weeks now. They were both away, but for how long? When he'd asked her ex — that dude who came to Club Fiore at least once a week — the guy had been kind of vague.

Shawna pulled over to the curb across the street from the blonde's building. A dim light was on, probably a table lamp on a timer. An idea wormed its way into Dave's head, buried deep within his psyche, and wouldn't let go.

Shawna's new friend Kyle was out of town for the weekend. But the last visit to the jerk's apartment late Thursday night had proved fruitful. While the dude was getting wasted on his way to seducing Shawna, she'd stolen his building key. Another key on the asshole's key ring was for the guy's apartment. She'd taken both and hidden them in her jeans pocket. Dave had to laugh. Shawna had flashed the guy her dick and hightailed it out of there while Kyle was left frozen, swearing and slobbering all over himself.

Now, if she wanted, Shawna had entry to the building and to the asshole's apartment. If he hadn't already changed the apartment door lock. Earlier that evening she'd checked the building entrance door. That hadn't been changed. Still, Dave had to take precautions. He couldn't be seen entering the building, for the tenants would grow suspicious.

Turning the throttle on the handle, Shawna made a one-eighty and then a right turn. The street behind Kyle's and the blonde's building was lined with a row of apartment buildings, old red brick ones, four stories high. Same height as the buildings on their street, only these buildings didn't look renovated like their loft building.

On a hunch, recalling that none of the tenants on the third floor was at home, Shawna parked in front of one, pocketed the motorcycle key and went into the alley beside the building. Just as Dave hoped, there was no fence between the two buildings, nothing to separate them but another alley filled with garbage bins. He looked up at the metal fire escape that zigzagged its way up the east side of the blonde's tan brick building. There was a landing outside the east-facing windows on each floor. The blonde lived on the third floor, the same as Kyle. If he could reach up and pull down the lowest handle of the mechanism, he'd be able to climb to that floor. There were no lights on each of the floors on the east side, so it was unlikely anyone would hear him or the fire escape clang down. It was barely eleven-thirty, so most people wouldn't be home or asleep this early on a Friday night.

Was it worth the risk? He had to know what the blonde knew. Kyle didn't seem to know much about her — the asshole was such a dud with women. But she seemed to have taken an interest in Shawna, the biker chick, yet she was into guys. That much he knew, though she might be between boyfriends. Her ex had a new girl every week when he came to Club Fiore. But Shawna didn't give a fuck about the blonde's ex, just what the girl might know or suspect about Sam and Dave. The idea that she could expose Dave and his brother plagued him.

The escape handle was a good eight feet up. He jumped but couldn't reach it and moving the large garbage bins was out of the question.

The bike.

He retrieved his motorcycle and parked it under the fire escape. Cautiously, he balanced himself on top of the bike seat and reached up. His leather-gloved hands grabbed the handle, and slowly he pulled it down after jumping off the bike. With an icepick in one boot and a pistol in the other, he wasn't worried.

Let someone try and stop me.

CHAPTER TWENTY-FOUR

It was five o'clock in the morning, so Athena quietly padded into the bathroom of Kas's Stargazer condo with her clothes and shoes. She showered with her long hair twisted and pinned into a roll on top of her head, then dried off and finished her grooming for the day. A part of her mind noticed the Antigua marble-tiled floor and shower walls, the mocha brown, plush rugs and matching towels. The condo had been professionally decorated, and every space reflected good taste and minimalistic elegance.

Could she live here with him? Her half of the loft apartment in Georgetown was perennially messy and strewn with sketches taped to the walls, half-finished canvases and paint supplies. Would he recoil in disgust at her work habits and grow weary with her lifestyle?

Kas Skoros's life was so different from hers. He'd become a successful businessman with Skoros Enterprises, but still had a folksy way with the tradesmen he dealt with daily. They appeared to admire his work ethic and the respect with which he treated everyone. Yet, she'd learned how organized and detail oriented he was. There was a prudent perfectionist hiding beneath a laid back but tough ex-military cop and ex-sheriff's deputy.

When she emerged from his bathroom, she was ready to meet the pastiche group for their shuttle to the airport and their flight back to D.C. Kas was sitting up in bed with his nightstand lamp on. He'd already put on his underwear and was shrugging on a pair of khakis.

"Kas, go back to sleep. There's no need — "

He waved aside her comments. "I'm seeing you down-stairs. Your suitcase is in the living room?"

She smiled. "Yes, all ready to go." As he slipped a golf shirt over his head, she stared at his chest and flat belly, and couldn't help but remember with pleasure how she'd explored every inch of his naked body over the past few days. Goosebumps moment. "Four days. Way too short," she said aloud.

He came over to her and took her into his arms. "You bet, it's too short. Hmm, you smell nice. That lavender scent — wow, it's . . ." Appearing lost for words, he bent down and kissed her instead. When he pulled back his head, "We don't have time for — " It was a question.

She gentled her voice and kissed him back. A long, wet kiss that made her head tingle. "No, 'fraid not. We leave in ten minutes."

"We better stop," he rasped. "Okay, one month, Thena. I expect you back here in one month. I'll give Valerie Thornton her notice and close the gallery. Meanwhile, think of ways to launch a re-opening of the Stargazer Gallery. Ways you'll improve it. I can order any materials you need before you return."

"Hold on, Kas. First things first. I do have some ideas for improving the gallery, and Martin does, too. He kept shaking his head at what Valerie was doing, or rather, not doing. I have lots of ideas. I just . . ." She faltered and left unsaid her lingering concerns about moving across the continent from D.C. to San Francisco. Moving into his condo and messing it all up. Taking a huge chance with Kas . . . again.

Her fears had surfaced again.

Still, there was no hiding how she felt about him. The love was plain on her face.

"Just what?" Kas held her at arm's length. "Just what? Are

you really having second thoughts about living here? With me?"

Who was the clairvoyant here? She had to smile.

"It's a gigantic move. Also, when I'm working, I'm spacey and messy. I'm not exaggerating, Kas. My work zone's a real disaster area. You'd come in and throw a fit."

He barked a soft laugh. "I don't throw fits. But you'll know if it bothers me. You saw my digs over the garage at the Loomis place. It's a man cave. This"—he swept an arm around him—"this apartment doesn't always look like this. I did a massive cleanup before you came. Wasn't sure you'd ever see it. I was hoping you'd like it."

She pressed herself against him, breathing into his shirt. "I more than like it and you, you know, ol' chap. Ever since I first saw you at the airport, when you and Alex picked up Mum, Chris and me. Let's see, how long ago? Three years ago, this November. Love at first sight."

"Oh yeah? You never told me that. How could you even notice me with my movie star handsome brother Alex there?" Even mentioning deceased Alex brought pain to his eyes. She felt the stab inside him, also. Felt his deep regret, his yearning to relive the past, especially that fateful night. Make things different.

"Oh, I noticed the strong, silent one. The ruggedly good-looking man with the big shoulders and the weight of the world on his shoulders. In my mind, I called you Atlas. Alex was Adonis, but you were Atlas."

He screwed up his face in an exaggerated look of dismay, which almost made her laugh. "Crap, not sure I like that comparison. Do I seem so solemn to you, Thena? When you're around, I feel like a kid again. A moonstruck teenager."

She glanced down at her watch, then looked up and playfully slapped his biceps. Before stepping out of his arms, she gave him one last peck on the lips.

"When one's in love, one feels like a kid at his birthday party. I feel that way, too. I'm jolly well thrilled we got together. Truly, I am."

"Well then, you'd jolly well better return here in one month," he said. "If you can make it sooner, even better. The month'll seem like a year. Any problems, you call me."

They moved out of the bedroom and into the living room, where her suitcase and lightweight jacket beckoned, draped across the black leather couch. "And watch your back," he reminded her, "Thena. If this threat my mother sees is real, call me. Better yet, call your cop friends, then call me. I'll be there as fast as a jetliner can take me. Understand?"

"I do, Kas. I shall be careful."

She pulled her jacket on and grabbed her satchel purse, all the while nodding dutifully.

Kas lifted the suitcase, gave her a long look of both longing and resignation, then led the way to the front door.

Athena took one look back at the city skyline out of the floor-to-ceiling windows. No fog that morning, strangely enough, just the growing light of dawn that gave all the buildings and the bay waters beyond a golden shimmer. Wow.

She sighed while Kas said, "Jeez, girl, I'm missing you already."

Pausing at the open door, she leaned into him and said, "I love you, Kas." It was the first time she'd ever told him that without the context of a tease or joke.

"I love you, too. Okay," he said, frowning, "so, dammit, hurry and come back."

By the time she arrived at her Georgetown loft apartment, it was dark already. The last of the artists to be dropped off by their shuttle van, she waved goodnight to Martin and Mark. She dragged her rolling suitcase up to her and Mikayla's third floor walk-up, feeling weepy and sad. Even though a nice fat check sat in her purse, her morose mood had lingered all day long as the group moved from shuttle van to airport to airport and another van. Even Martin had noticed, causing him and Mark to give her a pat and a brief hug. Martin had thanked her for such a successful and lucrative pastiche sale in San Francisco, as if she'd arranged it all.

"It was all Kas's doing," she'd told him.

"But it was his feelings for you that made it happen," he reminded her.

She had to admit that was true. Kas couldn't have won her back in a more compelling way. She confessed to the two men, "Kas is a smarter businessman than he realizes. He knows how to close a deal." They agreed wholeheartedly and it was then that she'd told them about Kas's offer and her possible move to the West Coast.

"In one month?" Martin was aghast, while Mark dramatically covered his face in horror. "What would we do without you? What about your D.C. street scene vignettes? What about your work at Visions? Omigod, she's going to leave us, Martin."

"It's not certain, really. I have a lot to think about. And I must take a trip to Milan to see my parents. There's just so much to think about." She assured them both that if she did leave D.C., she'd finish the vignettes, she'd continue to paint pastiches for GPWGP, and she'd miss them terribly.

Given the men's reaction, Athena solemnly turned the key in her front door lock. As soon as she stepped inside and turned on the hallway light, she froze.

She felt it. A presence of evil. As palpable as smoke. It almost made her gag.

Letting go of her suitcase, she rummaged around in one of the top pockets for her canister of pepper spray, grabbed it and pried open the lid. Then with her other hand, she dropped her purse on the floor and seized a walking stick umbrella from the umbrella stand to the right of the front door. The umbrella stand was the base of a tall, antique coat rack that Mikayla had bought recently. It held their coats, hats, rubber boots and umbrellas. Spring in D.C. was often rainy.

"Mick? Are you home?" Athena called out. There was no answer. She called out more loudly this time. Nothing. The last time they'd texted each other, Mikayla said they — she, her photographer boyfriend and the other two models — would be staying over in Bermuda two more days. Her roommate would be coming home Monday evening. That meant two more nights to be alone in their apartment, Athena realized.

Something was wrong. Her guts quivered it. Adrenaline swamped her, her head felt on fire.

Utter silence.

Trembling inside, she held out the canister and the umbrella like a gun and a sword as she moved to her bedroom. The door was closed, just like she'd left it.

"Anyone in there?" She'd heard of homeless druggies breaking into people's homes and ransacking the place, even homesteading while people were away on vacation. Summertime always brought out the crazies, especially since half of D.C. — the wealthy, elitist half, that is — took off for the Hamptons, Miami or Europe. But a middle-class loft? Desperate people did desperate things, she reminded herself.

"I'm coming in," she cried loudly, "I mean you no harm, but this is my place."

Silence.

Hot shivers ran up the back of her head, but she nevertheless opened her bedroom door. A wave of evil washed over her, like a splash of muddy water. She could smell the stench.

Athena flicked on the overhead light and scanned the room. No one that she could see. She went over to her nightstand and opened the drawer. The other canister of pepper spray, a larger one, rested there beside a paperback book. She dumped the smaller canister on her bed—the bedding looked the same, still made, no indentations, the pillows in place—and grabbed up the larger one. This canister held six fluid ounces of a spray that could blind an attacker for minutes, bringing him down to his knees in spasms of coughs and heaves. At least, that was what the hardware store owner had told her when she bought it.

Two and a half years earlier, she'd been attacked by Serbian mercenaries, had been hit by a ricocheted bullet fired from one of their pistols. Since then, before her parents left D.C. for her father's new posting in Milan, Italy, the security guys at the British Embassy had given her a cram course in self-defense. Now was not the time to let that go to waste.

Her sliding closet doors were closed, like she'd left them, also. Taking a deep breath, she stood in front of them. "If you're in there, you better come out. Now!"

Standing to one side, with the back of her left hand, she touched one door. Nothing came through her clairvoyant channel. She went over and touched the bed. Still nothing. There was no intruder in her room.

Stiff-armed, she made her way back to the foyer, then the large living room, the kitchen and dining nook. She noticed that Mikayla's bedroom door was ajar. It had been closed when she'd left on Monday morning, and she knew Mikayla hadn't returned while she was in San Francisco. She touched the door with the tip of the stick umbrella. A frisson ran up her arm. An evil, disturbed presence had touched that door.

She nudged the door open with her stick umbrella, ready for someone to jump out and attack her. Her left forefinger tensed on the spray button. The wooden door banged open, and when no one appeared, she moved inside. With the knuckles of her left hand, she flicked on the overhead light.

Her gaze roved over Mikayla's closet doors, both half open, but nothing emanated from them. The east-facing window, usually open when Mikayla was home but locked shut when she was gone, was open. There were about six inches between the casement frame and the windowsill.

Had Mikayla left it unlocked this time? Athena hadn't double-checked it before she left to meet the others a week ago.

The screen was no longer there. Discarding the umbrella on Mikayla's bed, she lifted the casement window with one hand and looked out at the alley below. The fire escape was in place, the lowest rung halfway up the wall of the first floor. Three floors below, something metal glittered. The window screen, perhaps? She took a moment to feel around the window.

She crinkled her nose. Yes, the stench was stronger here. Someone with a black heart and a twisted mind had opened the window and invaded their apartment. A man. But what did he want? What did he steal?

She closed the window and turned the metal lock on the casement. The lock wasn't broken so it appeared that the window had been left open. Her fault. She should've checked this window before leaving.

Mikayla kept her good jewelry in a jewelry cabinet inside her closet. Of course. Athena slid open the closet door, pulled on the light-bulb chain and illuminated the chest. Looked inside and shook her head. A mixture of emotions flooded her, but mostly puzzlement. As far as she could tell, each drawer was full and none of the jewelry had been taken.

Her next search covered their large living room. Mick's one painting, her expressionistic work-in-progress, sat on its easel, the painting supplies tucked away in a box on top of a nearby table. Her pretty roommate was so busy modeling these days that she barely opened her box of supplies. Modeling was paying well, and she'd become so preoccupied by her new boyfriend that her artwork had taken a back seat.

Athena's side of the large living room was cluttered with sketch books, sketches taped to any bare space of wall or window frame, and her painting spot. The canvas tarp on the laminated floor was a center base for her two easels, a small drafting table, a stool in front of it, garage-sale tables covered with supplies and jars of brushes. Nothing looked amiss.

Why break in if you're not going to steal something? Her troubled gaze fell on one of the two sketches of the biker chick she'd drawn one day in charcoal. This sketch showed the back of the young woman astraddle her motorcycle, her head partly turned to the side, her face obscured by a mass of dark hair ballooning out in a breeze. The other sketch, half-finished, had revealed the woman's face in three-quarter profile. This second sketch was missing.

She'd sketched both from a series of photos from her vantage point beside the loft's picture window one morning as she sipped coffee and looked down at the corner bagel and coffee shop. The young woman was sitting on her bike at the curb, getting ready to enter the shop. For a moment, Athena's heart in her throat, she'd thought the girl had looked up at her window. As if the girl knew Athena was watching her. When the biker chick turned away, Athena had grabbed her camera and begun clicking away. One of the photos she'd taken when the girl emerged from the shop, coffee in one hand, bagel in the other. If she was aware of Athena's camera, she gave no indication. Moments later, however, the biker chick happened to look up at Athena's window before donning her helmet and riding away.

Now the missing sketch drew all her focus. The place on the wall next to the windowsill was glaringly empty. She set the pepper spray canister down on the kitchen counter and went over to stand in front of the empty space. Whoever broke into their apartment had taken the sketch, that was certainly apparent.

The sketch was the model for one of the vignette paintings Athena planned to do for Martin's gallery. But why? It was the only sketch that showed the strange biker girl's face. That was true. Realization slowly dawned on her. The thief wouldn't know that the sketch was based on a photo, one of many Athena kept in a cardboard box under her bed.

Three other sketches of D.C. street life were also taped on a nearby windowsill, waiting for her to translate them onto canvas in vivid colors. These street scenes were also based on photos taken by Athena.

With sickening fear, she touched the empty space of wall, and then the remaining sketch of the biker chick's back. An image vibrated through her clairvoyant channel and into her mind.

A man with long hair and the face of a young woman had touched the sketch, leaving behind a trail of suppressed rage, the intensity of the rage making her insides quiver. Hatred and fury hit her like powerful ocean breakers. The emotions flooded her with their ugliness and power. This man was filled with the kind of rage that drove him to kill. The biker chick's face touched her mind, but what replaced it was the soul of the man behind the female mask.

The killer. Palomino's and Ochoa's serial killer.

He was back.

And now Athena knew what he looked like.

Somehow he knew who Athena was. And felt threatened by her.

Now he was *her* threat.

Chapter Twenty-Five

A sleepless night left Athena feeling groggy and with a pounding headache. She'd found Detective Ochoa's card and called the number, only to get the Metro Police Station's house phone. The Watch Officer had asked her name and number and had promised to contact Ochoa's private cell phone. While she waited for Ochoa's return call, she texted Kas, telling him she'd arrived back at D.C. and all was fine. There was no way she was going to blurt out all her fears when there was nothing he could do about it. No, absolutely not. Hadn't she kept insisting to Kas that she was a big girl and could take care of herself?

Instead, she slept intermittently on the floor by her bed, facing the closed and locked bedroom door with pepper spray clutched in one hand and the walking stick umbrella in the other. Fear had swamped her and she'd wept, even sobbed, for many minutes. She'd never felt so alone in her life. So alone and so frightened.

Still, she wasn't about to give in to despair or self-pity. If the intruder returned, she was ready to attack him with her imaginary gun and sword. By morning, still wearing the clothes she'd arrived home in the night before, Athena was determined to overcome her fear and get better prepared.

When Detective Ochoa finally called later that Sunday morning, she was close to tears. Her emotional summary of what she'd found in her loft fell flat. He was less than helpful.

"Was anything taken?" His voice was officious but concerned.

"No—well, one of my sketches. A sketch of the man who broke in."

"Nothing else was taken, Miss Butler?"

"No." She knew what he was thinking. Not much to go on.

"And you think the perp's our serial killer from three years ago? The younger brother of the electrician? Yes, It's possible he's had his face reconstructed. Plastic surgery, maybe hormones to make him look like a woman. Have you seen this younger brother anywhere else?"

"Yes, several times. He works at Club Fiore as a server. As a woman. I'm positive now that the woman called Shawna is the younger brother."

"And how do you know this woman at Club Fiore was the one who broke into your apartment?"

"I just do. I had a vision. And a bad feeling.".

"From your clairvoyance?"

"*Yes.*" She knew a feeling and a vision were not enough for probable cause.

"Miss Butler, have you been drinking? Smoking pot? You and your mother were able to assist us once, but your tips led nowhere concrete. You know we've been ordered to drop this case. It's in the Cold Case files. Another team will take it up some day . . . maybe. You can call the B and E team at Robbery and see if they can lift some prints."

Athena felt tears form in her eyes. No, she wasn't going to get weepy. "No, he's too clever to leave any. You won't find any."

A lull of silence ensued. Athena inhaled deeply and strove to keep her voice steady and calm.

"Detective Ochoa, my mother and I helped you once. You know we're not frauds. I wouldn't be calling you and saying all of this if I didn't believe what I feel is the truth. Like I said, he works the evening shift at Club Fiore. The brother is back and looking like a woman. His alias is Shawna—don't know his last name. His face has been altered. His hair is long and he drives a motorcycle. He changed his looks so he could come back and be with his brother, but he's still a troubled, dangerous man."

"Well, I'm afraid I can't help you, Miss Butler. You see, Detective Palomino and I have moved on to new cases. After that search a few months ago ended up with nothing, we've been taken off that case. The AG has made it very clear that he will not be approving any more search warrants based on our so-called psychic consultants. Our captain has called off the surveillance team at the electrician's shop. We came up with a big *nada* there. Again. There've been cutbacks and we've been ordered to move on. I repeat, those girls that were killed, those are cold cases now. Another team might revisit it someday but I'm afraid we've moved on. Orders from above. Sorry, Miss Butler. Call nine-one-one and report a break-in. A uniform will come around and take your statement. I'm very sorry."

With that, Ochoa hung up. Athena dropped her pepper spray canister and umbrella, got up off the floor and went to her bathroom. She splashed her face with cold water and ran a comb through her hair. Then she placed a call to Martin Larsen. Five minutes later—at a little past eight o'clock on Sunday morning—she left her apartment. As she was running down the stairs, she spotted Kyle entering the building.

Her heart pounding in her chest like a jackhammer, she stopped him. He was carrying a small bag.

"Kyle, I must ask you. Have you seen Shawna lately? The girl on the motorcycle?"

Kyle averted his eyes down to the floor as though he'd just stepped on a kitten. Shamefully.

"Not since Thursday. I've been home all weekend. Home to New Jersey." For the first time, he lifted his eyes to hers. "Why? What has he done? She's a man, y'know. Had me fooled for a while."

Athena nodded gravely. "Yes, I know. I think he broke into my apartment while I was gone. He didn't steal anything . . . well, one sketch of mine."

Kyle's dark brows furrowed in anger. "Last time he was here" — he pointed up to his place — "I think he stole my keys. Not my car keys, the keys to the building and apartment. I told the super I'd lost them, but I know he took them."

She looked at the building's entrance door. "Has the super changed the locks yet?"

Kyle shook his head. "Nope, just tried the copy I had. Same old lock."

Taking a deep breath, she expelled it and swore. "Omigod! Tell him it's important that he change the locks immediately. Today!"

"Okay," he said with vehemence, "if you think it's that important. Who is this chick — uh, guy? Someone you used to know?"

She couldn't help but groan, "It's a long story. Just know he's a dangerous man. A killer."

"W-what? That transvestite?" Kyle leveled on her a doubtful look. "He seems harmless . . . he's just a fuckin' thief."

One hand reached for the building's entrance door while the other fished in her purse until she found the canister of pepper spray.

It might not be enough. "If you only knew — "

Leaving Kyle abruptly, she speed-walked the four long blocks to Visions Gallery. Above the gallery, in a gray brick apartment building owned by Martin's uncle, she located Martin's and Mark's shared apartment on the fifth floor. They opened the door, Mark in a velour bathrobe and Martin bare chested and wearing flannel bottoms with cats on them. Their three cats meowed their welcome before disappearing behind the kitchen counter. Mark went to feed them while Martin set her down on the sofa in the sun-splashed living room. One look at Athena's frantic expression, and Martin called Mark for some coffee.

"What, my dear Athena, has you so upset? Has that handsome hunk changed his mind already?"

For a moment, Athena didn't realize that Martin was referring to Kas. She shook her head fiercely. How to begin? Where to start? Was it so wise to involve her two friends? Would they even believe her?

One thing was certain. She couldn't call Kas. Poor guy, what could he do three thousand miles away?

For the next fifteen minutes, Athena held both men spellbound by her story. She paused to sip the coffee provided by Mark but continued almost immediately. They interrupted her only once to ask one question. "How does this work, this clairvoyance thing of yours?"

She recounted the threat at the British Embassy two years before, her father's and the Embassy's security team's roles in detecting the problem, her own role in revealing when and where the threat would materialize, how the threat was ultimately stopped. How her mother often helped the police in their investigations and how she'd been recruited by two Metro Homicide detectives to help in uncovering a potential suspect in a series of murders of young girls in the D.C. area. How she believed the serial killer had returned and was now passing as a female.

"A transgender woman?" Mark asked, his hand to his throat.

Athena had to shrug. "I don't think so. I mean, the vibes I get, he's totally male, has male urges, that kind of thing. But his looks are a disguise. He looks like a transgender female or a transvestite. But he's not. Does any of this make sense?"

While Martin slowly nodded, Mark shook his head. "Are you kidding, dearie? This sounds like the Twilight Zone."

Mark slapped his knees and laughed. Martin just sat and frowned.

"You're in danger, aren't you?" Martin said quietly.

Athena could only nod. "Maybe. He — the killer — thinks I'm a threat, that I have proof he's the brother of the electrician. That's the problem. I don't have proof, and the homicide detectives I worked with before have been taken off the case. Their captain has refused my help. No psychic consultants allowed, in other words."

"What electrical company is this that the older brother owns?"

Athena hesitated to reply. She couldn't take the responsibility of involving her two friends to any greater extent. Ace Electrical was the brother's business name. She hadn't helped but notice it on the garage door sign when she'd gone with Ochoa that day to search the interior of the shop and the brother's adjacent ground floor apartment.

"I can't say," she murmured, looking down at her slightly shaking hands. "I promised Detective Ochoa I wouldn't say anything to anyone. I would keep the man's identity a secret."

Martin's expression caught her eye. "Understood, Athena, yet here you are. We won't probe any further, but it's clear to me that you feel that man, that TV or tranny, is a threat to you. We want you to stay here until your roommate returns. Tomorrow, right? So stay here tonight."

Mark broke in. "Now I don't know how you feel about defending yourself, but where I come from — a small town in Oklahoma — I know."

Athena couldn't hide her shock.

Mark laughed. "I know, who would guess? A small town in Oklahoma. Well, where I come from, we pack heat."

Martin rolled his eyes and crossed his legs. "He thinks he's Rambo."

Mark slapped his partner playfully about the knees. "I

have a CCW permit."

At Athena's confused stare, he went on, "A Concealed Carry Weapons permit. For when I take gallery cash and checks to the bank, I have a gun permit. A fine nine millimeter Heckler and Koch pistol. Also, a .38 Smith and Wesson snub-nosed revolver. That's more your size, the revolver."

"Ohh, I don't know. I've never held a gun, just a pepper spray canister."

"Well, dearie, maybe it's time. I can take you to a shooting range in Virginia and show you how to clean it, handle it, shoot it."

She smiled weakly but suddenly realized this revelation of hers was a mistake. Both men meant well and were kind enough not to laugh at her revelations of clairvoyance, but getting a gun was taking the need for protection too far. Still, she appreciated their offer for her to stay with them. She told them as much.

Mark stood up and fiddled with the sash of his bathrobe. "You can stay in our guest bedroom tonight. For as long as you wish or feel the need to. Today, however, we have plans, and you're going to join us."

Alarmed, she stood up, also. "No, I can't possibly interfere with your plans."

Martin skimmed his gaze over her jeans, knit top and light-weight jacket. "You won't need to dress up. Just come along with us. Spend the day with us. Under our protection."

She was confused. "Dress up?"

Martin took her hand in his. "You said you can read minds with just a touch. So prove it. Where are we going today?"

His thoughts came through immediately. Her mouth dropped open.

"The Gay Pride Parade. At The Mall?"

Martin smiled. "Well, no shit. That's either a neat parlor trick, Athena, or you're what you say you are. Don't dress up.

198

I won't, either. I'm too conservative for that crowd. Mark loves to go as a Super Hero, Captain America this year. Last year it was Batman and the year before, Spiderman." He sighed loudly. "What can I do? He's a perpetual kid. You come as you are, a pretty, straight female spectator. We hope you won't be too shocked."

Mark whipped around to leave the room. "You shouldn't have told her my costume. I wanted to surprise her."

Martin's handsome Nordic face split in a wide, ironic grin.

Athena tried to smile.

CHAPTER TWENTY-SIX

A thena had only seen the National Mall this crowded before on the Fourth of July. From the Ellipsis south of the
White House to the Washington Monument, a sea of people
undulated like so many ocean creatures. She'd never seen so
many blue-uniformed police on horseback before, either.
Most of the crowd had left the 17th Street roadway adjacent
to the Washington Monument complex and was streaming
eastward onto Constitution Avenue. By the time Athena,
Martin and Mark arrived behind the Museum of American
History and took up position second-deep on the sidewalk,
the front of the Gay Pride Parade had already passed by. With
his multi-color Captain America cape and costume, including
blue, knee-high boots, Mark showed off his tall, trim build as
well as his inner little boy.

He spotted a large group of friends associated with his concert band and waved them down. Whipping out his trumpet
from a backpack underneath his cape, he proceeded to blend
in with the brass section and march away. She and Martin
laughed and waved him off.

"Thank heavens I've got you to hang out with," muttered
Martin. "I hate these things. Not the spirit or principle behind
it, no, but the—the spectacle of it. Look over there."

A nudist club promoting the worship of the naked body
was walking by. The men wore nothing but gaudy sneakers
and rainbow-colored ribbons tied around their necks or
around their penises.

Athena gasped aloud. "Is that even legal? I mean, there are

families of tourists in the crowd," she told Martin, staring at the naked men preening and swaggering by.

Martin shrugged. "Every year they get bolder and bolder, as if they're daring the cops to intervene. The cops've gotten smart and refuse to be baited. No one bothers them as long as the parade stays peaceful and there's no lewd conduct going on. Oh, here comes the Club Fiore float. The female impersonators. This year it's a big one."

Her heart tripping, Athena looked. The theme was Hollywood, evidently. The female impersonators, the show stars, were all dressed like movie star icons of the Twentieth Century—Marilyn Monroe, Ginger Rogers, Lana Turner, Bette Davis, Kathryn Hepburn, Barbra Streisand; others were dressed as more recent, ethnically diverse stars, like Diana Ross, Kerry Washington and Jennifer Lopez. Their costumes, wigs and makeup were impeccably done, she had to admit. Others flanking the float on wheels were apparently the support staff, dressed in various costumes. One masked dominatrix all in black leather from head to toe turned his or her head rather briskly and stared back at Athena.

She couldn't tell for certain, but an uneasy suspicion overtook her. A tremor washed through her. Was this that biker chick whose face was female but whose body appeared more that of a slim male of medium height? *The one who broke into my apartment and stole the sketch?* And though more difficult for her to accept, the younger brother whom Detectives Ochoa and Palomino had once suspected was their serial killer?

Their gazes locked together for ten more yards before Athena turned away. It was apparent that he recognized her as well, but she dared not give away what she already knew to be true but couldn't prove. Not even bothering to call 9-1-1 about the break-in, she'd decided to handle her suspicions by herself. One thing she could not do is let the killer know what she already knew. She needed a plan, a strategy, but no idea had come to her since last night. Her first instinct had been to flee to safety and keep Kas and her family far away until . . . until what?

Until she could find proof? Proof of what? That the younger brother had returned to the city that he felt was home. Where his brother, the only human being he cared about, could give him protection, comfort, solace? And who perhaps could calm the cruel and destructive urges inside his psyche?

And why exactly was this *her* job? The homicide detectives had already shelved this case. All she had to do was stay away from him, give Mikayla thirty days' notice, finish her paintings and pack up what little stuff she called hers. Then leave town, maybe for good. Get the hell out of Dodge, as the Americans would say.

"Are you alright, Athena?" Martin asked, his hand clasping her shoulder.

She looked up at her friend's handsome, concerned face. Good grief, she'd been staring at the ground, lost in thought.

"Yes, I was just thinking . . ."

"Let's move on. There're food tents down there, just past the ice rink. The parade's turning south on 7th Street, heading to the main part of The Mall. I don't want to follow it. I've seen enough and I'm hungry. Are you?"

"No, but something cold to drink would be nice," she replied. The sky was cloudless and the air warm and humid. She let Martin take her hand and lead her east on Constitution Avenue, following the route of the parade. A lesbian group was passing, all of them dressed in an array of workmen's uniforms. Plumbers, carpenters, Metro subway workers, gardeners, firefighters, cops. Some were in suits and ties and wore signs that announced they were politicians, lawyers, lobbyists. These women were throwing fake money into the

crowds bordering the Avenue, making people laugh with derision.

Despite her sudden change of mood, Athena joined Martin
in laughing at their antics.

She said above the raucous noise, "Look, I wonder why the
women are wearing more clothes than the men."

Martin guffawed. "Don't you know? Women have more
common sense. Men are exhibitionists, and I include my dear,
beloved Mark in that generalization."

A half mile farther they turned onto 7th Street, where the
food and drink tents lined both sides of the street. They
paused at one that sold Styrofoam bowls of teriyaki-flavored
chicken wings, and Martin bought a bowl. Athena declined,
having lost her appetite. Thirst propelled her towards the tent
next door. Martin pointed to a storage tent, covered with
bright blue, plastic tarp and located in a second row of tents
on the grass behind the main ones lining the sidewalk. Picnic
tables littered the front area and one side of this storage tent,
and nearby Plane trees lent shade and respite from the sun.
Other storage tents appeared in rows behind and alongside
that one, but that appeared to be the only one offering a place
to sit and eat in the shade.

Martin indicated with his chin. "I'll try to get us two seats.
Go sit. Meet you there in five."

Athena noticed the long line in front of the beverages tent.
"Make it ten." Martin nodded and wended his way through
the crowd in the direction of the storage tent.

Ten minutes later, she clutched her bottled water and had
tucked a small bottle of juice inside her hobo purse, which she
slung back over her shoulder. She set about to join Martin at
the picnic tables, but the crowd had thickened around the
tents. Behind the storage tents on the vast, grassy mall were
rows of Porta-Potties, standing like green stalwarts amid the
ebb and flow of the crowd. Parade goers and spectators had

peeled off to refresh themselves and all of a sudden, it seemed, she was caught in a vortex of bodies. For several minutes, she fought against the stream of humanity until she saw a small clearing. She elbowed her way through and stopped beside one of the storage tents to catch her breath and to reorient herself.

A bustling group of teenagers heading towards the Porta-Potties pushed her back against the outside wall of a black canvas storage tent. Her heel snagged on a clump of grass, so she bent over to pull it free. For balance, she used the corner of the tent, leaning against the metal support post.

It was then that she felt a clammy, cold dread trickle down her spine. She bolted upright and froze. *Run! Get away!*

Shawna, dressed in black leather from head to foot, looked through the eye-holes of her dominatrix mask as she made her way among the tents. Having used the excuse with her Club Fiore co-workers to find a toilet, she'd kept to the grassy area behind the row of food and beverage tents lining the sidewalk. Sure enough, her stealth paid off, for as soon as she'd moved to the shade of a Plane tree, she spotted the blonde artist whose loft apartment she'd broken into just days before. Whose sketch of Shawna had shocked him and made him feel panicky.

But now, Shawna was no longer present. Dave Millhouse had disposed of her, her voice, her female mannerisms. He'd grown tired of the charade, wanted his old, true identity back, no matter the cost. He'd told himself that this morning as he'd dressed in the costume set out for him in the Club Fiore dressing rooms. Jeannine had covered for him while he changed clothes as usual in the women's restroom. By now, the other female servers at the nightclub had all accepted Shawna as a transgender female, but only Jeannine knew the truth. That gave her power over him, which he didn't like but had gone along with . . . for now.

And now this other bitch had power over him. She'd sketched him in his disguise, full face and frontal figure in his casual biker outfit, jeans jacket over tee shirt, ratty jeans and boots. This artist bitch — if it was true what her ex-boyfriend had said about her, that she was psychic — probably knew who Shawna really was. The bitch was a threat. It was obvious she was working with the cops, helping them investigate his brother. After all, she'd helped that detective search Sam's shop and apartment.

With his last ounce of breath, Dave would protect his brother, just as Sam had protected him by arranging their parents' deaths years before. His brother was so smart that he'd made it look like an accident. In Sam's and Dave's world, ultimately all threats had to be eliminated. One way or another. But very carefully. He had to use his smarts.

He stepped over the grass carefully in Shawna's three-inch heeled boots. He'd groaned to Jeannine about having to wear the heels along the parade route, but the boss said they were sexy, and sex was what Club Fiore was selling. Better than going nude, she'd said, winking at him. Yep, Jeannine kept reminding him that she was the only one at Club Fiore who knew his secret — Shawna was not a tranny; she was a full-fledged male with a strong appetite for rough sex. Jeannine liked it, too, and had broken up with her boyfriend so that Shawna could move in with her. Dave decided to go along, crash at Jeannine's place for the time being, enjoy the fun but stay aware of what was at stake. The time would come when he'd take care of Jeannine before she could betray him, too.

Stepping behind a black tent, he spied the blonde bitch standing at the corner. She was bending over her raised sneaker, her hair spilling over both shoulders, holding on to the tent's metal frame. For a moment, he was struck by her looks, her slim body showing its curves in tight blue jeans and a fitted red top. He could wait and seize her, take her somewhere and have his fun with her, too. Then eliminate her, like all the others who'd disgusted him. All the little black girls and foreign whores with their pathetic, weak lives.

No, too dangerous. His brother had told him to be careful not to get into trouble and leave evidence behind. No semen, no saliva or hair, no fingerprints, no DNA. With any of that, the cops would trace him back to Dave and then the two of them would get locked up, separated from each other for the rest of their lives. He'd rather die than let that happen.

Dave entered the black tent. There were rows upon rows of stacked cardboard boxes waist high and filled with cans of soda pop, glass bottles of beer and plastic bottles of water. He glanced around and behind him. No one had seen him enter, he was sure of it. By the far corner of the tent, silhouetted against the outside sun, stood the blonde artist bitch. She was standing still like a statue.

He slipped the icepick out of its sheath inside his right boot, secured it in his right hand and silently approached the corner. If he could jab it under the back of her breastplate and thrust it upward, he'd stick her heart and kill her instantly.

One threat — gone.

He held the icepick, deadly point upward like a switchblade, like he'd seen his brother use it on their parents after drugging them. The fire afterwards had erased all evidence, Sam had told him, and he was right. Always smart, Sam knew how to eliminate threats. He would be smart, too.

He stepped forward quietly, so quietly up to the tent's fabric wall that he could hear the blonde's muttering out loud. He drew his arm back, ready for the thrust outward and upward.

Just then, the girl moved forward, springing out of the range of the icepick. The pick pierced the canvas cloth, but instantly, feeling the point hit air, he withdrew it. A moment later, a voice behind him made him spin around.

"What're you doing? Making holes in the tent?"

Dave stared with horror into the face of a young woman dressed in a Wonder Woman's red and blue costume. A gold crown sat atop her black wig and toppled a little as the woman's dark eyes fell upon the icepick. "Wh-what're you doing with that thing?"

In two long strides, he lunged towards the woman, grabbed her throat, closing off the gargled beginnings of a scream. Without hesitation, he plunged the icepick deep into her chest, under her left third-from-the-bottom rib, like he'd done to so many others. He felt the tug of tissue, felt the soft cushion of her heart give way as the sharp point entered. He plunged the icepick more deeply into the woman's chest. The gasp of air she'd taken a moment before rushed out, her knees buckled, and down she went.

He dropped her on the grassy floor and stood over her for a minute to wait until her twitches and spasms stopped. He pulled out the icepick, feeling it scrape against bone as it emerged. Cursing to himself, he wiped it carefully on her cape, then looked around cautiously. No blood on his costume or boots — good. Her blood would pool inside her chest, maybe gather at the point of entrance, but the kill was clean, if not expected. With one gloved hand, he tucked the icepick back into the sheath inside his right boot. He took a moment to study his black gloves. No blood — good!

Damn, but he'd have to tell Sam . . . or maybe not. His brother wouldn't like this. His head and pulse throbbing with alarm, Dave gingerly stepped over the woman and slipped out of the tent's back flap. He scanned the area, noticed a lot of commotion at one of the Porta-Potties — two naked men wearing Musketeer hats, capes and swashbuckling boots were arguing and shoving each other. Just what he needed, a diversion. A small crowd was gathering in front of the john, some of them taking photos of the scuffle with their phones.

Dave walked calmly away. He reminded himself of the occasions he and his Dutch partner in crime had slipped away from the scenes of their carnage. All they had to do was hide their weapons, act innocent and walk away calmly. Their bland expressions let them get away with a lot. It was not what people expected to see.

He rounded the tent and looked for the blonde artist bitch. A moment later, he spotted her, standing with a tall guy in ordinary clothes. She was pointing back to the black tent. Their eyes met for only an instant, then Dave turned away and kept on walking.

Slowly and calmly. Adrenaline racing like wildfire through his veins.

Stay calm. Don't run.

Sam, I'm sorry. I tried to help.

Five minutes later, he rejoined his Club Fiore group as it escorted their float down 7th Street on their way to Independence Avenue. Two long blocks after that and the parade would disperse. Most of the participants would stay for the drunken street party that followed, but not him and Jeannine. They had other plans. He'd keep on his dominatrix mask and costume but take off the leather pants.

Oh yeah.

Sam said to stay out of sight and under the radar. He was working on a plan. As Shawna, hanging out at Jeannine's digs, he was doing just that. Staying under the radar. Doing his job at Club Fiore. Just a little while longer. Then Dave could go home. A new home. A safe home. That was all he craved.

Finally!

CHAPTER TWENTY-SEVEN

The following morning, Athena washed and groomed herself as best she could under the circumstances. She'd brought one change of clothes in her hobo bag and nothing else, not even a toothbrush, but at least she felt safe at Martin's and Mark's apartment over the Visions Gallery. However, it was time to go back to her flat and do something. Hiding away was not the answer.

After a breakfast of croissants, fruit and coffee, Martin prepared to go downstairs to the gallery to begin his typical day at work, selling artwork. He paused before the doorway, a newspaper open in his hands. With a second cup of coffee in one hand, Mark left and a few minutes later re-entered the kitchen. He set on the kitchen table with the other hand a chamois-wrapped .38, snub-nosed revolver.

"Is it loaded?" Athena asked hesitantly.

"No, 'course not, sweetheart," assured Mark, grinning under his tousled, dark curls. "I'm going to give you a lesson in how to clean, handle and load a revolver. Then we're going to a shooting range in Bethesda where you can learn to shoot, get comfortable with this mode of self-defense."

Frowning with uncertainty, Athena put down her mug of coffee and stared at Mark's hands while he unwrapped the gun. "Now, follow me. This is the barrel, this is the stock that you hold in your hand. This is the hammer that you cock back like this when you're getting ready to fire. This is the trigger guard, the trigger, the revolving cartridge where you insert the bullets. That's why it's called a revolver, not a pistol."

Mark demonstrated each part of the revolver, then with a flick of his thumb, took apart the major pieces. With the chamois cloth, he cleaned the outer gray metal parts and then took a lightweight cleaning rod from a small box of gun cleaning supplies. Dabbing a nitro gun cleaner solvent onto a square patch of white cloth, he wrapped the cloth around a slim rod and inserted the rod into the barrel's bore. He turned the rod until he told her the barrel was clean. As proof, he showed Athena the dark residue that the rod and covering cloth had removed. "Never shoot before cleaning the barrel." He then reassembled the revolver and placed it into her hands.

Athena was surprised that it weighed so little, not too much more than her hammer for making canvas stretcher frames out of wood.

"During an attack, if you have enough time, you'd cock the hammer before pressing back on the trigger. If not, you have to exert more pressure on the trigger to cock the hammer, and there might be more recoil. The greater the recoil or kick, the less accurate your aim will be. Never put your forefinger on the trigger—just keep it on the trigger guard—until you are ready to fire. Aim before you fire, and allow for the kick or recoil to jolt the barrel upwards a bit. Do you understand that?"

Even though her head was swimming with all the new details, she nodded. "Yes, sir, Captain America." Referring to Mark's costume for the Gay Pride Parade made him smile broadly.

"Okay, time for some practice shooting in Bethesda. Do you have time? I'll drive you there now and show you the ropes."

Already, her confidence in her ability to protect herself had risen and she was grateful to Mark for taking the time himself. Should she text Kas and let him know what she was going to do? Should she let him know that she'd sensed the serial killer's presence at the parade yesterday—and even spotted him?

No, she couldn't. Why bother him and worry him to distraction? He'd fly over in a rush, and then what? Be forced to sit around and guard her when he had his work to do in San Francisco? She wouldn't tell Martin or Mark, either. They were doing enough to help her.

Decisively, she stood up. "Yes, let's go."

Mark was staring at Martin, who had looked up over the top edge of his newspaper and let out a loud curse. "Now what? You might disapprove, Marty, but it's for her own good. This is how we defend ourselves where I grew up. Little town, Oklahoma."

Martin rustled the paper. "Not that. A woman was killed yesterday during the parade. She was working in one of the tents. Stabbed to death, it says."

Mark swore. "Know what that means? Next year's parade might be outlawed."

His handsome partner shook his head. "Damn the parade. I bet there's a killer of gays on the loose in the city."

Athena gazed at them both. With awful certainty, she knew who the killer was. And he had meant for *her* to be his target. An innocent woman was murdered instead.

This murder was her fault.

As usual, Shawna showed up at Sam Millhouse's Ace Electrical by nine o'clock in the morning. The five electricians working for Sam had already taken the vans out on calls, leaving the office empty except for his long-suffering older brother. He was currently on the phone, drumming up business or arranging for advertising, something that he often delegated to his current "girlfriend," Shawna. He motioned her in with a wave of one hand, so Shawna clomped inside on her biker boots and unzipped her leather jacket. Her long hair draped down her back in a single braid, but even that was all part of her act.

Inside, Dave was roiling with fear. Had Sam read the Washington Post yet? He'd come across the newspaper on a newsstand kiosk by Jeannine's pad. There was an article on the front page about a woman who'd been stabbed to death during the parade. Her body was discovered later in the afternoon when one of the vendors had entered his storage tent. She was one of his female workers, all of them dressed as Wonder Woman for the day of the Gay Pride Parade. According to the newspaper, the Metro Homicide detectives were investigating and following various leads.

Inside, he was trembling, aware that he'd broken his cardinal rule. Never attack out of fear or panic. As a result, what happened? He glanced down at the deep scratch marks on his left forearm, the one he'd flung out to restrain that bitch and keep her from crying out. A big fuckin' mistake. He'd forgotten that his arms were bare—he'd always covered his entire body during what he called an *elimination*. He'd always been smart about exposing himself, even while in Amsterdam and eliminating those damned whores. He pulled down the long sleeve of his shirt. Now he trembled with fear that his brother would find out and disown him. Sam was all he had, the only human on the planet he could trust. Like a little boy, Dave was on the verge of tears.

As expected, as soon as Sam hung up the phone, he held up his copy of the Post.

"Is this you? Did you do this?"

Downcast, Shawna wrung her hands and shook her head. "No. I was with the Club Fiore float the whole day. Ask any of 'em." He knew Sam wouldn't check, but he also saw the doubt in his dark eyes. "Y'know, there's lots of crazies in this town."

His brother's relentless gaze pierced him, but he said nothing, his accusatory stare saying more than any words could.

Shawna hung her head in regret. He shouldn't have taken the risk. He was getting weak, soft—all those damned female hormones to keep his skin smooth. God, he was so fuckin' sick of being a woman!

Dave looked up at his older brother. For a long moment, Sam's expression filled with both love and hate, lingered darkly and then passed.

Sam finally sighed heavily as he threw down the newspaper.

"I say we should sell and get the hell outa here," came his reply. "Sooner rather than later. We can't wait any longer. Know what I'm saying?" Exasperation and bitterness hardened his voice. "I don't blame you, Dave. We've both done bad things. I'm just as bad as you, I know that. But things've changed. This town's getting too hot for us. I know a guy who wants to buy me out. With one phone call, it's done. I can keep one of the vans, keep enough equipment to do small electrical jobs, change the name. Change our names. It's time to leave town, start over. Before it's too late. Understand me?"

Dave looked up with hope and nodded fervently. His devotion to his older brother was boundless, and his eyes misted over with gratitude.

"Yeah, start over. Where?"

"A small town somewhere. Where the cops don't know anything about us. We'll change our names, get fake IDs and a license plate to go with it. Easy enough if you know where to look and who to see."

Hope, love and relief bubbled inside Dave. Yeah! A small town where no one knew them, no cops would search their place, where Dave could be a guy again—

"Can I stop being a girl?" he asked, forgetting to drop Shawna's higher pitched voice. He switched to his natural, deeper voice. "I don't like being a girl. I hate the makeup, all of it. I hate . . . this!" He raised a gloved hand and scrubbed his cheek with it.

Sam shrugged. "Sure, stop taking those hormone pills, and your skin'll go back to a normal guy's. You'll grow hair. Grow a mustache and beard. No one'll see the old you, not with the new chin and nose and cheekbones. Stop the stupid makeup and falsies. Maybe keep the hair and biker look, but we'll clean you up a bit. You can go back to being a plain ol' hard-working electrician, like me."

In a rush of love and gratitude, Dave fell on his knees at his brother's feet, hugged his legs, rested his head for a moment on Sam's knees. He wept silently until his brother began stroking his face and hair.

"We'll be together like always?" Dave pleaded.

"Yes," Sam assured him, his voice softening, "like always. I promised you I'd always protect you. I let you down when we were little. Not anymore. It's not your fault. Not your fault, not mine. We got a raw deal and it screwed us up. We're not normal, but it's not our fault. We deserve a chance to be normal. Like everybody else." He lifted Dave's wet face. "Just remember that. Go on with your normal routine, but lay low and stay out of trouble. Go to your job at the club. Today's Monday. By Friday at the latest, I should have this fucking place sold, all the paperwork done. We can leave sometime next week, maybe Monday. There's a small town in Colo-rado—you'll like the mountains and the snow. We can be happy there. Get us some rifles and learn how to hunt elk."

Dave sniffled and wiped his nose with a glove. He smiled and hugged Sam around the waist. "Yeah, we can have a nor-mal life. I like sex like a man. I hate being a girl. I'll stop those pills right away." He stood up and clapped his hands to-gether. "Next week, yeah. Soon as we can, huh? Mountains, snow, hunting with rifles—yeah."

Sam leveled a speculative gaze on him and waved him off.

"I'm okay here. The cops gave up on us a long time ago. Those surveillance cameras are long gone. No detectives hanging around. Just you lay low. Just until Sunday, okay? You meet me here Sunday morning. We'll put all our stuff in one of the vans. Then we're off."

Dave went to the office door just as one of the vans pulled into a garage bay. "Yeah, a new home. It'll be great." He waved to Sam, grinning and feeling on top of the world. He brushed his fingers against his smooth face. Yeah, time to be a man again.

After Saturday's stint at Club Fiore, he'd move out of Jeannine's slovenly crib and hit the road with Sam. Ha! He'd kill off Shawna. Maybe that meddling artist bitch, too. He had the key to get into her building. Not her apartment, though, but he could figure out something.

No. He promised Sam he'd stay out of trouble. Just one week. Not so long.

CHAPTER TWENTY-EIGHT

M ark Cochinelli parked his BMW sedan at the curb, two
blocks away from the northeast Metro Police Station,
the headquarters for the Homicide Division. They'd left the
thirty-eight revolver and Mark's Glock pistol in his car,
locked in the glove compartment, before setting off. The
shooting range practice had been productive, and Athena no
longer felt afraid of handling or shooting the small thirty-
eight revolver Mark had loaned her. She'd keep it with her at
all times, never mind the Conceal and Carry law — until she
left town in one month. As Mark had told her, D.C. was one
of the murder capitals of the world and had one of the highest
mortality rates by firearms despite its very strict gun-control
laws. As Mark said, it's an example of the old saying, "When
guns are outlawed, only the outlaws will have guns. Worry
about the C&C law after you've saved your own life."

There wasn't time to apply for one anyway. She needed to
defend herself . . . now! She could see the reason and logic behind Mark's argument.

Whatever — blimey!

She felt she had no choice but to defend herself for any
eventuality. Including an attack from a serial killer who suspected, thanks to Dan Grantham's big mouth, that she knew
that biker chick's dark secrets. Dan hadn't called her to tell her
anything. Athena knew he'd told the server, Shawna — the
younger brother, the killer — what she'd confessed to Dan
about her clairvoyance. Something she now wished she
hadn't done.

She'd be dead or gravely wounded from that attack at the parade if it weren't for her sixth sense. Her clairvoyance. For the umpteenth time in her life, Athena was supremely grateful for her strange gift.

She used to think of it as a curse. Not anymore.

Still, another woman was dead because of her. If not directly, then indirectly. She owed justice to that poor woman. The pain of that guilt settled deeply within her, like a heavy weight upon her heart.

From that point forward—she swore—she'd use her clairvoyance to keep herself and those she loved as safe as possible. How she could use her powers to help mankind? Well, that was a bigger question than she could answer. For the present.

They announced themselves, waited for the Watch Officer to call Detective Juan-Pablo Ochoa, and when Ochoa gave the word, she and Mark went through the metal detector and entered the elevator. It had been almost three years since Athena had visited Metro's Homicide Division's squad room. On the fourth floor, a frowning Ochoa greeted them as the elevator doors opened. They passed by another Watch Officer's desk after Ochoa punched in his security code.

"Athena, surprised to see you." His scowl broke and morphed into a wide smile as he shook her hand in greeting. She introduced Mark Cochinelli as a *concerned friend* and as part owner of GPWGP, one of her art dealers. Mark shook hands with Ochoa, who then led them past a noisy squad room of male and female detectives to a conference room to the right of a long aisle. There they could have some privacy. Athena knew Ochoa was trying to avoid ridicule from the other officers in his department by sequestering his visitors. She looked around, but Detective Gino Palomino was nowhere to be seen.

The three took seats around a table that could seat eight.

The room was windowless, its walls painted a dull beige. The table was metal, the chairs metal-framed with plastic seats. Familiarity permeated Athena's memory bank.

With stubborn clarity, she recalled examining a pile of jackets on that very table two and a half years ago. What she had seen in those jackets had disturbed her sleep for many months. The identification of a dirty, suede sports jacket had opened the way for a limited search warrant, had focused Palomino's and Ochoa's investigation into the two Millhouse brothers, and then had prompted an international manhunt for one of them—the younger one, she'd learned. Despite it all, the suspect had slipped out of their dragnet by jumping the cargo ship he'd worked on—the *US Bullworth*—and had vanished somewhere in Africa or Europe. Police across three continents, guided by Interpol, had no success in locating him. Like many others, they'd guessed, he'd managed to find false ID documents, pay off some border patrol guards in Africa and disappear past the open borders of Europe and melt into the teeming crowds.

She'd learned all this just months ago when Ochoa took her with him to search the electrician's shop and residence. The name Sam Millhouse had been on the Ace Electrical sign. Athena knew the man—Sam—had learned her true identity. Not once in the intervening months had she returned to that place, nor had she seen Millhouse again, but it was unnerving to realize a killer's brother knew who she was.

Now the killer, himself, knew she was the one who'd pointed the cops in his direction. And now the killer knew where she lived, and he was stalking her. And now he had access to her building.

"Gino wants me to find out what you want or need, Athena. He's busy running down some leads on yesterday's Gay Pride Parade murder." Ochoa's luminous dark eyes flickered over to Mark before returning to Athena. "The Watch

Officer said you both were there at the parade and had some information for us."

"Yes, we were there. We also read the newspaper account, Detective," began Athena. She paused to take a deep breath. Would Ochoa believe her? Well, bloody hell, she had to try. "We were there, Mark, me, our friend, Martin Larsen, who's also part owner of Genuine Pastiches." She glanced over at Mark. "Mark was with several friends walking in the parade. Look, here's a photo." She showed him her cell phone. He nodded. "As you can see, they—Mark's concert band—were all dressed as Super Heroes. Martin and I watched from the sidelines. When the parade turned onto Seventh Street, between Independence Avenue and Maryland Avenue, Martin and I stopped following the parade to get something to eat and drink. We went over to where all the refreshment tents and portable toilets were. I got my drink and went over to stand by this one tent to wait for Martin. It was partly in the shade by a Plane tree . . ."

She could see his gaze wander over to Mark, to the door, back to her. He was growing bored by her lengthy explanation, she could tell, but she had to narrate the events in her own way. To lend her experience credence, if nothing else.

"So . . ." Ochoa prompted. He had a murder to solve and appeared anxious to get back to working the investigation.

"I was standing by this tent and suddenly I felt a, uh, a presence, an evil presence. I knew that the serial killer, the younger brother you were looking for three years ago was back. He was there, near me. Standing near me. I left as fast as I could but when I looked back, I saw a rip in the tent—a hole."

"What color was this tent?" Ochoa asked.

She knew the color of the tent wasn't mentioned in the news article. "Black. It was black canvas. It was behind a small picnic area." She looked down at her hands. A hollow feeling in her chest made her feel ill. Maybe she should have stayed or screamed or done something. Maybe that woman would still be alive if she had. "I looked back and saw a hole in the tent and an icepick or something like it, stabbing through the cloth. I knew then I'd just escaped being stabbed. I guess I panicked—I didn't know he would attack someone else. I should've known, but I didn't. I can't see the future like . . ." She was thinking, *Like Kas's mother can.* "Anyway, I told Martin, who panicked, too, and whisked me out of there. I guess if I'd stayed and called attention to the tent, that woman wouldn't have been killed. She was killed inside that tent, wasn't she?"

Athena knew by the slight change in Ochoa's expression that she'd said the right words. *Black tent. Icepick.* Those details were not mentioned in the newspaper article.

"So what evidence do you have that the perp, the murderer, used an icepick?"

She told herself to be patient. "I saw the pointed end, the tip of it come through the cloth of the tent. Then it disappeared. By then, I was pushing past people to get away. I did look back once a couple minutes later and saw him. Or her. He's dressed as a woman, and I think he's had his face altered by surgery. He was wearing all black leather, a face mask, pants, a bra-type thing like a leather sports bra. Also, tall black boots with heels, gloves. A coiled whip was tied to his belt, like he was a dominatrix. He was with the Club Fiore float. One of the costumed people on that float saw me and stared at me, like he knew me. I think he followed me over to that tent area."

Ochoa stared at her strangely. "The same man who broke into your apartment?"

Bloody hell, yes!

She nodded soberly. Ochoa was bending forward over the table, his face clouded over with apprehension. Or was it disbelief?

"How could you see the woman's face — or man's face if he wore a mask? What concrete evidence do you have that the serial killer of those little girls is back?" he asked, scowling again. He extended his arm on the table and began tapping it with one forefinger.

She held his stare and reached to touch his hand. Ochoa didn't shrink away. That he didn't shrink away gave her tacit permission to read him.

"No physical evidence, Detective, but you know me. How my mind works. My mother and I are clairvoyant. This detail wasn't in the newspaper, either, but I know the Medical Examiner found skin scrapings underneath the murdered woman's fingernails. She tried to fight him off the few seconds before she was stabbed. Once you get those skin cells analyzed, I think you'll find the physical evidence you need. Get the DNA from a biker who goes by the name of Shawna. She works at Club Fiore as a server on the evening shift. I think you'll find a match to the killer's DNA. If you can't do that, well, then I guess he'll get away with another murder."

Ochoa looked at her, then Mark, before standing up and shaking both their hands.

"Thanks for coming in and trying to help, Athena. I know you mean well. My hands are tied, sorry to say. Palomino and I are not allowed to use any tips except physical evidence. A new captain's in charge of homicide, and he's not a believer of, uh, ESP, clairvoyance and all that. I would have no reasonable claim, no probable cause for a search warrant, and I'd need one to get that person's DNA. Sorry, but all I can do is hear you out."

And her tips would go into the Looney Bin File. She took out of her hobo bag her sketch book. Mark had made copies on his home copier of a sketch she'd made that morning; it was close to an exact replica of the sketch of the biker chick. With excellent visual recall, as most artists had, Athena had focused on the biker chick's face this time. She also took out the photo that the sketch was based on, a distance shot that caught the biker chick's face in shadow. Not helpful, but the photo showed that the biker chick was hanging around Athena's apartment.

She gave the photo and a copy of the sketch to Ochoa and said, "Here's what the serial killer looks like today. Notice his facial features in the sketch. Compare them to whatever photos you have of the younger Millhouse brother. Also, notice that I took the photo from my front window, third floor. I think he's stalking me in his disguise as a woman." For emphasis, she tapped the sketch. "But the crucial test is the DNA. Get Shawna's DNA, then you've solved your murder case on The Mall."

Ochoa took the photo and the 81/2 by 11-inch sheet of paper. "This looks like a young woman in her twenties."

"That's no girl. Just her face. By the way, Detective Ochoa, this job's giving you chronic insomnia and IBS. I'm sorry about that. You're a good man. Metro needs more men like you."

Having failed to change his mind, Athena and Mark stood, bid their goodbyes and left the conference room. She paused outside the door as Ochoa stayed behind to make a phone call. What she overheard gave her a little hope.

"Gino, that psychic girl, the artist—yeah, she was just here. You won't believe what she told me . . ."

She and Mark left the squad room and walked to the elevator. Mark patted her shoulder. "Hey, you tried, Athena. That's all you can do. Now your job is to protect yourself. Their job, it seems, is to chase their tails and let a killer run loose."

Athena stepped into the elevator and finally gazed up at his boyishly handsome face. "Thanks for coming with me, Mark. You probably felt foolish, but I appreciate the support."

He punched the ground floor button. "Hey, gay men get used to the cops shrugging them off with a joke. Guess that's your normal, too."

She hadn't connected the two — psychics and gay men — before, but his remark made her smile.

"Yes, it's my new normal."

CHAPTER TWENTY-NINE

Seeing the lights on in her loft apartment, she had Mark drop her off. Before he did, she had to agree to keep the revolver he'd loaned her loaded and inside her hobo bag at all times. Athena thanked him and told him to thank Martin again for putting her up for two nights and for helping to boost her self-confidence. Martin and Mark were good friends. She no longer felt so alone or so frightened.

"Thanks for the gun and showing me how to use it."

"Keep it close at hand. You never know . . ." Mark left it at that and drove off.

Mick was back! Her heart bounced along with her steps up the wooden stairs to their floor. When she turned the key and unlocked the front door, she was greeted by an exuberant Mikayla. They hugged each other, hopped around a little and squealed out greetings.

"I've missed you, Mick! How long has it been — two weeks? Wow, you look great! Guess a couple of weeks in Bermuda was the ticket."

"You, too. I see joy in your eyes — no, it's love and lust. I got all your texts and photos with hunky Kas Skoros. So, whatcha gonna do? Move out there and live with him? Wow, girl-friend, that's a big step."

Athena became subdued. Just thinking about that "big step" made her heart leap in her chest. "I know."

"Big, big step. Not to mention, I'd miss you like hell. Well, me, too. I have a big step to make, too, 'Thena."

Mikayla waited while Athena hung up her lightweight

jacket and hobo purse on the tree stand. Her best friend from the Art Institute looked different. Mick's mocha complexion had taken on a shiny, bronze sheen, her usually curly black hair was flat, straightened and, though caught by a jeweled clip, cascaded down her back. There were stripes of reddish brown that drew one's eyes to its silky drape. She wore a bright rose-colored cotton tunic over white leggings and white sandal heels. Her mind was still in Bermuda, clearly.

Her flat mate handed her a goblet filled with white wine and invited her to sit down on one of the stools at the kitchen counter. She joined her at the counter, sliding into the stool next to Athena, bubbling with suppressed excitement. Her wide smile shone as brightly as her top. Mick's joy spilled over as she stretched out her left hand, splaying fingers tipped with perfectly manicured and polished nails. A single, big diamond blazed by the knuckle on her ring finger.

"Oh. My. God. Mick, he didn't!"

"He did. And I said yes. Me, Mikayla Richards, who vowed to never get married! Listen, I want to throw an engagement party for friends. Here in the loft. Think you can get your California hunk to come?"

"Wait a minute. We're talking about you and your photographer boyfriend? Or is this someone else, someone new?"

Mikayla laughed. "No, it's Barry. After one of the photo shoots, we hung out by the hotel pool and just talked. That night, we did the deed and that was the start of a lot of serious talking. You know what I mean, talking about life, love, kids, money, our dreams, our goals. We discovered we had a lot in common. We want the same things. He likes that I want to do more with my life than modeling. He likes my new line of fashion accessories and wants to invest in my company. So we're going into business together. How more serious can that be?"

They hugged again and then, settling back down, clicked

their goblets together.

"Cheers and happiness!"

"Cheers to you, too!"

Mick's expression sobered. "The thing is, we're moving in together at the end of the month. I'm moving into his place in Alexandria. I know, it's not at least thirty-days advance notice. I can pay for next month if that leaves you short of money. Money's not a problem. This photo shoot paid us both well. It was for a Neiman-Marcus catalogue. Barry's got a couple more assignments with them, so we're both flush. So is this okay or am I leaving you in the lurch?"

"No, not at all. I'm leaving town, too. I'm not certain where I'm going."

"What? Tell me your news. What have you decided to do?"

Athena sipped her wine—a nice Riesling—before trying to capsulate all that had happened in the last week, even the last forty-eight hours, that she hadn't texted her friend while in San Francisco.

"Well, to start," she said before pausing to take a shuddering breath, "You know I need a full-time position to renew my work-visa status. I'm afraid painting is considered a hobby, and the income isn't guaranteed. So Kas wants me to manage the Stargazer Gallery." She erupted into a squeal of delight. "I think I texted you, Martin's pastiche painters sold most everything at Kas's gallery, and everything turned out better than we expected. There's an incredible market out there in San Francisco. Lots of affluent people in the tech industry, and they're hungry for culture and good art."

They clicked glasses again.

"Congratulations to you, to all of you! You're all such great artists!" Mikayla glanced a little guiltily at her one neglected, half-finished painting on an easel in her half of the living room work area.

Athena followed her friend's gaze. "And you're a great de-
signer. We all have to find what we're best at, don't we?" They
playfully knocked knuckles together. Mikayla had come to
terms with her lack of painting abilities during their junior
year at the Art Institute, then had turned to design and modeling as compensations.

"So? You and Kas connected again, and I'm happy for you.
I hear a *but* at the end of your sentence. What's the problem?"
Mikayla asked, her big hazel eyes widening with surprise.
"And, by the way, what happened to Dan? I know you broke
up, but you two had so much in common."

In keeping with her promise to Dan, however, Athena
would not reveal Dan's new illegal art forgery enterprise.

"Long story, won't go into it now. All I can say is Kas and
I never stopped loving each other and — " She shrugged. "now
he's willing to take it to the next level. Sounds trite, but that's
where we are. I don't know if I want to take that chance."

"And move to San Francisco? What, are you nuts?"

Athena couldn't help but nod and grin. "That's where the
gallery is and that's where Kas is. I know, but I'll be further
from my parents in Milan." Another thought occurred to her.
"My brother, Chris, is going to Stanford University this fall.
That's just about forty miles south of San Francisco, so I'll
have one family member out there near me. He's flying in to
DC Saturday morning. Is it okay if he stays here with us for a
few days before flying on to the West Coast?"

"Of course. He can bunk on the couch. He must be a big
guy by now."

Athena laughed. "He's six-two to my five-nine. Tall like
my father. Good-looking guy, too. Looks Italian, like my
mother." She thought of her family in Milan, her Italian
grandmother and uncle in Como. Christmas would be her
next visit to see them all. Unless she chucked San Francisco
for a while and went to Milan to see how her father was doing.

But Kas was depending on her to help renovate his gallery.

Mikayla looked thoughtful, a look that Athena recognized. She was seeing problems in Athena's future situation. The same possible glitches that Athena wondered about, too. If only she had Lorena Skoros's powers of precognition.

Frowning, her friend said, "Well, that's good to have your brother close by at Stanford. But living with your boss, basically — well, that could be a little tricky. What if you change your mind about him? About living with him? You know the fragile male ego. You could lose your job. Everything could fall apart."

"I know." The potential for failure nearly overwhelmed Athena. There was another thing to fear besides losing a gallery management job — losing Kas for good. She put down her wine goblet and sank her face in her hands, her elbows firmly planted on the counter. She felt like weeping again. This time she held back the tears and swallowed down her fear.

She felt Mikayla's hand on her shoulder. "Then again, everything could work out and the two of you could live happily ever after."

Athena snorted softly. "If it all blows up in my face, I'll suck it up, move to Milan and, like a lot of our generation, bunk in with my parents. I'll continue to paint pastiches for Martin and keep improving my work. Life will go on. The main thing, Mick, I need to move as soon as possible. Either San Francisco or Milan, it's got to be soon."

Mikayla smiled. "You texted you had a commission from Martin? Your own original work?"

Athena turned in her seat and pointed at the sketches she'd taped to the wall on the far side of the living room. "Yes, finally. Four cityscapes." There was an empty space on the wall where a sketch once hung, the sketch depicting a young woman gazing faraway while sitting on her motorcycle. She doubted that Mikayla missed it.

228

The serial killer.

"Kas would like the new gallery reopening by the first of October. In time for the Christmas shopping season. A lot of work needs to get done there before then. The current gallery manager has done a poor job. If I do this, I'm going to borrow some of Martin's great ideas from the Visions Gallery. You know, invisible partitions, an open look, a feeling of space that emphasizes the artwork."

Almost simultaneously with Mikayla, she surveyed the open kitchen and living room area of their shared loft apartment.

"Dude," Mikayla breathed, "it sounds like you've already made up your mind."

Athena dropped her hands and exchanged a long stare with Mikayla. "It does, doesn't it?"

Her friend grinned. "Strange, we'll be leaving this place at the same time. How uncanny is that? Leaving here and moving on with our lives. Here's to good luck in our future!"

They clicked glasses again. Athena's thoughts turned to the recent break-in and the security precautions they still had to take before moving out. Tomorrow, she would arrange for an alarm system to be installed.

"Come with me." She led Mikayla the arm into Mikayla's bedroom, flicked on the light switch, and pulled her over to the lone sash window. "Did you notice what I did?" Athena pointed out the nails she'd driven into the windowsill through the wide, wooden window frame.

"No, why did you nail it shut? What happened?" Mikayla asked.

"We had a break-in while I was in San Francisco last week. The screen was removed, and somebody got in. Came up the fire escape outside and broke into our flat. You must've left the window ajar, 'cause the lock wasn't broken. Just the screen. I noticed this Saturday night when I got home. I made a thorough check of the apartment. Nothing was taken except one thing."

Mikayla's slim hand flew to her throat. "This freaks me out. Did you check my jewelry case? The closets? The kitchen?"

Her friend had a precious collection of Lladro that she adored, given to her by her mother and grandmother, both of whom lived in Florida. The expensive porcelain pieces were stored in one of the kitchen cupboards.

"I checked everything. The only thing taken was one of my sketches. Not paintings, not the landscapes. A sketch of a biker chick. It was taped to the wall by one of my easels."

Mikayla's dark eyebrows shot up. "I know that sketch. You were going to make a painting from it, right? Why would someone take just that?"

"Because the biker chick was the one who broke in." Athena waited for her words to be absorbed.

Mikayla's black eyebrows furrowed.

Athena rushed to explain. "She's not a chick. She's a man, a dangerous man. A killer."

"What? How do you know all that?"

Athena sighed.

"Ohh." Mikayla murmured. "Your clairvoyance. But are you sure?"

"Oh yes, I'm positive. You and I are both in danger."

How could she explain that her powers were increasing, that she was now not only clairvoyant, but also clairaudient and clairsentient? She didn't need to touch someone anymore to read his or her thoughts. At least, not all the time. She could see, hear and feel what others could not. She was a descendant of the Delphi Bloodline.

Mikayla sank down on her bed and stared hard at her.

Athena inhaled and ran her hand over the windowsill. Even now, she could sense his evil presence. The acrid emanations flowing off the places he touched in their apartment—

despite his wearing gloves—were unmistakable and as palpable as a skunk's stench.

Athena couldn't help but shrug. "The bloodline, it's a long story."

Mikayla stood up. "I've got all night, but I have a feeling I'll need some wine to hear this."

Athena went to retrieve the bottle of wine from the kitchen. When she returned, she was carrying the canister of pepper spray.

"This is for you. I have another form of self-defense."

CHAPTER THIRTY

It was past midnight when they gave it up and hugged each other good night.

Athena's heart felt lighter than it had for over two days, ever since she'd arrived home and become enmeshed in the evil miasma floating about her apartment.

At one point, Mikayla had stared into space and said, "Y'know, I knew something was different about you. That you were helping the cops, not just as a sketch artist."

"I'm so sorry," Athena had told her, "but I promised my mother I wouldn't do it anymore."

Athena made a small noise in the back of her throat. "I did today again. I gave them a similar sketch to the one the killer stole. Ironic, but I guess I'm a witness of sorts. Whether they believe me or can do anything about it is another story."

She and Mikayla were both drowsy and a little drunk. When Mikayla stood up, she swayed a bit.

"Wow, you've not only been painting these great pastiches, you've been fighting crime in your own way."

Athena stood, too. "Yes, well, a lot of good that's done. The homicide cops can't act on any of my visions or feelings."

Mikayla looked at her speculatively before hugging her again. "Don't give up, 'Thene. You'll find something, some concrete evidence. Just don't put yourself in danger doing it."

Too late for that.

Mikayla wended her way past the kitchen on her way to her bedroom. "Hey, it sounds like we're going to be super busy over the next few weeks. I think Barry and I should throw that engagement party this weekend. How about Saturday night? I'll get that caterer over on Wisconsin. They do good work, don't they? All we have to do to clean up the place and call people. Yeah, Saturday night, seven. Work for you?"

Athena went over and hugged her friend. "Great idea! Tell me what you need, I'll help."

Fifteen minutes later, dressed in a loose nightgown, Athena climbed into bed. She'd locked her bedroom door—had double-locked the front door—and had positioned her satchel next to her nightstand. Nestled inside at the bottom of her bag was the snub-nosed revolver. She was struggling to be brave, ignore her fears, but it was difficult. The stench of his presence was still perceptible, so much that she set up her portable fan on her chest of drawers and turned it on. The cool, circulating air helped to dissipate the smell of evil.

She scooted down under the covers. Immediately, a vision assailed her. She grabbed her cell phone and punched in Kas's number. When a groggy voice answered, she hastened to apologize.

"I'm sorry to call so late, Kas. I could see you were in bed but not asleep."

"How did you know—ah, never mind. Of course, you knew." She heard his deep chuckle, followed by a stifled, guttural yawn. "Your powers are growing, babe. I was lying here, thinking of you, wishing you were here in bed with me. Can't get back to sleep."

"The same here." She sighed with longing. "I'm thinking, Kas. Maybe I could wind up everything here in the next few weeks and fly out there before the end of the month. Martin said I could mail him those four cityscapes, so I could finish them at your place, like you said. And I could take that small condo you were talking about. I could probably afford to rent it, not buy it."

A moment of silence followed, then he drawled sleepily,

"Sure. That condo is small, but the living room is fairly large. It'd be a good work space for you. The windows are like my condo's. Tall, lots of light."

"Wonderful. That wonderful view will inspire me."

"I could inspire you, too, if you gave me a chance."

She had to chuckle at his sexual innuendo. "Oh, you'll have lots of chances to inspire me." Switching mental gears, she asked, "How's the gallery doing?"

"Same. Bad as ever. No business. Hey, I got the name and number of that artist you asked about. I called him and said the Stargazer Gallery would like to feature him in a one-man show as part of our October re-opening celebration."

"Oh, good," she gushed, "I know he'll sell very well. I can't wait to see his other work."

"I gave him your email address so he could send photos of his other paintings. You can get a head start and pick what you want for his one-man show. Hope that's okay."

"Great! Thank you so much, Kas."

There was a lapse of conversation as their thoughts revolved back around to their mutual longing for each other. His thoughts were coming through loudly and clearly, making her warm and aroused. Another thought sidetracked her.

"Chris is flying in early Saturday morning. He's staying a few days on his way to California."

"Yes, I know. My mother knew, too. Guess that'll make you feel better, to have some family out here on the West Coast."

"Oh yes, that'll be super." It was no mystery that her mother and Kas's mother communicated frequently. She suspected that the two distant cousins of the Delphi Bloodline made telepathic head hops with each other, just as she was able to do with Kas.

Her thoughts turned on a dime. She could see him sitting up in his bed and turning on the lamp on the nightstand, his dark hair spiking out on top as he rubbed a hand over his face.

He was wearing a white tee shirt and white briefs. With piercing recall, she remembered how he looked in bed the last night she'd spent with him. All big shoulders, hard body and bare chest, warm flesh and the heat of his sex filling her up.

Gorgeous, all six-foot-three of him. His arm muscles bunched as he bent over his raised knees. She saw him so clearly, she wanted to reach out and touch him.

"Thena, are you seeing me ?"

A warmth spread throughout her chest and curled into a ball of heat between her legs, making her shudder with desire. "Oh, yes."

She thought of the break-in and how she'd felt so violated and vulnerable. But no longer. Her eyes flitted over to her satchel. She'd warned Mikayla and tomorrow—rather, later this morning—she'd call to get that alarm system installed. Worrying Kas by telling him what happened and what measures she was taking to feel safer was pointless. And cruel, since there was nothing he could do about it.

Kas chuckled softly. "We could stay on the line and I could talk dirty to you . . ."

She laughed. "Or we could get some sleep. I have a cityscape to paint tomorrow and you . . ."

"Two meetings with two different realtors. We sold two more condos, but one of the buyers wants a total makeover. And good news, my Stargazer general contractor might be available for the residential tower in Berkeley if we start it six months sooner than planned."

"Great." Athena considered what Mikayla had said, her reservations about Athena living with a man who was also her boss. Outside of marriage, she'd meant, when there was no commitment. "Kas, I've got some savings. If I wanted to buy that small condo, what would it cost me?"

The following silence was prolonged. She realized he'd misunderstood. He'd thought she would rent the small condo to work in, not live in.

"I'm not saying that I don't want to live with you," she said, "I just might need my own space. Day, maybe some nights."

Across the ether, his thoughts and feelings came clearly. *I may not be clairvoyant, sweetheart, but I know why you're asking this. You're afraid we're going to crash and burn, like last time. You're afraid I'll cheat on you, that it'll be like last time when I hurt you and married Nikki. That's okay, baby, can't say I blame you. Okay by me if you don't want to live with me, just so long as you live nearby and I can keep an eye on you. Damn . . . You're backing out already . . . not a good sign.*

"Well, that same nine hundred and fifty square foot condo, one bedroom, one bath, hasn't sold, it's so small. I could sell it to you for seven hundred thousand and that's a steal. Or you could rent it—I'll give you a big discount. When you come, you can take a look at it."

Kas was keeping a stiff upper lip and not saying how he really felt. What could she say? She had to admit she *did* have qualms and doubts that he would be the kind of man she needed and wanted. Someone totally loyal, someone who could handle exclusivity in a major way. Kas's track record was anything but. He'd been a player all his life. Maybe living in separate units but within the same building was a good compromise. That way, if their relationship fell apart, she could just retreat to her place. Maybe keep her job at the gallery.

Or maybe not.

"Okay, I could handle the rent."

Maybe she doesn't really love me. Maybe she just needs the gallery job for her visa. Don't push her, Skoros, you'll scare her off.

"I'll give you a good deal, 'Thena. On the rent. I know a place, you can rent furniture. This little . . . whatever it is, doesn't have to be permanent."

She heard the unmistakable edge in his voice. How had

their cozy, warm conversation turned so cool and business-like? She mentally smacked herself on the forehead.

"Well, let's wait and see when I get there." She quickly added, "Mick got engaged, so she's moving out, too. Her photographer boyfriend, he proposed while they were on the photo shoot. They're planning to get married soon."

A long silence ensued. She smacked her forehead again.

This time, she didn't bother to read him. Didn't want to.

"Okay, well, tell her congratulations. She's one brave soul. Who said marriage was not for the faint of heart? It's the biggest gamble in the world."

"Well, Kas, you would know. I guess if I'd married someone I didn't love, I'd be jaded, too."

They'd had this argument before. Two and a half years ago in the boat house, and the wound still felt raw. But, at least, the Skoroses and Kas now had joint custody of little Alex. Maybe it was worth it for them . . . and Kas. In the long term, maybe for the boy, too.

Just remembering that pain made her want to provoke him. "Hmm, weren't you the one who told me just last week there's no such thing as a safe love?"

Kas harrumphed softly. "Yeah, well, it's true. I'm jaded about marriage. But not love. I was talking about love, passion, not marriage. Even those who start out crazy in love and tie the knot end up just . . . crazy. And minus half their assets. Lots of guys I know are right there already."

She began to see red. *So money plays a role here.* Kas and his family had lots of money; she and her family were middle class in England. Instantly, she changed her mind about inviting Kas to Mikayla's and Barry's engagement party. It would be pointless to invite him and torture for him even if he agreed to come.

"Who said anything about marriage? I don't even want to share a condo with you."

"Well, that's a relief. I'm sure we both want our privacy. I damn well need mine."

Blimey, how did this conversation deteriorate so fast? My fears have made me just beastly. But he's being beastly, too.

Aw, rubbish.

She saw him throw back the covers and lurch out of bed. He went over to the bedroom window and looked out, trying to calm himself down. The fog was swirling about in gray mists. He remained angry.

So did she. Kas Skoros was impossible! How had she ever agreed to move across an entire continent to be with him? What an arrogant, stubborn heel he was.

Well, bugger.

A moment later, he came back on. "Gotta get some sleep, Thena."

They coldly said goodnight a minute later.

CHAPTER THIRTY-ONE

Four days later, after finishing her first cityscape, Athena swung her satchel over one shoulder and tucked the wrapped canvas under the other. The day before, she'd spray-varnished the signed acrylic painting and then dried it with her hair dryer. She'd stayed up nearly all night for two nights to get it done, feeling the necessity to show her good faith to Martin and to reassure him that three more were on the way. She walked the four long blocks to the Visions Gallery, struggling to keep aware of her surroundings. The threat, she knew, was always present, and she knew relying on Ochoa and the other detectives in the Homicide Division was essentially a hopeless endeavor. A killer was stalking her, and there was little she could do about it except carry a loaded revolver with her every moment of every day.

Part of her mind dwelled on the phone conversation she'd had with Kas late Monday night. They had texted each other since then, but neither called the other in the intervening days to apologize or make up. Kas had inquired whether she would be taking the gallery manager's position and she had replied with a terse *yes*.

In her own mind, she vacillated from yes to no, with explanations and reasons on both sides. She knew Kas was hurt that she wanted to live in another condo in the Stargazer Tower. He knew she was having second thoughts about moving to San Francisco, and rightly so. What would happen if his eyes wandered and she broke up with him? He was her boss, and her management of the Tower's gallery could disappear in a flash if he chose to be vindictive. And what did her doubts say about their relationship? Did their relationship stand a chance if she was already doubting its success? Of course, her doubts were based on their history so far. He'd already broken her heart once. Why was she so eager to go back for a second round?

The day was sunny, but clouds were gathering overhead. She had to make her visit brief and get home before it started to rain. Minutes later, having stowed her bag on a chair, she unwrapped the stiff shipping paper and propped the canvas upon a nearby easel in Martin's office at the rear of the gallery.

Martin clicked off his phone and came over to stand in front of the easel. As usual, he stood silently, stroking his chin with one hand while the other supported his elbow. Athena held her breath. She'd decided to paint the first cityscape with a Georgetown street scene, its focal point the corner coffee and bagel shop by her apartment. There were several patrons sitting at tables on the sidewalk in front and there was a clear perspective of the intersecting street that vanished into the distance. On that street, sitting on a black, Harley motorcycle with iridescent green fenders and metal saddlebags, was a young woman in a unisex outfit of black leather. Her brown hair flowed down her back and she was smoking. Her head was partly turned away, but the motorcycle's license plate showed its numbers and letters.

She titled this painting simply, "A Georgetown Street". In her way, Athena was giving the cops a way to track their "person of interest" in one of the latest murders in the city, other than shouting from the rooftops who he was and one of the places he could be found, loose on the streets. If anything happened to her, the license plate was a clue.

"What do you think?" she asked Martin. Still the handsome blond Dane, he practically shone in a silky gray suit and black dress shirt.

Finally, he nodded and smiled. "Yes, I like it. It's a blend of romantic realism and expressionism. The colors are vibrant, your figures express a certain discomfort or distrust of people. I get that. The details, expressionistic, but like a miracle of artistic license, it all comes together and makes me want to visit that place. Sit down and people-watch over a cup of macchiato. So who's the girl on the bike? She looks familiar."

She hadn't told Martin or Mark that the intruder who broke into her apartment was the girl on the bike, a man dressed as a woman and a serial killer who'd evaded police for years. All she'd revealed was her knowledge, her clairvoyant sense that the intruder was a man she'd seen in the neighborhood.

"She was in the Gay Pride Parade. You probably saw her there."

"Ah, yes. The one dressed as a dominatrix, all in black leather. Okay, Athena, I think you've done a good job here. I'm going to ask a cool ten thousand for it. The other three, I intend to ask a similar figure, so keep the size the same. You know how customers are about the size of a canvas. I think we should make prints of this one and the remaining three. Maybe an initial run of two hundred and fifty. Sell the giclée's for seven hundred ninety-nine, maybe more depending on how fast the original sells. You could make a trip back and embellish the APs and SPs. Do you agree to that?"

Artist Proof and Studio Proof prints sold for a little more than prints with no embellishments, without the artist's personal touches of paint over the printed canvas. The artist's signature on the canvas copy, the giclée, always added to its value and the embellishments always brought in more money. Martin knew the business of displaying and selling original or one-of-a-kind artwork as well as selling the printed copies of the originals. She'd learned a lot from working at Visions Gallery.

The prices he'd ask were disappointing, of course. What could she say? She was an unknown artist whose original work had no established price tag or market value in the art world.

"Amazing, Martin. My pastiches sell for fifty thousand and more, yet my original artwork less than ten each."

He shot her an ironic but sympathetic smile. "Yes, well, you're not yet famous, dearie, and you're not yet dead."

The droll way Martin put it made her smile. "That's true on both counts." *Let's hope the former happens but not the latter.*

"Maybe in ten years, if these cityscapes take off, your originals will sell for more than your pastiches. Or because you'll be famous, the pastiches will be worth so much that I'll be able to retire. By and by, let me know if and when Mr. Skoros would like to book another pastiche sale. I've already announced to the other pastiche painters to start work on another round. Next June or July, we might be ready. We can arrange a showing again in San Francisco."

Even Martin was counting on her keeping the relationship with Kas going. She agreed, picked up her bag and hugged him tightly.

"Athena, you know I wish you the best in your new adventure in San Francisco. And I hope you and the Greek hunk will be truly happy. You have decided, haven't you?"

"Yes, I think so," she said, forcing a smile. "I shall miss you and Mark, so very much."

"You must stay in touch, my dear girl." He looked pointedly at her bag. "I hope you're carrying Mark's . . ." A customer walked into the gallery. " . . . you-know-what for your own safety. Before you leave town, just drop it off for Mark. His grandfather gave that to him, so it's of sentimental value."

"Of course. Thanks to both of you, I feel safer."

He moved to his open office doorway, bent over on impulse and pecked her cheek. He whispered into her ear. "If I were a straight guy, you'd have to beat me off with a stick."

She was chuckling as she stepped out of the gallery and started her walk back home.

The little crush she'd had on Martin had started two and half years ago when Martin, all gorgeous seventy-four inches of him, had modeled in the nude for their figure painting class at the Art Institute. She'd even entertained the fantasy of hooking up with him and letting him become her first lover. How naïve and foolish she'd been! Now, nearly twenty-three, she sometimes felt very old, indeed. So much had changed since she was nineteen and met Kas Skoros for the first time. And then he broke her heart and married someone else—his dead brother's fiancée. Dan Grantham became her lover and friend, sharing so much of her love of art that they spent many dates perusing the museums and galleries in the area. Even that common passion wasn't enough to hold them together. Still, nostalgia made her yearn for one last contact.

Impulsively, she punched in Dan's cell phone number while she walked. It went straight to voice mail, so her message was *Hi Dan, it's Athena. I'm moving to San Francisco soon. Look for some of my originals in the Visions Gallery. Drop by and say hello before the end of the month if you can.*

Feeling foolishly sentimental, she dug her phone into the front pocket of her jeans. They were so over and done with, but she still admired his talent. A nostalgia for the place that had been her home for over eight years welled up inside her. She would miss the people more than the place, however. The neo-classical architecture and size of the buildings in DC left her cold, although she had enjoyed the small town feeling of Alexandria and Georgetown. But the people she'd met and grown to like and love would stay with her forever.

Her thoughts jumped to Chris's arrival later that night. Excited to see her brother again, she let her nostalgia fade as she looked forward to hearing the latest news about her parents and the Consulate her father ran in Milan. She'd filled her fridge with some of Chris's favorite comfort food.

With a start, she realized where she was. The corner coffee and bagel shop loomed ahead at the end of the block, just a few yards ahead. She scanned the exterior, the sidewalks around the shop. There was no motorcycle in view, not on her street or the side street. There was a black panel van, however, parked along the side street's curb, but that was common. The coffee shop was a favorite with the tradesmen in the area.

The pedestrian light turned green and she crossed with a group of people. Instantly, the hair on the back of her neck rose. The bugger—he was inside the shop! She knew it, sensed the evil vibes streaming from that direction. For a moment, she stopped dead in her tracks on the sidewalk outside the coffee shop. Immediately, she switched her bag from her left shoulder to her right, unzipped the top and tucked her hand inside. When her fingers touched the cold metal of the revolver, she felt a little reassured.

If worst came to worst, she had something lethal to defend herself with. What if he had something more dangerous than an icepick? Like a gun? She knew the greatest danger was the element of surprise. Most people didn't have an antenna for danger, like she had. Maybe that instinct for survival had lessened in people as mankind evolved. Maybe she had it because of her clairvoyance.

She'd called several alarm system companies, but they were all experiencing booming business. The earliest they could come out to install a system was over a week away. She'd scheduled an installation for the week after next. Until then, she and Mick would have to be extra cautious. The super still hadn't changed the downstairs entrance lock. The lazy bugger.

Picking up her speed, she passed the coffee drinkers sitting along the sidewalk before crossing her street to the other side. Without slowing her steps, she continued to the middle of the block. Only then did she stop outside her building's entrance and look back at the corner. She wasn't paranoid. Although she couldn't see the guy, she knew he was there.

Why was he so obsessed with her? The cops would do nothing with her tips, so she was no threat to him. If only she could tell him that. But then, of course, he would know with absolute certainty that she knew who he was.

Dave lowered the newspaper and folded it. He stared through the plate glass window and frowned. From where he sat, he could see the blonde bitch stop at her building. There were little brass-colored mailboxes by the door, but no alarm system. Now that he had Kyle's building key, the only locked door was the front door to her apartment on the third floor. He had seen the one dead bolt and chain lock on the front door when he'd searched the flat.

He glanced at his watch. Sam had packed their van with suitcases filled with their belongings in addition to tool chests and electrical equipment. There was space for Dave's motorcycle inside the van, but all he had to do was wheel it out later. The sales contract for their electrical business was already signed, and early Sunday morning he and Sam were off.

Right now, he had to drive their black van to the detailer's shop on East Second Street. The detailer would paint it overnight, a rush job that Sam had paid a chunk for. His brother had stolen the license plates off a van he'd found parked near North Capitol and M Street, and they would put them on while on the road somewhere in rural Virginia. Sam was one smart sonuvabitch. He'd planned it all.

No cop was gonna follow their tracks. No cop was gonna bother them again. This small town they were going to—no one would know them from Adam. They'd start new lives there.

Shawna hadn't said a word to anybody at Club Fiore. Hadn't explained a damn thing to anybody, not even Jeanine. That very day he shut the bitch up. When he was packed and leaving her apartment and she started yelling and cursing him, he shut her up. Dave found himself shaking a little from that rushed killing. He should've just kept walking, but her voice, the yelling and cursing—he couldn't let another damned broad treat him that way. Never again! It was time to shut the bitch up.

Shawna wouldn't show up for work at the night club that night, and neither would that stupid slut. It'd be days before anybody would start looking for them. Dave didn't tell Sam what he'd done, hell no. His brother would get mad at him for risking their getaway, but Dave was glad to be rid of them both. Jeanine and Shawna.

That Sunday, Sam and Dave would be long gone.

Just one more bitch to take care of.

CHAPTER THIRTY-TWO

It was eight o'clock, but dusk hadn't yet fallen. Athena had drawn the drapes but continued to stare out of their tall front windows, a cup of hot black tea in one hand. The aromatic steam tickled her nostrils, reminding her of home and hearth. But where was home and hearth these days? Not Milan, although her parents lived there, but like all her father's diplomatic postings, it was a temporary place of residence. Like Lyons, France. Like Zurich, Switzerland. Like Washington, D.C. Did it matter where she lived if she was with the people she cared about the most? As long as she was able to pursue her artistic career?

However, between her frequent moves as a child and the awful transparency of people's minds, Athena had never kept friendships for very long. Everything and everyone in her life seemed so transitory. Never lasting. Was that why she was so afraid of being so vulnerable? Of giving other people the power to hurt her?

Perhaps this was a deeply seated fear she would always have to live with. And if she moved all the way to San Francisco, would her love affair with Kas Skoros be just as transitory as her relationship with Dan?

In anticipation of Mikayla's and Hal's engagement party the following night, she'd already cleaned up her workspace, had stowed the two easels and worktables away in her bedroom. Her boxes of paints, brushes, palette knives and solutions were safely tucked away in her closet. Never a great cook, she'd even prepared a few of her brother's favorite comfort foods, like pub pies and mac and cheese. Her eagerness to see Chris again kept her mind humming and her nails clicking on her cup.

A yellow taxi pulled up at the curb, causing Athena's heart to leap into her throat.

Chris!

She glanced at her watch. Chris's arrival at Reagan International was over an hour ago. What had kept him at the airport so long? Three car doors opened. In addition to Chris's dark head, two others emerged. The driver headed to the car's open trunk, dwarfed by a taller man with broad shoulders.

Kas!

She flew down the three flights of stairs, thrust open the building's entrance door and flung herself into the solid wall that was Kas's body. Wrapped her arms around his neck until she felt his arms encircle her. They embraced like lovers who hadn't seen each other in months. They'd been apart one week, which seemed to her like a year. They embraced and kissed. Long and soulfully. She made mewling sounds between their kisses. He was breathing loudly. Traffic noises disappeared, the world receded. All she heard was the pounding of her heart and each other's noisy passion. The only emotion racing through her — unmitigated joy!

Visceral and immediate, Athena's emotions over-rode her clairvoyant channel, but a few of Kas's thoughts transmitted, riding the wave of his joy.

I don't want to lose you, 'Thena . . . don't leave me . . . give me a second chance . . .

The cabbie's noises behind them and Chris's presence reminded them that they were not alone. Never mind the one passing car whose owner honked his horn. They broke apart and with tears streaming down her face, Athena turned to her brother.

"Oh, Chris —"

"Hey, I feel left out of this lovefest," he said, grinning and opening his arms. His eyes looked moist, too. Her younger brother appeared taller and more muscular than the last time she'd seen him, last Christmas. His dark brown hair was longer, curling over the collar of his rugby-style striped shirt. He appeared confident and excited to be on his way to a new adventure, Stanford University.

They hugged each other, giving the double-cheek kiss that they'd grown accustomed to since their formative years in England, France, Switzerland, the USA. In no time, the three had climbed the wooden stairs, each pulling a wheeled suitcase.

"This isn't all my stuff, Sis," Chris informed her. "These are my clothes and a few books. I mailed a box of soccer gear and my high school competition ball and — what else? Oh yeah, my tennis racket. I might get new skis or a snowboard, so I didn't ship the old ones I got years ago. Kas invited me up to the mountains to ski with him this winter."

Chris, as voluble as ever, continued chatting about his upcoming school year at Stanford, his hopes to play college soccer or, at the minimum, intramurals.

"I have to try out for the team next Friday, so I can stay only until Tuesday. My flight's at noon on Tuesday. I want to get settled into the freshman dorm. Go to some parties. I hear girls in California like British accents."

Kas laughed, and so did Athena.

"Well, that's something I never tried," Kas joked. "What's your major? If it's engineering or business, I've got a job for you in four years."

He was going to major in International Relations, like their father, Chris said, or maybe computer science. He was fluent in French, Italian, passable in German, so maybe a career as a British Intelligence officer would be even more exciting. He'd been impressed by Max, who was head of security at the British Embassy. Chris added, "Yeah, sis, not like Max or even James Bond, but analysis with some field work. I've checked into it."

Smiling the entire time, Athena oversaw the two men getting settled. She pointed Kas and his one small suitcase to her bedroom, over-riding his expressed concerns—*I can bunk on the living room sofa*. She gestured to the short hallway leading to her bathroom and bedroom. For Chris, she'd already stacked sheets, blanket and pillow on the edge of the living room couch, an old Mid-century Modern piece. She and Mick had bought it at a consignment shop for a song, but it was sturdy and faced the tall windows. She watched Chris place his bags along the wall, where once her easels and supply tables had stood. She couldn't stop grinning like a foolish teenager bursting with happiness. Minutes later, her two favorite men filled her living room with their broad shoulders and manly scents.

She served them cold sodas and sat down with them, herself next to Kas on the couch and Chris dangling his long legs off one of the nearby kitchen bar stools.

"Nice place, Thene. Where's this hot flat mate you talked about?"

"She'll be back later tonight with Barry. Her fiancé."

Settled once again, she had a chance to really look at her brother and how he'd changed over the last eight months. Although Chris's physique was tall and slim like their father's, his dark hair and eyes and facial features resembled their mother's. Still, masculine imprints were evident in his jawline, his long Roman nose, his high forehead. Even his hairline had changed a little. He walked with a bit of a swagger that hadn't been there before. Doing well in his academic subjects at a college prep school in Milan as well as winning a soccer tournament and Most Valuable Player had added a hitch to his step.

His personality, outgoing and talkative, was like Anna's, also. Genes were a funny thing, she decided while listening to Chris talk about his college plans, his dormitory assignment and all the rest. You never knew which gene of your parents you'd get. She had her mother's mental powers but didn't inherit her physical looks. Strange, but there it was.

She and Chris were as opposite but as complementary and compatible as her mother and father. Polar opposites that managed to love each other and get along.

Meanwhile, Kas held back, staying in the background as she and Chris caught up on family news. Yet she remained keenly aware of his stares, sometimes bemused, sometimes smoldering. He said little to her personally in Chris's presence, but showered her brother with an older male's attention that Chris apparently relished.

An hour later, Athena served them a heaping chicken and kale salad and pub pies filled with beef, potatoes and peas — just like home in London. And, of course, the best English ale she could find in Georgetown. Over their meal, the three capsulized family news. Mother (Mum to Athena) was translating a bestseller from French into Italian and English; Father had recovered from pneumonia and was back at work in the Consul General's office in Milan; Uncle Terence would be joining them for Christmas in Como, Italy, where her Nonna and Zio Giancarlo and his family lived.

During her stay in San Francisco, she had asked about his family, the Skoroses. Two and a half years ago, during Thanksgiving week, she'd met them for the first time. And the last time she'd seen them had been at his brother Alex's funeral. That whole day had been filled with heartache for everyone.

Now, she wanted Kas to update her on what she'd neglected to ask before. His aging parents were hanging in there, diligent in their daily walks around their estate in the Loomis hills; little Alex was talking up a storm, just like his biological father and namesake. The little boy loved to play in the family's swimming pool and had two new best friends, Kas's dogs, Spartacus and Cassandra.

Kas's mother, Lorena, on weekdays had begun giving readings to people, against her husband's wishes; weekends were spent keeping two-year-old Alex entertained. The two German shepherds at the Loomis hills estate frolicked with the little boy around the property, playing throw and fetch all day long. Kas's father, the old-school Greek American, was holding his own at eighty-two and went into the Skoros Enterprises office once a week. Kas's two older brothers, George and Leon, did their best to bring their father up to date on building projects and their other commercial properties.

"I'm taking a short break from the Stargazer, but mainly I'm here to help you pack," Kas told Athena pointedly after she and Chris got his updated news. "I'm hoping it won't be no for an answer, Thena."

She smiled. "I never said no, Kas."

"But your yes was always hesitant."

Inwardly thrilled that he'd flown across a continent to change her mind, she strove to play it cool. "True, but I did say yes. And you don't mind if I rent another place? I mean, one of the other condos? I know how busy you are, and I'll be busy, too."

Kas shrugged before explaining. To take his place for the long weekend, George and Leon were covering for him at the Stargazer Tower, managing the final construction and sales of the last ten condos on the top two floors; hiring a manager of the Stargazer hotel, since the hotel bookings had increased; supervising the vacating of the gallery's former manager and the closing of the gallery, itself, until Athena could take over its management.

"Most of the work is done, but I'll continue to live there during the week. Weekends, I'll be in Loomis. 'Thena, I don't plan to monopolize your time. I know you want to paint when you're not managing the gallery. I respect that."

She beamed at him. "Then I don't see a problem. If it doesn't work out or if you don't like the way I run the gallery, we can go our separate ways. Stay friends but move on."

Chris looked like he was at a tennis match, his head swiveling back and forth. He kept his counsel as Athena and Kas hashed out the terms of their peculiar arrangement. Kas grinned and nodded.

She loved him but felt the need to save face in case their romance crashed and burned.

"Always friends, you bet," Kas assured her. He took Athena's hand, and she smiled warmly at him in reply.

His eyes big with resolve not to interfere, Chris sat and sipped his soda. The look he exchanged with Athena said it all. He approved.

All talked out and drowsy with food and ale, Chris excused himself and headed to Athena's bathroom. Athena's and Kas's voices fell to whispers as she cleaned up the kitchen and made up Chris's bed on the couch.

Kas told her that after Mikayla had called to invite Kas to her engagement party, he had been undecided, not sure if Athena wanted him to come—their last phone conversation in the middle of the night had been so strained, after all. The need to see Athena had ultimately over-rode his caution— was she upset with him?

"No," she said, coming over to stroke his cheek. They were sitting on the kitchen bar stools, facing each other, their knees touching, but she could tell he was holding back. They had some things to iron out first. "But your words about marriage and commitment were so cynical, I thought you might find the engagement party silly. Boring."

One side of his mouth turned up. "Not if you're at the party." He caught her hand and lifted it to his lips. He pressed his mouth against her knuckles. "I missed you. And I worried that I'd turned you off to the idea of living with me. I knew I said the wrong thing on the phone. I was wrong, Thena. That's not how I really feel. Not about you, anyway. That whole idea, marrying Nikki for the kid's sake — good in theory, lousy in practice. It left me soured on forced relationships. It made little Alex a Skoros, but was it worth it? I don't think so."

It was now or never, she determined. She had to be forthright with him, for both their sakes. She nodded at him, then looked away. He held her hand and she let him, wondering if he would drop it like a hot potato after she said what she felt compelled to say.

"Don't feel forced to do anything, Kas. I know how independent you are. I am, too. I won't be your typical girlfriend. Yes, I want to manage your gallery and live there at the Stargazer Tower. It's a beautiful building, and the location seems perfect for me, for someone who's new to San Francisco. The management job is a wonderful opportunity and I'm grateful. But . . ."

"But you don't want to live with me," he stated flatly. "I know that."

"But do you truly understand why?"

"It's too soon for you." Strangely enough, Kas was smiling tentatively at her. "I'm not upset, Thena. We fell in love with each other again . . . or maybe we never stopped. But I began to realize I was rushing you, pushing you into an arrangement you weren't comfortable with. I get it."

"You do?"

Kas let go of her hand and cupped her shoulder instead. He looked her in the eye.

"Hey, I'm thirty — thirty-one in one week, by the way —

you're twenty-two. You're too young to settle down, get married and all that. I'm jaded, sure, but I want to be certain. About me, about you. If I ever do marry again. Marriage with Nikki gave me a glimpse of a kind of legal prison I wouldn't wish on anybody. Sure, I didn't love her, but like I said, even the guys I know who started out in love ended up miserable after five, ten years of marriage. The rules, the obligations, the, uh, limitations on your private life, your work. I don't know if I can handle that. So, baby, you're off the hook. I'll give you a great discount on that small condo. It's move-in ready. You can rent or buy, I don't care. You can rent some furniture or buy some. It's your call."

If it was possible to feel utter elation and utter disappointment at the same time, Athena felt both. On the one hand, she'd have the alone time and the space to pursue her work. On the other hand, Kas was not offering her a commitment or any kind of future together. She didn't know whether to smile or weep.

"You sound like you're trying to talk me out of it."

"Isn't this what you want?" he asked.

She couldn't smile or frown. "Yes, I think so."

"Is it enough right now that we love each other? That we want to be together as much as possible?"

She nodded, mesmerized by the pulse in the vein at his temple. His dark brown eyes never left their focus on her face, his stare intense. At that moment, she realized how important this frank talk was to him. It was an honor bargain.

"The thing is, Kas, I want an exclusive relationship with you. I don't want to share you with any other woman. Understand that. But I don't want to pressure you or me into anything. Because, truthfully, I don't know what I want . . . other than a career as a painter."

"Thena, I may be further down the road in life than you but I understand completely. So, we're of one mind. So to speak?"

"Yes." Standing up, she offered her hand and drew him up with her. "I'm just happy you understand. Once you see all my work stuff, you'll be so relieved I didn't clutter up your beautiful place with it."

Chris emerged from the bathroom, bare chested but wearing flannel pajama bottoms. His favorite, sporting all the flags of European soccer teams. She kissed him, then made sure the front door was locked. The dead bolt. The chain link. She turned to Kas as she started to move down her hallway. "Let's go to bed, shall we?"

When at last she led Kas into her bedroom and locked the door, he surprised her with a passionate, no-holds-barred kiss. As he came up for air, she felt as though every muscle in her body had turned to Yorkshire pudding. He ground his hips against hers as he pressed her flat against the closed door.

"You can always change my mind, y'know," he murmured into her temple. "You have that kind of power over me."

Yes, but for how long? Will you ever be truly mine? Am I setting myself up for the biggest fall of my life? If so, God help me.

She shifted her hip bone to snuggle her mound against the soft part of his crotch. Not for long, though, for he immediately adjusted his body so that his erection could rub against her. Her hands slithered down to his zipper.

"Do I," she muttered simply. What was he really telling her? Their raging lust had numbed her mind. "Do I have power over you?"

"How can you not know? You read minds."

They both chuckled and made their way to her bed.

"Yes, but I don't always understand emotions," she said, "Why people do what they do. It's often a mystery to me."

"You're not alone there, sweetheart, and I'm nearly a decade older than you." He grinned as he pinned her back on the bed. Then he removed her top, closed his eyes and trailed kisses up and down her torso.

She knew, despite her ability to read minds, men were always puzzles, and Kas Skoros, the greatest enigma of all.

CHAPTER THIRTY-THREE

All day Dave had stewed over his dilemma. While hiding like a runaway mutt in a back room at the detailer's shop—under his brother's order—he pondered over the threat the blonde bitch posed to him and Sam. If she hadn't done so already, he was certain she'd go to the cops and rat on him, tell them she'd seen him at the Gay Pride Parade by the black tent, tell them about Shawna working at Club Fiore. Soon, they'd track down Jeanine, find her body, put a BOLO out on him. Sam had warned him about that. He should've kept his nose clean. Might even ditch him and leave for Colorado alone. Then where would Dave be?

That was what Sam warned him against. Not thinking straight, losing his cool and control and letting the thunderous rage take over. His brother understood what happened to him every so often.

The rage. The rage. It filled his mind and body.

He couldn't help it. Dave glanced around the storeroom. It smelled of motor oil, paint, solvents—they made him gag. The detailer, a pal of his brother's, was getting ready to paint the black van, make it white and change the signs on the sides to read "Rocky Mountain Electrical". That was Sam's idea, after he'd had their IDs altered. Enough to throw off the fucking cops, anyway. His brother was one smart dude. Dave was a dickhead, a screw-up compared to his older brother, the one clever enough to keep them both out of prison. So far.

No more fuckups, Dave, he told himself.

Yet the worries over that blonde bitch gnawed at him. He

258

was sure she had what his mother used to call "the Third Eye." It was what his crazy bitch of a mother used against him and Sam. "I've got my Third Eye on you two. You stay put in this closet and don't you come out until I say so. If you do, I'll tan your hides, and when your father comes home, he'll beat your brains out." She'd touch the middle of her forehead. The Third Eye.

The evil bitch.

And now the blonde with the Third Eye. She knew it was him inside that tent with the icepick. That was why she froze, then straightened up and moved away quickly—she knew!

Worked up into a lather, he jumped up and went to the shed where they painted the cars. The van wasn't sealed off yet. The detailer was in his office on the phone. Just his worker, a guy in dirty blue overalls, messing with the paint sprayer, was inside the shed.

"I got errands to run. I need my bike out of there."

The guy shrugged and opened the back doors. Dave climbed up a metal ramp to the cargo hold. His mind was already made up.

Athena awoke from a dream, a horrible dream. Her mother had been trapped inside a burning building, screaming for her to wake up and save herself. Instinctively, she knew her mother had shouted a warning across thousands of miles. Jerking suddenly to consciousness, she sniffed the air. The smell of something smoky and foul invaded her senses moments before she fully awoke. Her skull seemed on fire with her mother's screams.

He was close by—the killer!

Faint sounds down the hall alarmed her. Chris was up and moving about in the middle of the night. Someone was at the front door! Chris's muffled voice could be heard. The foul smell increased. Athena sat up and swung her legs over the end of the bed. Her digital clock shone the time, a little after four o'clock.

Mindful of her nakedness, she went over and grabbed her flannel bathrobe off the hook of her bedroom door. Kas stirred.

"Thena?"

She said nothing but unzipped her satchel, which sat in a heap in front of her nightstand. The gun felt cold to her fingertips.

"What's going on?" By now, Kas had sprung to his feet in the semi-darkness, a night light limning his naked figure. Another sound again, this time inside the apartment. Chris cried out.

No longer hesitant, Athena seized the revolver and sprang to the door.

"What the hell—" Kas scurried out of bed.

Kas moved behind her as she opened the bedroom door and rushed down the hall.

A loud pop—like an exploding champagne cork—went off, then another as she began to round the hallway's corner. Two loud thuds hit the wall near her head. She gasped and ducked back behind the corner wall.

Someone was firing a gun at her!

Chris!

She peeked around the corner—the entry way and living room were lit by one source, the dim light in the vent over the stove. Enough light to see Chris on the floor crying out again and holding his arm. He was kicking up his good soccer leg, connecting with the intruder's legs. The long-haired figure buckled, his head crashing into the wall.

"Stop, stop!" Chris yelled as he cowered and tried to cover his head.

Adrenaline pumped through her, clouding her thinking.

She had to stop the shooter. *Chris! He's hurt!*

Crouching near the floor, she aimed the revolver at the figure against the wall and tried to pull back the hammer. Her hand was shaking so much that she had to cover her right hand with her left. Just then, Kas appeared behind her and knelt down to her level.

"Let me." He seized the gun. "Stay down!"

"Chris is on the floor. A man with a gun."

He pulled her back just as another thud hit the wall above them. Barely a thought registered in her frantic mind except this—a former deputy sheriff, Kas could clearly aim the revolver better than she could. Kas pushed her behind him, moved in front of her, and stepped away from the hallway.

"No, Kas!"

She sprang up close behind Kas, saw the dark figure by the door aim his gun at Chris. She screamed as loudly as she could. The figure turned to them, his arm outstretched, about to fire again.

What sounded like a small explosion erupted from the revolver in Kas's hand. The long-haired figure screamed, fell back and crashed against the wall. Athena looked around the corner, rose to her feet and ran to Chris.

Her back to the figure by the door, she bent over Chris. Her brother appeared unconscious, his eyes closed, his right arm bleeding. She glanced back as Kas approached them.

The intruder was halfway down but struggling to stand up. He clutched his right leg and dropped something as he did. It landed with a clatter on the wooden floor. An icepick. The acrid smell of gunpowder hung in the air like a thin cloud. Her eyes smarted and teared up. Suddenly, the intruder lurched to his feet. His left hand held something that glinted in the dimness of the entryway. A pistol. He switched the gun to his right hand and pointed it at Kas.

"Stay back! Or I'll shoot 'em!"

Athena didn't recognize the male voice, but she was certain it came from Shawna, the biker chick. It was him. Dave Millhouse. The serial killer from two and a half years ago. She froze as the pistol swung her and Chris's way.

Why was he here? In her apartment?

A second later, she knew. All of it. The flood of thoughts from his deranged mind made her sick. *He wants to kill us! But he's afraid, didn't expect the men to be here.*

Kas stepped further into the entryway. "You fire that gun and I'll drop you dead." His voice was cold but trembling. "Don't do it."

The open door registered suddenly to Athena. The killer must've persuaded Chris to open the door, maybe passing himself off as a female friend.

Again, the intruder swung his arm in Kas's direction, then back at Athena. The gun barrel pointed at each in turn. She saw the icepick on the floor where he'd dropped it. The killer's leg was bleeding, a dark stain spreading on his jeans leg. Drops splattered onto the floor. Kas had wounded him.

There was a smear of blood on the wall next to the open doorway. His head must've bled, too, from where he'd crashed twice against the wall.

"I'll kill her! I'll kill all of you!" the attacker screamed. His pain-glazed eyes scanned over them, back and forth.

Athena cradled Chris's head against her. She felt something warm and sticky on his arm. Kas, not a stitch on him, stepped in front of them, putting his body between the killer and her and Chris on the floor, drawing the attacker's attention away from them.

"You want to be a dead man," Kas hissed. His voice sounded menacing but strangely calm. "You want to live? The door's open. Make a run for it. You stay here and point that gun at us, I'm going to shoot you. This time, I'm aiming for your head."

Athena ignored the killer bent over at the doorway, sensing his weakening resolve, hearing the frightened thoughts in his mind. He was already cursing himself for disobeying his brother. The pain was building in his leg. Kas's aim had hit the mark. A bone was broken. Now the killer was scared.

With the killer's gun pointed at them all and Kas's gun pointed at the killer, Athena couldn't tell what was going to happen. But she focused and did something she'd never done before. She sent a telepathic command to the killer.

Run away! You'll die here if you stay. Your brother's waiting for you.

A second later, she felt the killer caving, his fear spiking. His brother was going to be furious! He was fucking everything up. He needed Sam to help him!

Then, Kas's voice could be heard, eerily steady but as sharp as a razor's edge. His deputy's voice, calm and cold but quaking with emotion held in check.

"Leave now and you get to live. Drop your gun, or I'm taking you down. Do you understand me?"

The voice she heard next was that of a little boy, half sobbing, half hysterical with anger and fear.

"Y-you fucker! You hurt me, you hurt me!" The killer backed up to the open doorway and dropped his pistol, the hand relinquishing it, flying to press against the side of his leg. The pistol made a thud when it hit the floor.

Kas kicked it to the wall and lowered the revolver.

"Get the hell outa here!"

With his bloody left hand, the killer clutched the doorway as he lurched out and down the stairs. He screamed once, "You motherfuckers, I'll get you, I'll get you!" His steps sounding like hammers on the wooden steps, there was a crash as wood cracked and a body fell. Kas, tall and naked, followed him, the revolver in his hand thrust out in front of him.

"Kas, don't!" she yelled. "I know him! He's a killer!"

Oh God, she couldn't lose him. She said a silent prayer as Kas ignored her and ran down the stairs after the attacker.

Other noises invaded the open doorway. Neighbors in the building were opening doors, one shouting, "There's a naked guy with a gun. He's running after a girl! The girl's hurt and bleeding. Call the police!" Another neighbor yelled, "I'm calling now—nine-one-one. Get inside and lock your door!"

Athena turned to Chris. Rivulets of blood ran off his arm onto the wooden floor of the entryway. She ran to get a towel, came back in a flash and wrapped his forearm. Helping him to the kitchen, she turned on the overhead lights and washed his wounds. Two puncture wounds on his right forearm confirmed the killer's use of his icepick. Only then, after wrapping Chris's arm in a dish towel, holding back hysterical tears, did she run to get her cell phone from her bag. She placed a hurried call, this time to Detective Ochoa's private cell phone number. There was no answer, so she left a message.

"Ochoa, the killer—the younger brother was here tonight. He attacked my brother, tried to kill us. He's wounded. Come quickly, please, and you'll catch him. It's The Mall killer."

She disconnected and dropped the cell phone on the counter. Haltingly, mixed with spats of swearing, Chris tried to explain what happened. He'd heard a knock and gone to the door. A woman's voice pleaded with him to open up. She was a neighbor and in trouble. Half asleep, Chris had opened the door and the figure in the dark hallway—why wasn't the landing light on? The woman lunged at him, wielding the icepick. Chris thought the woman—whoever it was—was expecting Athena to open the door and had instead stabbed lower on Chris's body. Chris hadn't realized the distressed female voice on the other side of the door would turn out to be a man with the strength of an obsessed killer. Chris's athletic instincts took over and he flung up his arm in self-defense, getting a second stab wound. When he fell backwards on the floor, he'd kicked out like any good soccer player would.

Athena heard the roar of a motorcycle engine, then minutes later, police sirens down the street. Kas reappeared before them in all his nakedness. His skin from forehead to belly was slick with sweat. He was breathing heavily.

Chris muttered, "Well, bloody hell."

"He got away, but not far. He tore out of here like the hounds of Hell were after him. How he rode that bike without passing out is beyond me. Hurt but functioning. I heard a skid and a scream, so I think he's down. Thena, you said you knew this guy? Who the hell was he?"

Athena could see Kas didn't have a mark on him and gasped. *Thank God!* She went over to him and touched his arm. "It's a long story."

"Well, I wanna hear it. First, I better get some clothes on." He headed for her bedroom.

She watched him go, grateful that he hadn't tried to pursue the killer. She marveled at his cool demeanor during the entire episode. He'd had training in the military and as a sheriff's deputy, but still, facing a killer with a gun pointing at you was a heart pounding freak-show. He'd risked his life to save them.

Kas had left the front door open so the police would know where to go. No need, for at least two of her neighbors were only too happy to point the cops to the apartment the naked man had disappeared into. Kas reappeared, dressed in tan khakis and royal blue polo shirt. He was still barefoot, his dark hair tousled, dark whiskers clouding his face. But he was fully awake and staring at Athena. He went over and placed the revolver on the floor by the doorway. The killer's pistol lay against the wall.

He came over to her and Chris. "So that's the threat my mother was talking about? You could've given us a heads up, Athena. A man looking like a woman. What's that all about?"

She grimaced and looked down at Chris's arm, now covered with two towels. She wrapped her arms around Kas's waist.

"I'm so sorry." Fighting off a welling up of tears, she sank to the stool beside Chris. She was still trembling. All she could do was shake her head.

Noises below distracted her. The commotion downstairs was getting nearer as police officers clomped their way up, calling out their approach. Outside the loft windows, flashing lights indicated several cop cars had pulled up to the scene. Wasn't there action somewhere else in this crime-ridden city? Or was her apartment the only magnet that night for sociopaths? Her pulse rate was slowing down, and she was finally able to link halfway coherent thoughts together.

Detective Ochoa! He needed physical evidence. She took another dish towel and quickly swiped the drops of blood off the floor, then placed it back inside a kitchen drawer. Kas and Chris silently watched her do this, frowning all the while. She slid the drawer shut just as the first officer appeared in the open doorway.

"What's going on? We had a call." His eyes flashed to the two guns on the floor. His hand palmed the holstered gun at his belt. "All three of you, hands up!"

Kas threw up his hands and looked at Athena's and Chris's puzzled faces. It took but a second for them to realize the cop was talking to them as well. Their hands flew up. Or rather, both of Athena's and one, the uninjured arm, of Chris's.

Minutes later, Detective Ochoa showed up, his badge displayed openly in one hand. The uniformed cops appeared to defer to him.

"Well, Athena, there's an unconscious man or woman lying in the street next to an overturned motorcycle. Has a bullet wound in his leg. That wouldn't have anything to do with you and some naked man with a gun, would it?"

She looked from him to Kas, then to Chris and back to Ochoa.

It was going to be a very long night.

CHAPTER THIRTY-FOUR

It was nine o'clock that morning when the last of the cops, including Detective Ochoa, finally left. Their statements had filled all of one of his little notebooks. All the weapons had been confiscated, but Athena was assured that Mark's revolver would be returned to its rightful owner with a stern warning about lending guns to friends. Even though that gun, wielded by a man who knew how to handle it, had likely saved their lives.

The responding officers had called a medic when they heard what had happened, and Chris's arm had been tended to. So far, it didn't appear that any permanent damage had been done. Athena had given Detective Ochoa the killer's blood sample, saved on her cotton dish towel. Crime Scene techs had supplied him with photos and would give him any trace evidence that they could collect. With the testimony of three witnesses and their attacker in custody, the detective would get the DNA match he needed.

The problem—the older brother, Sam Millhouse, had disappeared, dropped out of sight. Evidently, the killer's leg wound wasn't life threatening, but from his hospital bed, he wasn't saying a word. His older brother had escaped the cops' dragnet around the neighborhood of Ace Electrical. Dave Millhouse, aka Shawna the biker chick, appeared to be staying loyal to his brother. The cops had no clue where the other brother had gone, or even if he was still in town. The State Police all up and down the Eastern Seaboard were alerted, and BOLOS would be sent out to every police station in the country.

Ochoa told them, "We'll keep looking now that we have the prime suspect in custody." He nodded at Kas. "Thanks to your friend here, the Gay Pride killing just got a major lead." He'd turned to Athena and shaken her hand. "We'll get the other one, Athena. I'll let you know when we do. Meanwhile, our serial killer is no longer on the loose."

Gazing at both Chris and Kas, she walked back to the kitchen. She sensed that the threat—for her and her loved ones, anyway—was over. A uniformed cop in his cruiser had been stationed at the curb for the remainder of the weekend and police surveillance posted in her neighborhood around the clock. If the killer's brother returned, they'd catch him. They'd use his younger brother as bait.

Before Detective Ochoa left, however, he asked Athena if he could recommend her services to his cousin, a detective inspector in San Francisco. She'd sighed with misgivings but ultimately nodded and gave Ochoa her forwarding address at the Stargazer Tower. They shook hands before he departed. Kas watched disapprovingly but said nothing.

What Ochoa had unwittingly begun for her by that ill-timed search of the Millhouse premises that day, he had finally ended. She hoped so, anyway—hoped that justice would be served.

Though, for Athena, it wasn't soon enough.

Thank God we're all alive.

But, blimey, what a nightmare.

CHAPTER THIRTY-FIVE

Despite the yellow crime scene tape crisscrossed over Athena's front door — which she had permission the next day to tear down — Mikayla's and Barry's engagement party on Saturday night for their twenty or so closest friends and work pals went off without a hitch. There were still smudges on the wall, doorjamb and apartment door where a forensics team used powder to find fingerprints. Neither she nor Chris noticed whether the attacker wore gloves; Kas claimed not to have seen any, so prints were lifted. She, Chris, and Kas had given their fingerprints for the elimination process.

The presence of the tape, powder smudges and bullet holes in the walls elicited a lot of excited conversation, and everyone drank much more and became even merrier. Chris stole the show for a while as he recounted everything that had transpired early that morning, with Kas filling in the remaining details. Mick and Barry got to hear it for the second time after they showed up Saturday morning and inquired about the police cruiser downstairs and the crime scene tape across the door.

Athena felt subdued. Still in a state of shock and distress over the attack and how close they came to getting killed, she remained quiet and contemplative. Kas stayed at her side, a comforting and strong presence. Little by little, her sense of well-being returned and she began to enjoy the party.

Chris looked dazzled by all the beautiful models present and appeared to revel in their attentions over his wounded and bandaged forearm. He wore a sling covered by one of Mikayla's colorful Caribbean-styled scarves. The painkillers he'd taken in Emergency hadn't worn off and continued to slur his speech and lent him an air of merriment that Athena knew he didn't really feel. The only thing he worried aloud about was whether he'd be in strong enough form to try out on Friday for the Stanford soccer team. Both she and Kas had to field concerned phone calls from their respective mothers. Athena felt remorse for bringing them such grief, although, as Kas kept telling her, she was not to blame.

Kas glanced appreciatively at the models present—all friends of Mick's and Barry's—but spent most of his time at the party on one of the kitchen stools, sipping his whiskey sour, his arm around Athena's waist. She returned his gesture of affection with an arm around his shoulders. Never once did she leave his side, her proprietary drape an unmistakable message to all the singles present that they were a couple. Every so often, their gazes would lock and they would smile at each other. She read his mind freely, so there was no need for him to speak, except when someone came over to converse.

I'm glad I was here, baby. I did my part with that creep . . . and now I'm going to help you pack and get you out of here . . . Can't wait to get you in the Tower . . . close by . . . see you every day . . . hold you . . . make love to you . . . that's all I want . . .

The emotions inside finally erupted and she leaned close and kissed the side of his neck.

"Oh, Kas. You're fearless, gutsy. I can learn from you about overcoming my fears, being brave. You give me courage."

Just then, Mick and Barry made their formal announcement, clicked their champagne glasses together, and then kissed passionately. Their guests cheered and took turns hugging Mikayla and pounding Barry's back. Athena and Kas stayed where they were until finally her roommate came over. Dressed in a sexy bright red dress, Mick looked at the two of them, their arms around each other, unwilling to split apart.

"Maybe you'll be next," she teased, her pretty red lips widening in a big, beaming smile. Red glossy nails flashed as she fluffed up her hairdo.

Athena felt Kas stiffen under her arm although he grinned back at Mikayla and was quick with a wisecrack. "I wouldn't wish myself on any woman, poor thing. Thena can do much better than me."

"Not true, Mick," Athena said. "He's the bravest man I know."

Mikayla turned a speculative smile onto Athena before moving on to another guest. Waiting until her friend was well out of earshot, Athena lowered her voice. What she said was meant for his ears only.

"Like you said, Kas, one day at a time."

His thoughts flowed through while he gazed at her and smiled.

The day might come when I'll change my mind. Then what, Thena? Will you be ready to commit? My mother keeps telling me, like storm warnings, our problems are still ahead of us . . .

A little taken aback, she pretended not to read him. She asked the bartender to refresh her drink. The vodka martini helped to numb her churning thoughts.

Kas's mother, Lorena's prophecies were always, always correct. Why hadn't Kas told her? *. . . like storm warnings, our problems are still ahead of us . . .*

Now, amid Mikayla's engagement party, she found herself leaning her head on Kas's shoulder. He looked as wiped out as she felt. The answer to her question came to her. *He's afraid of losing me.*

"Are you exhausted?" she asked Kas. He bent down and kissed her forehead.

"Sorry I'm such a dud, but I feel like I've run twenty miles, then ran into a dumpster. Go and mix if you want."

A glance at her watch told her the party was likely to continue for hours. She spied the gleam in his eyes and beat him to it.

"Oi, luv, fancy a shag?"

Kas laughed softly. "If that's Brit-speak for what I think it means, I'm all yours." He picked up his drink and, holding her hand, led her to the bedroom.

A week later, her and Mikayla's apartment looked as vacant as when they'd first seen it over two years ago. Mick had moved her furniture into storage before relocating to Barry's flat in Alexandria. Everything except her kitchen supplies and cookware had been packed and moved. The remaining boxes held her precious Lladro figurines and china. The only furniture Athena had brought into their household had been her bedroom set. That along with her art supplies and clothes had already been shipped to San Francisco. Her two suitcases contained clothes, books and a few personal items of jewelry, like her gold medallion of the goddess Athena, which she now wore for good luck. She'd decided to never take it off.

She and Kas had already seen Chris off at the airport on Tuesday, the police had returned the revolver to Mark, and she had promised Martin the other three cityscapes before Christmas.

Now she was sitting on one of the suitcases, waiting for their cab to show up. Kas was standing by the window, insisting on remaining vigilant in case the killer's brother came back. He refused to accept her insistence that the danger was over. When her cell phone buzzed, she knew who it was.

Detective Ochoa identified himself and then said, "Athena, you were so right about this. We did a rush on the analysis of that blood sample. The lab confirmed a DNA match to the DNA found in the skin cells under the murdered woman's fingernails. That man who broke into your apartment and attacked your brother — one and the same as the woman's killer. The search warrant from over two years ago had the older brother's DNA on file — enough similarities in their genetic markers to conclude the killer is a relative of Sam Millhouse. Our prime suspect is under guard in a prison hospital while his leg heals, but his accomplice after-the-fact is still at large."

I tried to tell you, ran her frustrated thoughts. "You have no idea where he might've gone?"

"All we know, he's in the wind."

And a dangerous sociopath is free to possibly wreak havoc on another town. A shame. But no longer my personal problem, no longer my responsibility.

"Listen, Athena, that cousin of mine, the cop who lives in San Francisco. I relayed your information and he said he'll contact you."

She wanted to laugh bitterly but couldn't, her ingrained politeness restraining her.

"I'll be very busy ... trying to balance everything in my life, you know, but ... maybe. We'll see."

When hell freezes over.

"Good. Well, as you know, your gift is very helpful. The Stargazer Tower, the gallery?"

"Yes. Good luck, Detective Ochoa," she said, then hung up. *I can always say no, thank you.*

Kas glanced over his shoulder at her. "Cab's here." He took one of her suitcases and his own. "You, okay, Thena? Glad to be leaving?"

She shot him a rueful smile, which instantly turned hopeful. "Oh yes, on my way to the city by the Golden Gate. With you. What more do I need?"

"Ready for new adventures?" He paused to give her a peck on the lips. She smiled and returned his kiss.

"Always." *Ready for balance in my life. Only you can show me the way.*

Athena closed the door behind them and proceeded down the stairs after Kas.

The End

About the Author

Donna Del Oro is an award-winning author who lives in Northern California near the Sierra Nevada Mountains.

www.ingramcontent.com/pod-product-compliance
Lightning Source LLC
Chambersburg PA
CBHW061552170626
46811CB00001B/171